TOWARD THE SEA

WITHDRAWN

TOWARD THE SEA

Stanley Middleton

Thorndike Press
Thorndike, Maine USA

This Large Print edition is published by Thorndike Press, USA.

Published in 1997 in the U.S. by arrangement with Century, one of the publishers of Random House UK Ltd.

U.S. Softcover ISBN 0–7862–1128–8 (General Series Edition)

The text of this Large Print edition is unabridged.
Other aspects of the book may vary from the original edition.

Set in 16 pt. New Times Roman.

Printed in Great Britain on acid-free paper.

Library of Congress Cataloging in Publication Data

Middleton, Stanley, 1919–
    Toward the sea / Stanley Middleton.
        p.   cm.
    ISBN 0–7862–1128–8 (lg. print : sc : alk. paper)
    1. Large type books.   I. Title.
[PR6063.I25T69   1997]
823′.914—dc21   97–13096

To John and Pauline Lucas

Go up now, look toward the sea.

I Kings xviii, 43

... the growing good of the world is partly dependent on unhistoric acts; and that things are not so ill with you and me as they might have been is half owing to the number who lived faithfully a hidden life, and rest in unvisited tombs.

George Eliot

CHAPTER ONE

John Henry Shelton walked down the foggy street.

He moved quickly past semi-detached villas at the top, along a string of town houses, a new complex, three shops, a small one-storey factory and finally terraces of Edwardian urban cottages, each respectable with its neat front garden, before he reached the narrow main road in the valley.

Over the other side of this, the land rose more steeply. From his present vantage-point, and he stopped to stare, he could see his own house, marked by three steepling poplars, and a lime tree. In the mist these lost their clarity of outline, took on something of the appearance of a children's fairy-tale illustration or the towering castles of the dentifrice advertisements of his childhood. The poplars, he thanked God, were not on his property but in the garden of the house on the street well below. The fog softened the outline of buildings, translated their shapes from provincial brick boxes to interesting, shifting oblongs fit for a painter's eye.

Henry glanced at his watch. Three-fifteen and almost dark-hour. Though this day was almost the last of November the weather seemed mild enough for October. He paused,

1

one hand on a stone garden wall, looking towards the trees. A few steps further and the tops of the poplars would disappear behind the dull row of houses fringing the main road. He resumed his progress; at the bottom of this hill he would have to turn right or left before beginning the upward climb to his home; there was no straight way. He decided on a right turn and a call at the newsagent's for an evening paper. This errand completed, with a word on the unseasonal weather to the man behind the counter, Henry Shelton stepped off again. The shops on one side of the main road and the Victorian houses on the other had lights in their windows. He stared in. Nobody spent Saturday afternoon in untoward activity, but he did not expect it. The blue light of the television screen played in appointed corners. He could not make out whether anybody watched. The pavements, on main and side-roads alike, seemed deserted; shopping for the day was over and done. A young woman with a push-chair and infant, and a man wearing a blue flat-cap with a top button represented humanity. Neither spoke to him. Cars, lights on, swished by on the damp roads.

Henry turned left and uphill, among newer houses on an avenue, built between the wars, and tackled the fiercer slope. He began to whistle between his teeth, swinging his bag. As he increased his pace, he felt no breathlessness as yet, and congratulated himself that he'd reached his present age, fifty-nine on Boxing

Day, without serious illness. He stopped again to watch a boy in a lighted front room playing his violin. Carefully listening, his ears were sharp, he could make out no sound. The window, criss-crossed with lead, must be double-glazed. The boy leaned forward to his stand to turn over his music. A sheet fluttered to the floor. The player laid the instrument on a chair and used both hands to restore and straighten the copies. He nodded, solemnly, bent to pick up his instrument, and began again, bowing hesitantly. Henry Shelton left him to it.

His own street consisted of fairly superior terraces of three-storey houses, with variations of design. His was the exception, double-fronted and detached with a narrow stable to one side. The front garden was protected by stout iron railings, removed during the war and replaced within the last twenty years by Shelton's predecessor. These were painted black and topped with ponderous spear-heads. Henry unlocked his front door, and turned about. Lights blazed in a window opposite, but revealed no movement or sign of occupation. That must be the place with shelves packed with cassettes, and a print of Picasso's *Child with Dove* on the far wall framed but invariably hung askew. He had seen young, indistinguishable people emerge from time to time as they found their way to shabby cars parked along the street, half on, half off the pavement.

The hall of his house struck warm; the central heating had come on while he was out. He put down his two bags, which were heavy, filled with potatoes bought from an allotment-holder some two miles away. He did not immediately switch on the light, but removed his anorak, and hung it on the hall-stand. Yawning he went to retrieve the bags, noticed a yellow envelope on the floor, delivered by hand. An advert, he guessed; a new tandoori, fish-and-chip bar, pizza-delivery service, supermarket. He moved forward, stashed the potatoes as they were in the pantry, and did nothing about the lights until he reached the kitchen. Then he filled and plugged in his electric kettle, lifted down a mug, dashed in a tea-bag. His arms ached from the humping of his load; he did not know why he went to so much trouble. The produce tasted better than that from the shops, but he had an hour's walk to fetch it; the grower, moreover, treated him with ironic respect as a connoisseur of potato-culture. Henry stretched, opened the knife-drawer to find means to slit his envelope. He had strong objections to ripping letters with his fingers, leaving a jagged tear. Henry used the knife, put it by the sink to be washed up. 'You don't know where it's been', his mother had warned him often in childhood. He grimaced. He was becoming, with his little compulsions, an old woman himself.

With no sense of urgency he extracted the

4

letter. He had not recognised the handwriting on the envelope. 'Dear Mr Shelton' and just over the page the signature: Helena Gough. Deliberately he refrained from turning the sheet and reading. He did not know any Yours sincerely, Helena Goughs. He looked along the knobs of his kitchen cupboards. Slightly annoyed with his behaviour, he allowed himself to read the address: 23, Stansfield Road. He did not know where that was, either, but he did not permit himself to consult immediately his A to Z Street Atlas of Beechnall. The script was neat and well formed, while the address had commas and full-stops in the right places. Unlike modern office usage. Modern secretaries had no time to spare for punctuation.

Dear Mr Shelton,
    You won't recognise my name but I'm the daughter of Marion Ball (née Meeks) whom you knew at one time. She would like to meet you again if that is possible. She has been quite ill, but is now much better. I don't wish to spring this message on you by telephone, and so I'll deliver it by hand, and then ring you later. We don't live very far away. I am sorry to trouble you, but my mother has talked a great deal about you these last months, and so I suggested you might meet.
                Yours sincerely,
                    Helena Gough

The kettle boiled; he made his tea.

Marion Meeks he remembered well, but it must be over forty years since he had seen or spoken to her. She had married, and gone away, to Bristol, Worcester, the West Country. He recalled a small, smudged photograph of her wedding in the local paper, with the husband towering over the bride. She must have been sitting down, for she was a tall girl. He had been fond of her, no, loved her, but with national service and university to complete he had not thought seriously of marriage. She was older than he was, in more of a hurry, foolhardy. Since her departure from the district he had not seen or heard of her. Her sister, Bessie, he had passed in the street from time to time. She was a stoutish, bustling woman, quite unlike Marion, and she never acknowledged him by so much as a nod. Perhaps she did not connect him with her family. The Meeks parents he had not thought about for years, though he carefully read the obituary columns of the evening paper. These announcements with their ham-fisted verses left him curious, and dissatisfied. When he taught English at a nearby grammar school he used to read out these stumbling rhymes, and ask for comments. His pupils would laugh, roughly, but he could silence them by demanding if they could do better in such circumstances. They never quite knew where they were with him; he was a quiet man, 'weird' they said, known for his explosions of temper. 'With him,' one fourth-former pronounced, 'you don't know whether to laugh or cry. But you have to be careful. When he hits you, it hurts.'

Marion Meeks.

He carried his mug of tea into the back room, a dark, north-facing oblong where he kept the television set. He took to the rocking chair, holding the mug in both hands in front of him. He had switched on neither television nor lamp, so that place, ill-lit by the one window only, was dark. He held his cup, stiff as a priest at an altar, thinking of nothing, allowing the murky dusk outside and his surprise at the letter to set a mood, but without using words to modify it. The dim space throve on his silence. Henry Shelton took a swig at his tea, half-emptying the mug.

' "Oh! she doth teach the torches to burn bright",' he said out loud, without much volume, but intensely, surprising himself. He found he was holding out his tea at the end of a straight arm, ridiculously.

He had quoted the line to Marion Meeks. She had laughed, but softly, self-admiringly, easily applying the compliment to herself. He was seventeen, still at school, and she, twenty-two or -three, worked in the office of an insurance firm. They had been walking in the

7

cold darkness of a wood, arms round each other, and she had been singing. He had spoken his words to match the clear delicacy of her voice.

'Who said that?' she had asked.

'Romeo.'

' "Romeo, Romeo! wherefore art thou Romeo?" '

That had deserved a kiss. They swayed in ferocity.

He replaced his mug, and opened the letter again, read it with scrupulous care, but made no more of it.

At the time Marion had been engaged. What was the man's name? Stephen? Stephen Slater, his father had kept a large greengrocer's, and he was an excellent cricketer, opened the innings for the town in the top division of the Border League, a big, graceful man with black hair. Why had she needed a schoolboy to embrace in the dark? She spoke of Steve with scorn, dismissing him. 'He can please his dead aunt,' she'd say. She invariably wore his ring, but did not marry him in the end. Slater had died a few years back, respected businessman, father, grandfather, taken to rest in God's garden.

It meant little now. Henry Shelton prepared himself for the football results. That seemed suitably decorous behaviour for a man of his age, especially one who had no interest and did

8

not fill in a pools coupon, to see the names, and the scores, and hear an educated voice, lifting for victory, slumping for defeat, raise hopes and dash them at the fag-end of Saturday afternoon.

Marion Meeks. He scratched his face.

They had met at a dance. She had chosen him in a ladies' excuse me. He invited her to a spinning quickstep, and at the end of the evening he had walked her home, as she lived not half a mile from him. She had made the pace, leading him a long detour across the common, amongst the gorse-bushes. He would not have dared to suggest this. In the dark she had pulled him in to kiss, quite wildly. Back home in his bedroom at midnight he had found his face daubed with her lipstick. His parents had gone to bed. Oddly, for them, they did not mind his staying out late, provided it was not too often, and he made no noise on his return. Marion had delighted and shocked him. She had unbuttoned her dress, guided his hand to her naked breast and then complained that his fingers were frozen.

'Still, that's the place to warm them,' she had said.

To him in what he now recognised as innocence, she seemed grown up, a woman, and this flaunting availability of her body unexpected. Strangely, they did not meet often, perhaps once a week, when she would name the venue and the night, usually a Thursday. He

9

arranged his homework so that the time was clear. When he asked why she needed him in this underhand way, she frowned, licked her lips, muttered, 'How about charity?'

In the end she had seduced him, slipping a note through his door commanding him round to her parents' home that Saturday evening at six-thirty. The old folks were away for the weekend. She had taken him up to her cold bedroom, invited him to play Adam and Eve with her. He remembered to this day his goose-flesh and the ripples of fear that flayed his back. They had clung together under her sheets, she manipulating him.

'Have you brought a french letter?' she had asked, bluntly in his groaning ecstasy.

'No.'

'Never mind. I've got some of Steve's. You can pinch one. He won't miss it.'

She had leapt out of bed, run naked downstairs, returned with her handbag. In the end it was she who had fitted his contraceptive, gently grumbling that he didn't know much.

'No,' he'd answered humbly.

'But you're a big boy, though,' she had said.

Marion had sent him home no later than ten-thirty, accompanying him to the back door clothed only in a dressing-gown. He remembered her naked feet pink on the red quarry-tiles of her kitchen floor.

The whole affair had lasted no more than three or four months. He had visited her home

10

only on one more occasion, and had walked out with her perhaps a further dozen times. Their meetings depended, he presumed, on the absence of her parents and Steve, and the freedom of her bed on the absence of all three. Just as suddenly as she had taken him up, she dropped him, announcing that she wasn't at home next week, but she'd let him know. A month later he received a postcard from Worcester, a view of the cathedral; it read, 'Have moved here. New, better job. Love M.'

They corresponded into the spring, when his exam-preparation and her lack of fervour put an end to it. It must have been the following winter when, on his first army leave, he had seen the photograph of her wedding in the newspaper. That meant she had been married from home, at St Mary's, her local church. In her letters she had made no reference to returning to Beechnall; her relationship with Steve, and with him, he considered ruefully, must have been killed off in the first week or two of her stay in Worcester.

He had no idea why she wanted to meet him again. Nor how she had found his present address. Henry could not be bothered to offer explanations to himself. Somewhere he had kept a photograph of her. He remembered her kisses, the skimpy underwear even in that cold winter, her superior air as she livened him, her genuine, or so it seemed now, affection for him. It mystified then, but was all too long ago to tinker with. He cooked and ate his supper in due course, took a turn up the black garden, merely to enjoy coming back in out of the fog.

Next morning at about ten o'clock, he received a telephone call from Helena Gough. He had finished his breakfast, washed up, tidied the room and was reading the review section of the *Observer*, undecided whether to accompany this with music from Classic FM.

'Mr Shelton? This is Helena Gough.'

'Yes. Hello.'

'I've got the right Mr Shelton?'

'I suppose so. Henry Shelton.'

'You knew my mother? Marion Meeks?'

'Yes. Over forty years ago.'

'Here in Beechnall?' Helena asked. She spoke clearly, with the accent of an educated Midlander.

'Yes. But for a few months only. In the winter of ... Oh. Early Fifties.'

'Before I was born. I'm thirty-eight.'

They chatted in this constrained, jerky way for five minutes before she invited him to Stansfield Road that afternoon for a cup of tea. Helena seemed to take it as very natural, but he felt bound to lodge an objection.

'I didn't know your mother all that well,' he said, grudgingly.

'She speaks of you with some affection.'

'We haven't been in touch for something like forty-two years.'

'Yes. Life's like that, isn't it?'

12

'You've no idea why your mother wishes to see me again?'

'She's back in England again. She was married twice. To Eric Blake, my father, and then later to Edward Ball, who lived in the United States. She lived there for thirteen years. But now Edward's died, she's back and has been for some time. And she'd like to make contact.'

'Your grandparents are dead, I take it.'

'Yes. For many years. And my mother's only sister died two years ago.'

Henry would have sworn that he had seen the woman in the last six months.

'There's the odd cousin about, I suppose.'

They both repeated the time, three-thirty, of the afternoon's reunion, so that there could be no possibility of error, when the woman rang cheerfully off. He returned gloomily to his newspaper. As usual, he had been too pliable, too polite. He did not want to meet this woman, nor could he see any advantage for him or anybody else. Sunday ought to be a day without shocks.

CHAPTER TWO

Henry Shelton walked out to Stansfield Road. The journey occupied twenty minutes along still-foggy streets. Mrs Gough's road seemed very like his own, built early in the first decade

13

of the century, without garages so that both sides were now lined with cars. He was glad he had left his in the garage-stable. Parking would have been impossible. Glancing at his watch, he found he was three minutes early so he retreated from No. 23, spending the time in examination of curtains and sooty, damp shrubs. Exactly at three-thirty he rang the front doorbell.

The summons was not promptly answered. He cleaned already clean soles on a doorscraper.

'Mr Shelton? Do come in.'

Helena Gough looked younger than her thirty-eight years as she stood in the narrow hallway. Perhaps that was a comment on his own age. She stood back to usher him into the front room, where a gas-fire already burned, relieved him of his coat, invited him to sit down. She immediately went out, presumably to hang up his anorak, but again kept him waiting for her return. Henry sat nervously listening to the hiss of the fire.

Helena appeared, and with a swift, silent movement closed the door. She perched on an armchair opposite him on the other side of the hearth.

'I'm glad you could come,' she said.

He nodded solemnly.

'My mother has spoken of you so many times lately.' This drew no reply from him. 'In the end I asked if she would like to meet you again. She had read your novel about Robin Hood.' A children's book, published twenty years ago, it had been recently reprinted. 'I saw your photograph in the paper, and my mother thought it might be the young man she knew. She's been quite seriously ill, pancreatitis, since she came back to England from America.'

'Does she live in Beechnall now?'

'No. She has a bungalow at Sutton-on-Sea. She settled there near a cousin. I was about to part from my husband. I've now divorced him, and I bought this house about eight months ago. The reason I'm talking to you now is that my mother is having a nap. She gets very tired.'

'How long has she been here? With you?'

'Six weeks.' Helena placed elegant hands on her knees. 'It was clear she couldn't go back home straight away. So here she is. They say she is cured, but she needs time. She's sixty-four.'

'Are you at home all day?' he asked.

'No. But I work close enough to call in at lunch-time.' She did not mention the nature of her work. 'It's company. For us both. Divorce saps your confidence. Are you married?'

'No.'

'Divorced?'

'A widower.'

She apologised. The room seemed to shake with heat. He felt positively dizzy.

'Let me make you a cup of tea,' she proposed.

'I'd prefer a glass of water, if you don't mind.'

'Lemonade? Orange?'

'Water, please.'

Henry sounded ungrateful, especially to an attractive woman. Again it took long enough for Helena to bring back the glass. Perhaps she had checked up on her mother.

'Are you still working, Mr Shelton?' she asked, after he'd taken his first sip.

'Yes. In the mornings only. I teach Latin in a private school.'

'Do many want to learn Latin these days?'

'Want to learn? That's a moot point. But you don't need expensive laboratories. A classroom, a blackboard, a book or two, pen and paper.'

'You sound defensive?' she suggested. He did not answer. 'Do any do Greek?'

'No. In small schools you have to make up a class of fifteen or more. There's no one-to-one teaching. They can't afford it.'

'Do you teach boys or girls?'

'Mostly girls.'

From the next room came a thin call of 'Hel, Helly'.

'That's my mother. She must have woken up.'

Again she left him on his own. He played with his glass and examined the room. The ceiling and walls had been recently painted, a bluish white, a cold choice in this heat. Five

16

water-colours, all cloudscapes, in off-white mounts with thin black frames. Henry walked across to look more carefully; they were originals, not prints, but unsigned. All seemed interesting, the one above the mantelpiece especially so. It showed wind-driven clouds over a dark-green, foam-touched sea and a pale beach divided roughly by low breakwaters. The sun shone and the sky was a hard blue in the spaces between the clouds. The sands were half-shadow, half-bright. No humans appeared. The light on the thin-running tide gleamed silver-pale. He wondered at the odd shapes of the clouds; one had an almost straight base. He guessed the season as early summer.

Helena opened the door quickly and quietly as he stood in front of the hearth.

'You'll scorch your shins,' she warned.

'I'm just admiring your pictures.'

'Do you like them?'

'Yes. Really interesting.' He coughed. 'Are you the artist?'

'No. My father. Eric Blake. He took it up after he and Marion parted. When he died, five years ago, he left me these pictures.'

'What did he do for a living?'

'He was a quantity surveyor.' She waited for further questions which did not come. 'I think my mother will be ready to see you now.' He inclined his head. 'I'll bring her in.'

Henry moved away from the fierce heat of

17

the fire, but remained standing. He recalled Marion, the violent young woman with the wet mouth, the searching hands, and wondered what he would find now.

Again the door opened, slowly this time, and Marion Ball eased her way in, guided from the crook of her arm by Helena. She walked upright and firmly, unlike a sick person, but stood at first just inside the room, partially excluding her daughter.

'Here's Mr Shelton,' Helena called in a bright, social voice.

'Henry.' Marion extended her hand. He stepped forward to grasp it. 'It's a long time. But I would have recognised you.'

He would not have recognised her, would have passed her in the street. The face seemed thin, lined, haggard with recent illness. Her hands were ugly, knotted, thickly spotted. She had dressed fashionably, as though she could afford the time and money, and in youthful colours, which suited her for she had not grown fat or shapeless.

'Let's sit down,' she said, pointing Henry to an armchair. She occupied the settee, queenly centre-stage. Helena hovered, still on her feet.

'How long is it since you last met?' Helena asked. Henry calculated.

'Forty-two years.'

'Is it as long ago as that?' Marion said. She seemed to be searching round herself for a handkerchief, a tissue she had dropped. 'Yes, it

18

must be.'

'Mother saw some reference to you in the local newspaper. That was before she was ill.' Helena waited, but Marion did nothing to help her out. 'I think it was about a play you'd written for television.'

'Radio,' he corrected.

'Was it? About Blake, the poet and painter. That was my single name.'

Marion stirred.

'Both my husbands had the same initials. Eric Blake and Edward Ball. Eric was Helena's father.' She jerked up fiercely. 'They both died the same year. That's five years ago, now. I'd been divorced from Eric a good period.'

'I was fourteen at the time,' Helena said.

'Were you? I thought you were younger.'

Helena now sat opposite Henry, her skirt high on her elegant crossed legs. She questioned him about the play, about his present writing, about the rewards. During the cross-examination, which went on too long for his liking, the mother sat back on the settee, upright but uncomfortably, as if she was in pain. She interrupted only once to croak, 'I always knew you'd make a name for yourself.'

He nodded, smiled in her direction. Marion was as uninterested in the conversation as he was. She perhaps had the life knocked out of her by illness, and could not make the effort. To him nowadays talk of his writing grew boring after a sentence or two; he did not

19

understand his industry at sitting down at a table arranging words, ideas, sorting himself out into fictional characters.

Helena bore the brunt of talking. She described a friend who wrote verse and novels and this led, easily enough, for she spoke with an interesting clarity, about her own attempts at water-colour painting. Her father had sent her a book on the subject, some sheets of Bockingford paper, four brushes, ten tubes of paint and a small Dutch palette with five round and five oblong mixing spaces.

'It seemed little enough,' she said.

'I didn't know Eric had any interest in painting,' Marion grumbled.

Helena pointed to the pictures on the wall.

'And he did those?' Marion asked stupidly.

'Yes. And the one in the middle room over the fireplace, and those three in your bedroom.'

'Bedroom? You know, I hadn't noticed them. I wonder if that's typical of me? Or Eric, painting pictures nobody noticed?' Her face for the first time grew animated.

'Why do you say that, Mother?'

'Why? That's why.'

Mrs Ball's face set itself again into grey concrete. She leaned forward, sighing heavily.

'Did you write when you knew my mother?' Helena, determined to make an occasion of the meeting.

'Poems. Short stories.'

20

'Were they any good?'

'I doubt it.'

'Were they published?'

'In the school, and then college, magazines.'

'Have you never gone back to them, reread them?'

'No. Emphatically not.'

Helena sat straight, pulling a comical face at the strength of his denial.

'Can you remember any one line from your poems?'

Henry thought, arms dangling suddenly apelike.

'Yes,' he said. 'One. "Religion plus Victorian sentiment plus Una".'

'Is that it?'

'I'm afraid so.'

'Why have you remembered it, rather than any of the others?'

'I've no idea.'

'Who was Una?'

'A name I took. I didn't know any girl of that name. Nor do I remember what the poem was about.'

'Why have you remembered that particular line?'

'Not a clue. Certainly not for its merit as poetry.'

Henry felt he had answered honestly, and Helena pressed him no more. She now encouraged her mother to talk about her periods of residence in the United States with

21

her second husband, Edward Ball. Marion loved the people, and the great distances, she said. She spoke with enthusiasm for a sentence or two, and then drifted into hesitation as if she had not retained enough physical strength to vocalise more words. This feebleness belied the smartness of her dress, the sheer tights, sheen of shoes, the elaborate coiffure. She held her hands in her lap, palms upward. Her most lively movement was to lick her lips.

Helena spoke now of a trip to Stratford where she had seen *Love's Labour's Lost*, which had considerably intrigued her. It seemed neither here nor there, she said. She went on, fearing silence, to describe her attempts to make her house comfortable.

'It's a bit of a comedown,' Marion grumbled. 'After your last.'

Helena smiled, by no means put out.

'I was unhappy there. At least, for a time.'

Neither woman offered more information. Henry now felt uncomfortable. Helena seemed to preside, not wanting her own way, but willing to nurture and support theirs once they knew what it was. They offered nothing apart from some by-play with a handkerchief from Marion.

'You met at a dance?' Helena asked, harassed at last by their silence.

'Yes,' Henry answered. 'We were taught dancing in the sixth form, and now and then I tried to put the lessons into public practice.'

'Was he good?' Helena asked her mother.

'I think so. He didn't trample on my toes. We whirled round, if I remember. It was ballroom dancing. And then he escorted me home.'

'Romance,' the daughter said sarcastically.

'I don't know about that. I was engaged to another man.'

'My father?'

'No. I didn't know Eric then.'

'And where was he? Did he dance?'

'Not on these nights. Was it Thursday? He attended some sort of snooker or billiards competition. Nothing could interrupt that. He was very good at sport.'

'But not at dancing?'

'Oh, he was light enough on his feet. When he wanted to be.' Marion stroked her forehead, as if massaging ideas into being. 'Henry was different. He could talk to you.' She stared across, none too friendly.

'What did he talk about, Mother?'

'Poets. Music. There was no stopping him sometimes. He seemed to know a great deal. He wasn't like other people. He told me about Virgil, and Milton. You see,' she spoke accusingly at Henry, 'I haven't forgotten.'

He lowered his head, touched.

'Do you read Virgil now?' Helena asked him.

'No. I mean I have to read pieces of the *Aeneid* or the *Georgics* with some of my pupils. But never at home. For my own pleasure.'

23

The talk idled on for another half-hour, Helena leaving her elders to embark on new topics. They did so awkwardly. The fire hissed loudly as if in disapprobation. In the end Henry Shelton shuffled to his feet, saying he would detain them no longer. The women seemed unsurprised. He invited them to visit him, to high tea, or lunch on Saturday or Sunday. Helena said they would be delighted, but that they could not decide at the moment on account of her mother's medical appointments, which might well change. She would, she promised, give him a ring.

Henry moved across to shake hands with Marion Ball. Helena had left the room. The mother took his hand in both of hers, and smiled, wrinkling her eyes.

'You haven't changed all that much,' she said.

'I'm glad we could meet again,' he lied, but bent to kiss her cheek. Her eyes were dull and bloodshot.

'I liked the way you used to tell me things.'

'About the poets?'

'Yes. And about yourself. But you were too young. I couldn't wait all that while to be married.'

She shook her head. He wished her goodbye. Out in the passageway Helena waited, smartly shook hands, said she would phone as soon as she had sorted matters out.

'It will have done her good,' she concluded,

24

ushering him quickly into the foggy street. 'Don't get cold.' She closed the door quietly but with speed.

CHAPTER THREE

Henry Shelton shut the last exercise book, glad to be done but pleased with the work he had marked this Sunday evening.

The little dears, twelve—thirteen now, had completed the final revision exercises after one term's Latin. They had bothered to learn what he had taught them, and put the rules correctly into practice. In many ways the class seemed grown up beyond their years, tall, some with well-formed bosoms, shapely legs, womanly behinds, but in Latin lessons they were children again, would soon begin to face wide-eyed the complications of the third declension, hanging trustfully on to his clear instructions, liable to tears if he corrected them over-harshly in public. In other words a good class. He had lost nobody so far. How long they would persist with the ever-growing lists of irregularities he did not know, but in the ten, eleven weeks so far he had not put them off.

He packed their books into a briefcase, ready for the Monday morning rush.

He had heard nothing from Helena Gough about the invitation to lunch. Perhaps his visit to them had counted as a disappointment. He had received the impression that Marion Ball would stay with her daughter at least until the New Year. He put their name on his Christmas card list.

Marion had lacked all sparkle. He would have passed her, smart clothes and all, in the street without a second glance. The energetic young woman who had seduced him, tumbled him naked into her bed, kissed him with tongue and violence in the cold woods, had no connection with this dull widow. There was no resemblance in the voice; he thought some pattern of intonation might have been preserved there, but it was not so. She had knocked about the world too long, in the US, in Canada, in Worcester, Bristol, Manchester, Lancaster, Sutton-on-Sea. Perhaps if she had written to him he would have recognised the handwriting. That invariably amazed him; old gentlemen wrote exactly now as they had in their late youth. He did so himself.

Helena Gough had been attractive, though quite unlike the younger Marion, but she had no interest in him, her mother's old flame. She had picked him out of her mum's boring snippets of conversation, a blunted point of interest, had ticked him off, raked him in and now regretted it.

The invitation had disturbed him because it had roused memories of the seventeen-year-old boy entangled beyond expectation with a passionate woman, one who made no pretence of hiding her feelings, her sexual energies, her demands from him. She had snatched him up from his school-desk, his books and rugby football and had dragged him into another world, mode of emotion without so much as a by-your-leave, and then after a month or two had walked away from it all to Worcester. He had, he considered, never recovered. The initiation had been both too easy and too intense. Why she had found him so attractive he had never fathomed. Fine, he had shared her with Steve Slater, that athletic cricketer, but that was part of the deal, all determined by her. That was the attraction, moreover. She was no virginal ideal, but a woman who flaunted her sex, who did not keep herself intact until she married, but shared her favours out wantonly with two men, both of whom she dropped in due course. He saw it, then and now, as a time when the rules, the provincial conventions of love were deliberately ignored and flouted, when a woman led him where no woman should, had lifted him into an ecstasy beyond price.

And now she was a smartly dressed skeleton with barely a word to offer him.

What did he expect? Marion Meeks had been for years a changing figure in his imagination, a goddess, not a sexually enlightened secretary trying her hand, if that was the word, at cradle-snatching. She would

27

be more important to him than he to her because she was his first. In these secret months he had still kept up his courtship of a girl at school, two years below him. They met at socials, school dances, kissed, held hands. Sometimes he fondled the clothes over her breasts, and sometimes Sylvia allowed it, sometimes not. They walked home together on occasion, or sat close on the bus when she had strolled the half-mile to his stop. He did not mention Marion to her. By the end of his second year in the sixth form they had each, though not without pain, taken new partners.

Sylvia Cross of Crossley Street. He had not seen or heard of her since he left school. He wondered what sort of showing she had made of her life. She had taken science in the sixth form with the idea of training as a pharmacist. What would he have to say to her?

Henry often took a turn in the streets in the evening, even though it was dark. He rarely met anyone he knew, did not call on friends, or drop into the local pub, merely walked, peeking into cracks in drawn curtains, or at bushes in front gardens. Even as late as this in the year, and as cold, one or two roses bloomed still, miscoloured in the amber streetlights. As he walked, not quickly, he turned over in his mind the next episode of the book he was writing. He found this enjoyable, for he had no final decisions to make, merely to consider alternatives, or decide when and how he should set about the next necessary snippet of research.

A man strolled past.

'Henry Shelton, isn't it?'

Henry turned. The man, darkened in the street light, was unrecognisable.

'I can remember you when you were a demon fast bowler.'

'That must be long enough ago,' Henry answered.

'I've seen you about here several times, and I've thought to myself, "That's Henry Shelton. I'm sure it is. I'll speak to him one of these nights." So now.'

'You have the advantage of me,' Henry said.

'You don't know me, do you? I was at school with you.' The man gave him a second chance, directing the beam of a torch he had taken from his pocket upwards at his face. The result was extraordinary; the shadowed human features became an ugly caricature, a mask, a shot from a horror-film. Henry did not answer.

'Naylor. Ted Naylor.'

'My eyes aren't good in this light.'

'No. We're none of us as young as we once were.' Naylor's voice had a Midland twang. 'I come up this way to visit my mother. She lives on her own.'

'She must be a good age?'

'Ninety-three. And spry. You should hear her when we suggest she ought to have a flat or move into one of these warden-aided complexes. "I've lived here sixty-eight years," she says, "and I'll die here." They moved in when they were first married. It's where I was born. And I'm thinking of retiring next year when I'm sixty. I'm manager of Redgate's, the wood-yard in Basford.'

'Have you always worked there?'

'No. The last twenty-three years.'

'Will you be glad to go?'

'Go? Yes and no. I haven't made my mind up yet. I'm on top of the job, though the recession has made it harder. But I'm not afraid of graft. The question is: What shall I do? The wife has ideas, and the children are all away now, but I'm not sure. We shall see. Have you finished?'

'I do some part-time teaching at a private school.'

Henry remembered Naylor, E.M. at school, a quiet boy, always on the edge of everything, a grudging creature, toadying to masters and bullies alike, too nondescript to be bothered with, always there, following his own devious road. In the 'A' form of their grammar-school year, he'd manage good examination results, but would not consider staying on into the sixth form, would have disappeared into the world of commerce. The masters would have condemned this as the waste of a good brain, but would not have struggled very hard to encourage him to continue with his studies; he was not that sort of boy.

'I've seen your photograph in the papers

from time to time. Do you live about here?'

Henry offered the name of his street, tentatively.

'Oh. Some nice houses there. If I remember right. I live a bit further on. Stansfield Road. Do you know it?'

'I visited some people there quite recently.'

'Who'd that be?'

'A Mrs Gough. And her mother.'

'Gough? Gough?'

'At number twenty-three.'

'I think I know who you mean. A good-looking young woman with one of these blond, page-boy haircuts. Drives a smart, blue car. Don't know her to speak to. She's newish. Ours is a street of shifting population. She looks a cut above it.'

Shelton offered no comment, so that Naylor edged closer, head forward.

'I often think of the old days at school. I shall be sixty next year,' he said. 'I've been left forty-four, -five years. Doesn't seem it. And I wonder what happened to some of them.'

'There's an Old Boys' Society,' Henry interjected.

'After I did my National Service I swore to myself I wouldn't join a bloody Christmas Club, never mind anything else. I saw "Whacker" Crewe the other day in town. Looked very smart with an attractive wife.'

'What does he do?'

'No idea. I didn't get the chance to speak to

him. Dirty bastard he was at school, if you'll excuse my French. But grey hair now, neat moustache, kid gloves. "By God," I thought to myself, "you've come a long way."' Naylor smirked, rubbed the back of his hand along wet lips. 'Are you married?'

'Not now,' Henry answered.

'Divorced, eh?'

'No. I'm a widower.'

Naylor pulled a sympathetic face.

'And his friend, Whacker's, Conrad Powell. Very pale boy, white skin. He's in prison. And do you know what for?' Naylor waited his time.

'No.'

'He murdered his wife. Four or five years ago. You'd think at that time of life he'd be past the dangerous stage. It was in all the papers.'

'I didn't see it.'

'No, you poets wouldn't. It was down south somewhere. Portsmouth. I knew his wife slightly. In fact, I went out with her a time or two. Joyce Twells.' The name meant nothing to Shelton. 'Joyce Berenice Twells. Unusual. That's what drew my attention, in the first place. Berenice. Powell had been fooling around with some younger woman. His secretary.'

'What was her name?'

'I can't remember that. What do you think I am, the Memory Man?' He spoke with

32

exasperation, which melted as he reached his climax. 'I shall have to push on, or my wife will be murdering me. Or thinking about it. Nice to have met you again.'

They did not shake hands. Naylor sidled away as Shelton stepped back. Naylor coughed at length as he walked off.

To be remembered as a fast bowler at cricket was unexpected. In the darkness he whirled his bowling arm round. He could just about do it, though what he'd manage with a ball he could not guess. He grinned, mirthlessly, settled himself to his usual methodical pace. Few cars or pedestrians disturbed him. He examined a crumbling front wall, stopped outside a house where the television banged over-loud from behind closed curtains, watched a cat crouch by a front door, decided the fog was thinner.

He had turned into his front gate, and was fiddling in his pocket for the door-key, when a woman's voice hailed him.

'Where have you been at this time of night?'

He recognised the voice, that of Jennifer Speed, who quite well knew his habit of walking round the streets.

'Constitutional,' he called, continuing to unlock the door. Jennifer pushed through the gate, closed it, approached him, heels clicking.

'I was just going down to the beer-off,' she explained. 'I've run out of ciggies.'

'Are you coming in?' he asked.

She followed him through the door.

'That's better,' she said, slamming it shut. 'Keep the night out. I could do with a bit of company.'

'Isn't there anything good on the telly?'

'If there is, I haven't noticed it.'

Jennifer Speed, in her thirties, was short, round, stoutly handsome, with cropped hair. As she removed her coat he noticed that her dress was too tight, too low-cut at the front. Her well-shaped calves gleamed in sheer tights.

'God, it's cold,' she said.

'Put more clothes on.'

'I'm not proposing to hang round the street corners.' Her full face, with its large pale eyes, assumed an air of mischief. She ran a plump hand through her hair with determined ferocity. As she moved, her round breasts bounced.

'Coffee?' he asked. 'Or gin?'

'How about both? It's a bad night.'

He pointed at the bottles, having flicked open the cabinet door.

'Help yourself.'

He closed the curtains quietly before moving into the kitchen. When he returned with the coffee she had turned on the gas-fire, made herself at home in one of the armchairs, her gin and tonic on the nest of tables on her right. He put her cup alongside. She had set him a drink, he noticed.

'I didn't expect to see you,' she said. 'I thought you spent Sunday marking

34

exercise books.'

'Work complete.'

Jennifer drew her short frock higher to expose her shapely, large legs to the heat of his gas-fire. She massaged her thighs with both hands, paying no attention to Henry.

'That's better,' she said, kicking off her high-heeled shoes and holding her feet comically towards the hearth. 'I'll say this for you: you do know how to keep yourself warm.'

'What are you doing out?' he asked.

'I told you, search for tobacco.'

'Try again. You can buy cigarettes rather nearer home than this.'

'I was fed up,' she said, almost hesitantly. 'But not for my usual reasons: nothing happening in slow time. They fetched me out to see a corpse.'

'Who? Where? When?' He tried to trivialise it.

'This morning. A few doors up. An old man. He'd been there for three or four months.'

'Where was he? In bed?'

'In an armchair. He was dried up.'

'Suicide?'

'They don't know yet, but they think he just died.'

'What about neighbours? Hadn't they heard or seen anything?'

'They thought he was away.'

Jennifer now massaged her thighs with long, smooth strokes from crotch to knee to calf.

'And how was he discovered?'

'A daughter came down. She hadn't been able to make contact by phone, she said. She hadn't tried very hard. But she happened to be this way, couldn't get in, asked round the neighbours, got one of them to climb in with a ladder. And they found him.'

'And how did you come into the act?'

'I'm connected in their minds with hospitals and social work, so they sent for me.'

'Did you know the old man?'

'No. Can't ever remember seeing him. Bit of a recluse.'

'Wasn't there a bad smell?'

'No more than usual, apparently.'

'And it upset you?'

'I did all the right things for them, police and so forth. The neighbours were old and dithery, and his daughter half-daft. The young man who'd climbed in for a start, and actually found the body, was in a state. He's a nervous case, anyway. But it wasn't pretty, the corpse. Not human. It did me no good. So I thought I'd come round this way. I might even have knocked on your door, though I knew you wouldn't be pleased if you were marking books. But I might have risked it. And, then, there you were in the street.'

'There'll be an inquest?' Henry said.

'Certainly. Though this sort of undiscovered death is more common than you'd imagine. No milkman; he fetched his own when he wanted it. There was a great pile of free newspapers and junk mail inside the door, but that couldn't be seen from outside. The windows weren't too filthy; quite a few others dirtier. This weather neither the old man nor his neighbours went out, so it was nothing new not to see each other for days on end. People don't bother. They're not even curious.'

Jennifer sipped her coffee. A spasm crossed her face.

'But the sight of him.'

'Was he dressed?'

'Yes. He had a top coat on. And a cap. He must have been on the point of going out. But, ugh, the face and the hands. Dried and shrunken. I didn't stand staring, I can tell you.'

'But he sat naturally?'

'Slumped in the chair.'

'Couldn't he be seen from outside?'

'If anybody had looked. But his back gate would have been locked and bolted to keep intruders out. And it's a darkish room. I'm used to seeing people in trouble, but this, in his cloth cap. His glasses were on the ground; they must have fallen off. And he had his gloves ready on the table.'

'You didn't know him.'

'No. Not at all.'

Jennifer pulled down her skirt, then stroked her chin with her left hand.

'How are you keeping?' she asked.

'Fine. For an old man.'

'Ready for Christmas?'

'Ready for anything.'

Henry looked across at her. She had now regained her composure, but sat neatly for a heavy woman, with a kind of prettiness. She drummed on her chair arm with the bent fingers of her left hand, as if seriously considering some matter.

'I don't see much of you these days,' she began.

'No. I'm busy. End-of-term tests. Reports. Parents' evenings.'

'You're only half-time.'

'Makes no difference. The school expects me there in the evening.'

'Don't know why you do it.'

'Make ends meet.'

He had retired from full-time teaching in the education department of the polytechnic some four years ago. He had not much liked the job, and his visits to schools to oversee students had been a farce, so that when in the course of one of the college's many reorganisations the authorities had offered him advantageous terms on which to retire, he had not hesitated. He was a widower, without children, healthy, not short, with private means. He would make the most of his life while he could, travel the world, revel in sunshine or culture.

It had not worked out that way.

Three times he had visited Italy, and then Athens twice, once Jerusalem. He had taken

Jennifer to the Costa Brava for a fortnight where they had bathed, eaten, drunk, squabbled, made love. They had judged it good, but had only once repeated the venture. She had one evening told him that he had forgotten how to enjoy himself, and this had seemed not unjust.

She had finished her coffee and now toyed with her gin.

'This afternoon,' she said, and stopped.

'Well?' He usually had no need to encourage her.

'I was lost. I'd no end of things to do for next week. I was glad, because it would take my mind, I thought, off that ghastly corpse. I did them all, filled in my forms, shopped in the supermarket, prepared lists, cleaned through the whole house, and at the end of it I was just as fazed.'

'Good word,' he said.

'Bollocks to you. I thought I'd seen it all. Old people dying, deserted, cold, braving it out, caving in. But that brown-faced horror this morning. It didn't look human. More like a guy some kids had knocked together for the bonfire. It got at me. You never manage to come to terms with everything, but this was ... I don't know, different. It made me wonder if I was coming to the end of my tether. So I walked down your street. That wasn't sensible; you'd be inside and busy so that I shouldn't see you. But I did something. I didn't sit at home

39

horrifying myself.'

'No.' Henry sounded sympathetic.

'And I saw you. In the street just going in at the front gate. I ran down. I pelted, and I called out. It must have been my lucky day. You heard me.'

Jennifer Speed took a gulp at her gin.

'Ah,' she said, eloquently. 'Ah.'

'Have you been working too hard?' Henry asked.

'I suppose so.' She slapped her belly. 'I don't know how I can chase about so much, and carry all this flab.' She laughed out loud as if she'd come to terms with her vicissitudes.

'Help yourself to more gin,' he advised.

'I'll be drunk.'

'Ah, Speed, Speed. You're a puritan.' He had at one time called her by her surname when they made love. She approved. It acknowledged her status, she said.

'A case for the psychiatrists. Are you flattered that I decided just to walk past your house?'

'Touching the hem of my garment?'

That seemed wasted on her, but she rose, helped herself at the gin-bottle.

'I envy you and your Latin,' she said. 'A nice little subject, all the rules pretty well fixed; decent pupils from good homes; not too many in the class. All manageable.'

'It compares well with your daily capers?'

'It's driving me cracked. If I stayed twice as

long, I'd still be behind. There's no solving my problems.' She worked for social services, and was attached to the University Hospital. Jennifer was a bold woman, spoke her mind to superiors or clients alike, but she acted always with reason, could recognise a brick wall without a gate when she saw it. Henry had always believed that she relished the impossibilities of her job, that she could put aside her failures stoically. He had not realised that her work exacted such a toll. In his mind she had appeared a winner, more successful than her colleagues, and with her success duly recognised and without envy.

He walked across, sat on the side of her chair, put an arm across her shoulder. She did not respond at once but took another sip of her gin and began slowly to cry. He pulled her head into his lap.

After a time she sat up, dabbed her eyes, tried to grin.

'I'm sorry,' she said. 'I don't know what's come over me.' He stood, now, looking away. 'It's a bastard.'

'Life?'

'Everything.' She cleared her glass. 'I'm glad you're here, Henry.'

He felt ashamed.

'I don't know,' he answered. 'I've neglected you.'

Jennifer stood, threw her arms round him. He could smell the gin.

41

'Squeeze me,' she begged. 'Squash it out of me.'

He attempted it. They rocked together by the hearth, she so much the shorter.

'Be good to me,' she begged.

This was her euphemism for 'make love'. Even as he hugged her, his lips locking on hers, he wondered where the sentence had originated. She used it only in moments of importance.

He feared for her.

CHAPTER FOUR

'You don't consider full-time teaching?' the headmaster asked Henry, not for the first time.

'No, thanks. I'm nearly fifty-nine.'

'You don't look it, or act like it. If I could fill the rest of your day with a bit of English teaching, it would exactly suit my book. You know something about your subject, Mr Shelton, unlike these young women we take on. They're either decorative or dowdy, but between them they can't distinguish a comma from a colon. God knows what they learn these days at universities. So you see...'

'No, thanks.'

Henry stopped both the proposition and the flow of the headmaster's criticisms. He liked Arthur Kinglake, but had no intention of altering his way of life to oblige the man.

They were standing on the terrace outside the Victorian mansion where Kinglake's school was housed and stared down in misty winter sunshine at the dull stretch of lawn and the cherry trees doubly terraced below them.

Kinglake was perhaps ten years younger than Henry, a chemistry graduate, who had inherited this house from his grandfather, together with a substantial sum of money for its upkeep, and had decided with his wife, who taught at the primary level, to open a private school. This must have been nearly twenty years ago, and the experiment had prospered. 'Value for money' was the Kinglake motto, and, in spite of the times, he had done well. Now, with prices low, he had recently bought the place next door, another Victorian sprawl, to house the overflow of pupils. People were willing to pay to have their children trained to leap through acceptable educational hoops, to speak clearly and to be able to walk about inside a building without wrecking it.

'Good plain cooking here,' Kinglake told Henry Shelton, in whom he sometimes confided. 'This GCSE suits us to the ground because we'll see to it that they labour on, spend and be spent, fill in their folders and then have it properly marked and brought up to scratch. It's not the children, nor the parents who are to blame if anything goes wrong; it's the teachers.' He adopted an oratorical pose.

'Are they able? Not always. Brilliant? Never. Knowledgeable? Rarely. But as long as they're conscientious, and put the time in at home as well as at school, then that suits this type of student.'

'That's me. A dull dog,' Henry chaffed him.

'You're the exception. Old and shy and super-efficient. That's why I want you in more often.'

'If I taught longer, I'd do it less well.'

'I doubt that. But think about it, will you?'

'I've already done so.'

Kinglake sighed, immediately immersed in some other scheme, wasting no time on the impossible. Henry admired the man, cynically hoped that there would always be enough parents dissatisfied with the state system to fill his classrooms and keep him solvent. True, he paid below state levels to the part-time teachers: he knew who taught well and dismissed those who fell below his standards; he was not particularly kind to those who took time off for illness, but he was an excellent planner, and worked to draw favourable publicity towards his school. Not a cultured man, he occasionally read a novel recommended by the reviewers in the posh Sundays, and took his wife, an equivalent level-head, now and again to the theatre or a concert.

Mrs Kinglake appeared as Henry moved towards the gate. She led a troupe of perhaps twenty of the smallest children, boys and girls, smart in their uniforms, two by neat two in their crocodile, smiling not talking. He guessed they were on the way to a PE class in the house next door.

'Good-afternoon, Mr Shelton,' Sarah Kinglake called across. It must be after midday.

'Good-afternoon, Mrs Kinglake,' he returned. 'There must be easier ways of earning a living.'

She did not answer his pleasantry. The pupils looked wide-eyed at him but continued to march. There were at least five Indians or Pakistanis, and two handsome Jamaicans walking tall but saying not a word. They advanced towards the back of the building and disappeared through a gate in the dividing wall. Sarah Kinglake instilled the ethos of the school into them without trouble, and early. She walked silent as a nun now, and the little ones copied her. The pattern of the school was revealed.

He made his way home. The postman had called; he picked up the mail. His publishers had accepted two children's books he had submitted, one about a seaside holiday in Normandy, the other about a flight in a helicopter over the city. Their terms seemed acceptable, and they canvassed his ideas about illustrations. He felt pleased as he warmed up the remains of yesterday's beef casserole, cooked frozen peas and broad beans, decided against potatoes. He liked these small decisions and ate with relish because he was hungry. He had washed up, and was halfway through the correction of a Latin exercise when the doorbell rang. Annoyed, for he had forced himself to sit down immediately so that the rest of his afternoon and evening would be free, he placed a red tick beside *Caesar Gallis obsides imperavit*, 'Caesar ordered the Gauls to give hostages', and went without hurry towards the front door hoping the double-glazing salesman or religious proselytiser would have lost heart. The bell pealed vigorously again as he turned into the hall. Through the glass panes he could make out a woman's shape.

Frowning he jerked the door open.

'I thought you might be at home,' the woman said. 'You told me you only worked in the morning.'

Helena Gough. He invited her in.

'I'm not interrupting anything, am I?'

'The correction of Latin sentences.' He led her towards his table.

She picked up the book to read out, ' "The sun was so hot that the soldiers envied the fishes which were swimming in the river." What's the Latin for hot?'

'*Calidus.*'

She refused a drink, but sat at the table fiddling with the book, as if it held some fascination for her.

46

'Are these GCSE candidates?'

'They are.'

'I won't keep you long.' He lowered his head. 'My mother's been taken back into hospital, and I wonder if I could persuade you to visit her.'

He looked suitably puzzled.

'She seemed to be so much better when you came to see us. But then she collapsed one day when I was out at work, and they took her back immediately.'

'What's the trouble?'

'Cancer. Of the pancreas. There's nothing much they can do for her. They don't give her very long; she's so weak.'

'How long?'

'They won't, or can't say, but it's days rather than weeks. And she mentions you. She was looking forward to coming here to visit you. She would like to see you again. She's very poorly. I don't stay long with her.'

'When do you go?'

'In the evening. Soon after seven. I'm at work all day.'

They arranged that she should pick him up at seven-fifteen. He was not best pleased, because it meant he wasted another free evening, but his delight at the publishers' letter had left him generous. Helena slipped away almost immediately. Why was she not at work? Perhaps she had a flexible lunch hour, or could dodge out for half an hour. He returned to exercises on the dative case.

By seven o'clock he was ready, with a suit and a bunch of bought chrysanthemums, but Helena did not arrive until seven-thirty. She made no excuses for herself, merely remarking that her mother would enjoy the flowers. Marion ate little at all these days. In the car Helena appeared preoccupied, spoke only briefly.

The hospital was hot, as the pair used the lift, traipsed the short yards of rectangular corridor. Marion Ball occupied a single room. A nurse busied herself near the bed, though the visitors could not make out what she was doing.

'Hello, Marion. Are you awake?' the nurse called, straightening. 'You've somebody come to see you.'

The patient opened her eyes.

'Hello, Mother,' Helena said. 'I brought Mr Shelton.' Then, without pause, to the nurse. 'How is she?'

'Much the same.' In a louder voice, 'You're doing nicely, aren't you, love? I'll leave you to it now.'

She scuttled from the room.

Helena bent to kiss her mother, and signalled Henry forward. He bent, brushed her cheeks with his lips. For a second he smelt her sour breath. Marion moved her head from one to the other.

'Have you had a good day?' Helena asked.

48

'Yes, thank you.' There was no power, but the wasted face attempted to smile.

'Mr Shelton's brought you some flowers. Aren't they beautiful? I'll get a vase from somewhere. You talk to Mr Shelton.'

Helena took the chrysanthemums which he was holding rather stupidly upside down in front of him, and went out.

He smiled at Marion without response.

'How are you today?' he tried.

She made some murmur of an answer which he could not understand.

'Are you comfortable?' She made an indecipherable noise. Now and then she tried to open her eyes more widely. The conversation proceeded thus. With long pauses between, he asked questions and she murmured in reply. It seemed to him both unsatisfactory and yet all he could expect. He groped for further banal variations. Finally as he stated that this was a pleasant room, she made no reply. She was asleep.

Relieved he looked round the place, four-square, clean, blinds closed. Henry sat for a further ten minutes, though it seemed longer, before Helena returned, carrying his chrysanthemums in a glass vase which she placed on a tall locker away from the bed.

'She's asleep,' Henry said. Helena glanced across and raised her eyebrows, before slightly shifting the vase.

'I don't think she's in much pain,' Helena

instructed him. 'She's just worn out. I've been talking to the sister. It was terribly painful at first, I understand, but not now. Unless of course they're drugging her up to the eyes.' Helena was straightening the already tidy bedclothes, marching about, surveying her handiwork from the end of the bed. It seemed a nervous procedure, contradicting the elegance of her clothes. Marion, sheets up to her chin, lay, a bony caricature. The wrinkled parchment skin stretched yellow; her hair, thin and disordered, seemed dead already; the clawlike fingers hid under the bedclothes. 'She's uncomfortable, I guess. They're afraid of bedsores, which are very painful. She's hardly any flesh on her.' Helena went on to sketch the speed of her mother's decline. She sat down. 'Her constitution must be strong, for her to last like this.' She bounced to her feet, leaned over the body, and asked, almost fiercely, 'Are you awake, Mother?', then jovially, 'This is a fine way to go on. Mr Shelton comes specially to see you, and all you do is to drop off.' The patient did not stir. 'Oh, well, if that's how you want it.'

'Is she sometimes livelier than this?' he asked Helena, who had seated herself again.

'Not these last few days. She just lies there. She might take a sip of water, or one of these iced things to suck. I don't know how she hangs on.' She watched her mother, not a sign of emotion on her face, her fingers locked

50

together. Suddenly she smiled over at Henry, and called out, 'Are you going to wake up, Mother?' She kept her voice low. 'We're wasting our time here, I'm afraid. We'll give her another five minutes, and then we'll go.' The time dragged. The visitors did not speak; occasionally the daughter touched her mother's hand and Helena finally broke the silence with a question, unanswered, to her mother. She then stood, went over to the bedside cupboard, exchanged towels, nightgowns, flannels, jamming the dirty washing rather angrily into a bag, which she zipped up. Again she opened the cupboard doors to make a second check. She leaned forward over the bed.

'Now then, Mrs Ball, are you going to say anything to us?' No answer. 'Right, then, we might as well shove off.' Her words voiced anger or disappointment.

Henry stood up slowly. Helena bent to kiss her mother and smooth yet again the perfection of the bedclothes. He did nothing. They stepped out into the corridor, stopped at the nurses' room. Helena tapped. A young girl poked her head round the edge.

'She's asleep. Mrs Ball. Is there anything she needs?'

'I don't think so.'

'You'll let me know if there is any change for the worse?'

'Yes.'

Helena expressed muted thanks, the liveliness knocked out of her. She said nothing in corridors, lift, foyer and only when they were outside walking across to the ill-lit car-park did she remark on the weather.

In the car she sat tapping the steering wheel, drumming up something to say. She failed to find it, and drove off. They exchanged pitifully few words, as if both were enervated by the visit. Outside his house, he invited her in for a cup of coffee, and was surprised at her acceptance.

She sat straight, in front of his hearth, large coffee cup in her hands.

'That was a waste of time,' she began, still uncomfortable.

'You don't know. Though she looked half-asleep, she recognised us. She even made an attempt to talk.'

'They don't think she'll last long. I had a word or two with the sister when I was out chasing that vase up. They don't know, but she said she'd be surprised if she saw the week out. She's gone down very fast. Just over a week ago she was getting along nicely and they were thinking about sending her home after the New Year. Then suddenly ...' She snapped her finger and thumb ferociously in the air, leaving the cup steady in her left hand. 'My guess is she hadn't a great deal of resistance. But she's only sixty-four. That's no sort of age these days.'

'No. Had she always been something of an

invalid?' he asked.

'In the best of health. She wasn't ill when you knew her?'

'No. Not at all. I didn't know her for long. Four months or so. But she was full of life.'

Helena looked hard at him. She sat smartly straight, her hair shining, her clothes well cut, her shoes excellent.

'I hope you don't mind my asking this,' she said. 'How old are you?'

'Fifty-nine,' Henry answered, surprised. 'Nearly.'

'So you'd be five years or so younger than she was?'

'Yes.'

Helena frowned at the surface of her coffee. 'You'd be young, wouldn't you?'

'Seventeen,' he said, checking in his mind.

'And still at school?'

'Yes.'

'She left? Went to live somewhere else?'

'Worcester.'

'Didn't you hear from her? Didn't you write?'

'For a short time. And then it tailed away. I had exams that year.' It sounded weak enough. 'And she got married.'

'Did you go to the wedding?'

'No. I saw a photograph in the local paper some time afterwards. She must have come back home for the ceremony. But we weren't in touch any longer. I didn't know her husband at

53

all. She'd never mentioned him in her letters when we were writing.'

'That would be my father. Eric Blake.'

'Yes.'

He refilled her cup. She put it to the floor.

'She spoke, recently, as if you were lovers.' Helena did not raise her voice much beyond a whisper, but he could hear every word. He did not answer, but looked her brazenly in the face, staring her out. 'I wasn't born until three years after the marriage.' They fell into silence, considering implications.

'I never saw her after she left here.'

'And your wife?' She had little sense of tact.

'My wife died, oh, fourteen years ago. Heart failure.'

'I'm sorry. She couldn't have been very old.'

'No. Thirty-nine.' He decided to add detail. 'She'd been ill for some time.'

'When you were first married?'

'Oh, no. She was quite athletic. Tennis. Squash. Swimming. That sort of thing.' He looked grim. 'We never had children. It was as well, perhaps, as it all turned out.'

'I'm sorry. My mother didn't know whether you'd been married or not. And yet you've written some children's books.'

He shrugged, tired of the subject. She persevered.

'Did you live in this house at the time? The time she died.'

'Yes. We'd moved in, oh, four years

54

perhaps. It was a bigger house. She could have a bedroom downstairs.'

'This room?'

'No.'

Her curiosity stung him. What in hell did it matter? Perhaps these questions were the result of her unease at her mother's imminent death. He looked at her hard. She sat much at her ease, upright, attractive, well dressed, the expression on her face non-committal. Perhaps she was attempting to show friendliness towards him with these impertinent questions. Marion Meeks had been outspoken, from what he could remember, saying what she should not. He wondered about Helena's employment, but he would not ask. She spoke correctly, made herself pleasant, and yet there was a vulgarity about her questions, a quality his mother would have condemned as 'back-street'.

'It seems a pity that it all has to end like this,' Helena offered.

'Her life. Yes.'

'If either of you had known when you were young that this lay in the future, it would have made a difference to you then, I guess. It depended on things happening that hadn't occurred then. We don't know.'

'No.'

'It seems odd to think of her at that time of her life. So much younger than I am now. Would you have recognised her again?'

'Hard to say. Perhaps. I'm not sure.'

'And now she's dying.' Helena picked her cup daintily up from the floor. 'I think she knows, but I'm not certain. She's always been that bit awkward, obstructionist, so that people didn't confide in her very easily. So I can't guess how much the doctors have told her. She doesn't talk as if she's...'

'She didn't speak much this evening.'

'No.' Helena set off on a new tack. 'She liked reading. Always had a book to hand. That's one of the things she admired about you, she said. You'd read such a lot.'

' "That one small head could carry all he knew". Goldsmith.'

'I suppose so.' She looked puzzled.

She finished her coffee, refused more, put cup and saucer on the table. This involved standing, taking a step or two. When she had sat down again, she said, diffidently, 'Do you believe in an after-life?'

'No.' He had no difficulty with that.

'So once she dies that's the end of it.'

'Apart from the memories. And bits and pieces she left behind. A diary, perhaps. Objects she made or bought.'

'I don't think she was the sort to keep a diary. Except a small one: "Dentist, 9.30. Eric's birthday. Marbella, question mark. Pay car insurance." And she'd throw that in the dustbin at the end of the year.' She stood up. 'I must be on my way now. Thanks very much for

56

coming with me to see my mother. It wasn't much of a success, but you never know. And thanks for the coffee.'

'I'll go with you again, if you see any advantage.'

Helena did not answer, but stared at the carpet, with a sullen face. It reminded him of her mother, who would receive in this way some innocuous statement from him. Marion had seemed to withhold herself, as if she suspected some danger to herself, some drawback in what he had said. What had struck him then was that the silence could not have been caused by his remarks. It arose almost by chance, and perhaps had no connection with his words. She spoke sometimes with a brutal frankness to him, and often with an ironical insouciance or boredom in answer to some deeply held principle which he had outlined.

Helena led him from the room, but allowed him to hold her coat.

'Thank you again.'

'Let me know, will you, if anything happens?'

'I will.'

CHAPTER FIVE

Henry heard no more from Helena until late on Boxing Day, his birthday.

He had spent Christmas quietly at his home with Jennifer Speed as his only guest. She had arrived at midday when his preparation for the main meal was almost complete; the smell of the turkey in the stove filled the house, and a plum pudding bubbled in a large, rarely used saucepan. Jennifer helped him in the final stages. He did not object, as they laughed together, drinking sherry. She mocked him, saying he should have called her in earlier, as he had cooked enough food to feed a dozen. They ate with appetite, drank a bottle of muscatel, and after the pudding with its thick, sweet, white sauce, a Jennifer suggestion and concoction, sat for a further hour with brandy and coffee.

They decided on a walk, a sure sign, he said, that they were far from sober, for outside after a fortnight of west winds and mild rain the fog and frost had returned. They could only just make out the houses on the far side of the road, and traffic raised no noise.

'Not exactly festive, this street,' Jennifer said. She wrapped a light-blue scarf over her mouth. She looked well dressed in a simple tweed coat, and despite her size both elegant and spry walking without difficulty on high heels. 'Are there plenty of children about?'

'No. We're all elderly and middle-aged apart from the students, and they've presumably gone home.'

'One of the most enjoyable things about Christmas is to go outside replete and watch fathers giving their children a try-out on their new bikes or roller-skates.'

'You wouldn't expect that today,' he said.

'If I had a brand-new bicycle I should insist on being taken.'

'No wonder there are family rows.'

They passed a lighted steamy window, where hung a bowed banner wishing them a Merry Christmas. Bulbs blazed, blinked on a large, ceiling-high tree in the corner and glared from the hearth but no one moved inside, no shouts cracked the festive afternoon. Jennifer commented on the empty room.

'They'll all be at table,' he told her.

They moved out of the street, and into the main road, where a church stood black and shuttered.

'They've done their duty for the day,' she said. 'Now it's left to the pubs.'

Hoar-frost whitened the tops of gates, privet hedges, trees, the curbs and pavements. It grew infinitely colder, biting into their faces.

'Have you had enough?' Jennifer asked.

'Have you?'

'Yes. I'm freezing.'

They smartened their pace, and ended by running the last thirty yards to his front gate, hand in hand. Inside the house, the heat struck like an oven. They clasped each other in the hot hall, laughing foolishly, before they lit the rooms, drew curtains, made tea.

'Perfect,' she said.

They read, listened to music, watched a television show like a married couple. He made no mention of his birthday. The fog did not lift so that Jennifer decided against going home. They slept in the big double-bed in the guests' room, ate breakfast next morning at ten, sat about and talked. She had recovered from her shock at finding the old man; it had taken her a week, she said. She spoke rudely of the daughter who was interested only in what she could prise out of her father's pitiful estate. 'There are some bastards about.'

' "How beauteous mankind is",' he said.

'You can say that again.'

As she wrapped up to go, he thanked her. She was excellent company, quiet and lively. He watched her down the drive.

'Don't get lost,' he called.

'You could walk me home.'

'I never thought about it. Hang on. I'll come.'

He accompanied her in the fierce cold of the afternoon. She kissed him on the open street outside her front door.

'Now for the answer-phone,' she said. 'My

joy and delight.'

She closed the door on him, grinning, and he sang as he walked.

Back in his own house, in front of a fire, he was glad to be alone. He winked at the thinly decorated Christmas tree. He played with the sports pages of the day before yesterday's newspaper, ignored the radio, warmed his legs, fell asleep. He woke to find he had missed the news on both channels, cursed them for altering routine on high days and holidays. He tuned in to the wireless for the six o'clock news; they had their priorities right. There were still people about who wanted to know what was happening in the world. He did not listen carefully, but took comfort from a familiar voice reading the not unusual catastrophes.

He shuffled out contentedly to the kitchen where the telephone interrupted his brief preparations to make a cup of tea.

Helena Gough. Her mother had died that morning. She had tried to ring him in the afternoon. Twice.

'Are you all right?' he asked.

'Yes.'

'Would you like me to come round?'

'The weather's bad.'

'Never mind that. Shall I come round?'

'Yes, please. I don't like asking…'

'I'll walk. It will be as quick as by car.'

Her immediate acceptance of his offer surprised him; he did not want to venture out

61

again. He spruced himself up without enthusiasm.

Helena let him in, thanking and praising him. She set him down before the gas-fire where he had talked to her mother on his last visit. The central heating throbbed in a room blazing from five bright bulbs. He asked again after her health.

'I can't grumble,' she said.

She looked well, her face smooth, her modern hair shining, the clothes well cut, her perfume tasteful. She provided tea and sat opposite him.

'It's an awkward time to die,' she said, moderately. 'Boxing Day. Nothing's open. People are away. But everybody's been helpful, the undertaker, the hospital. They've explained what I have to do. And I've been ringing round telling people who should know. Neighbours in Sutton, and relatives.' She lifted her head. 'I expected her to die.'

'Did you see her yesterday?'

'Yes, I went in. She'd been moved into a different ward over the Christmas period. They had garlands, and a tree, and cards on the lockers by the beds. I don't think she noticed anything. She seemed to know me, and tried her best to speak. I'd wrapped her present up, but I had to unwrap it for her. She didn't know what was going on.'

'What did you give her?'

'Perfume. Talcum powder. Shampoo. That

sort of thing. Tissues. A new set of combs. I wasn't sure how long she'd last when I bought it. Anyhow, it might be useful to somebody else there.'

'But on Christmas Day?'

'She was very ill. They had curtains drawn. They thought she might go at any time. But she lasted the night. She died next morning while the day staff were taking over from the night.'

'They sent for you?'

'Straight away. They rang. But she was dead. I drove up. In the fog. But there was hardly any traffic about.' Helena shook her head. 'She didn't look like herself, I thought. Any old, dead woman.'

'Did you and your mother get on well?'

'What do you mean?' She bridled at his question, but calmed herself immediately. 'As well as most. To tell you the truth we didn't have a great deal to do with each other. We hadn't quarrelled. Don't get me wrong about that. We telephoned, oh, perhaps once a month; it might have been longer because time goes so quickly. We sent cards on birthdays and from holidays. We called in if we were anywhere near, but that wasn't often. It wasn't until Edward Ball, that's her second husband, had died and she moved to the east coast that we began to see one another a bit more frequently, and not until she started to be ill that I visited her regularly. And still not very often. Both her husbands had died in the same

63

year that my marriage broke up.'

'I suppose that's a common history nowadays.'

'Is it?'

Her question dropped cold, from an unsmiling mouth, denying the beauty of her gold dress. Small wrinkles formed in the corners of her eyes.

'I'm more upset than I expected,' Helena said. 'I've known for some time that her illness was terminal, though her death came more suddenly than I thought. But I've known since she was back in hospital that she might not have long, and for the past week or two that she might go at any time. So why am I so knocked about? I feel as if she had gone out of the door this morning in perfect health, and had been killed in a car accident. It feels as if I had done nothing to prepare myself.'

'We tend to take an optimistic view.'

'I don't know about that.' She took pleasure in contradiction.

'Do you regret, then, something you've done or failed to do?' He set his tone to match her cool politeness.

'No, I don't think it's that at all. It's that she's no longer alive. She wasn't old. She'd plenty to look forward to. And now she's dead.'

'Yes.'

'You think I read it as a warning to myself, but that isn't so. It's that this lively woman has

64

gone, vanished, disappeared. Didn't you find her unusual?'

'I did.'

'You had sex together for a month or two.' She paused. She had accepted her mother's story. 'Then she goes elsewhere. You write a few letters and then that stops. Whose fault was that?'

'I think I wrote the last two letters, and she never replied.'

'And you made no attempt, later in life, to get in touch with her?'

'No. How could I? I'd no idea where she was.'

'You felt disappointed about this?'

'Yes. I suppose so. Mildly. I often thought about her. At first. I never forgot her. She was always on the edge of my life. Somewhere.'

Helena settled back as if her cross-examination had in some small way calmed her.

'When you saw her the other night, or even round here, did she resemble her younger self?'

'Not really. Especially in hospital.'

Helena leaned over to a folder, placed to hand, and produced a photograph which she passed across to him.

'I've been going over one or two of her things.'

Henry looked at the photograph, then produced his spectacle case, donned glasses, and looked again.

A black and white picture brought Marion straight out from his heart.

He guessed that it must have been taken soon after her marriage. She stood by a hedge and tree in a silky summer dress, spotted with white circles, which clung to her limbs and breasts as if in a breeze. Marion smiled, lipstick prominently black, and her hair permanently, woodenly waved. Her left hand was outstretched at an angle of thirty degrees from the body with the fingers absolutely straight. This dramatic pose dug into his memory, for she often illustrated some outlandish or unexpected statement with an ironic, contradictory movement of head or arms. Here she indicated to the photographer, probably her husband, that standing in her Sunday dress in a rural setting could only be regarded as ridiculous, but she'd put up with it for his sake. The effect of dress on body, after all these years, fixed on this small piece of card, seemed incredibly erotic, needed no enlargement for old eyes. He turned the photograph over; it lacked inscription; no date or place. Henry looked again at the woman, Marion, shook his head; he could smell her face-powder.

'That's exactly her,' he said, in a dry voice, 'as she was when I knew her.'

'Would you like to keep it?'

'Is this your only copy?'

'That doesn't matter.'

'I'll have another one made.'

'There are a number of photographs. Plenty, I expect, when I get round to sorting them all out.' Helena pointed roughly at the rectangle that he was now tucking away in his wallet. 'I don't connect that with the old woman in the hospital.'

'No.' Nor did he. This depicted the dominant woman who had confronted him with her sex, who with her writhing invitation, wild tongue, her skimpy underwear, had altered his life, knocked it topsy-turvy. The photograph safely stashed against creasing, he stowed the wallet with care into his inside pocket.

Helena stood over him, the fingers over the folder white at the knuckles.

'I resent her death,' she said loudly, in a subdued shout. The force surprised him. He looked up suspiciously. 'She was not old. She'd had a decent life, most of it without me, and yet I can't accept her being taken out like this.'

'Well.' He dwelt on the sound, still in the world of the photograph.

'Don't give me any of that old cock about it coming to all of us.'

'Was *she* angry?'

'I don't think she was. She didn't consider dying when she was first ill. She didn't like pain and weakness and dependence on others any more than the rest of us, but she thought, she knew she was getting better. It was slow, her recovery, but certain. When she went back in dock she was so knocked about by the rapidity of the advance of the illness, she felt so ill, that in the end she didn't bother about death. She was too ill to think straight.' Helena turned fiercely away from him. 'I'm the one, I hate it. Him.'

'Him?'

'Bloody God,' she spat out.

' "Whatever brute and blackguard made the world"?'

Her face expressed her contempt for him and his quotation. She despised, he thought, his assumption that one could comfort oneself with a well turned insult. Immediately she became calmer, sat down to talk easily to him. She was going away on a short cruise into the Mediterranean at the end of January. She wouldn't need now to worry about having to cancel that.

They talked about travel. Helena sounded more friendly, even cheerful, unlike the woman of a few minutes ago. She laughed as she told of men on the lookout for wives or casual sex, and their idea of what would attract a woman.

'Do you blame the men or the women?' he asked.

'The men. But I see what you mean.' She frowned winningly at him. He made a few observations on his married life while she listened smiling. 'You've not considered trying again?'

'No. Not seriously,' he answered.

'Nor in any other way?' She enlightened his puzzlement. 'Unseriously?'

'No. It's fourteen years since Joanna died.'

'Do you regret that there were no children?'

'Occasionally. I would have been a different man. I probably would have been solely responsible for their upbringing.'

'And that might have encouraged you into remarriage.'

'She was only thirty-nine. It was heart.'

'Was she ill for long?'

'Two years. More, perhaps.'

'Did you continue working during her last illness?'

'Yes. She went into hospital in the end. She died there. After her last attack. It was the best thing.'

'You don't feel guilty about it?' Something of her earlier, awkward ferocity had returned to her voice.

'No. They looked after her exceptionally well.'

Helena clasped her hands between her knees.

'I asked you that because I feel uncertain about my treatment of my mother. She came here after her first spell in hospital, but I didn't give up work. I could call in at lunch-time, and she made no very big demands on me. She was very good, a self-sufficient woman.'

'Then why should you blame yourself?'

'It wasn't, isn't so much the end of her life. I did pretty well all I could apart from giving up work to concentrate solely on her, and that would have been a disaster for us both. No, I wish, in some ways, I had known her better. I left home at seventeen for good. She'd married again, and I didn't think my stepfather fit to clean my father's shoes.'

'Justly?'

'I don't suppose so. All in my silly adolescent mind. At eighteen I began to train as an accountant.'

'Is that what you do now?'

'Yes. But my firm was in Stoke-on-Trent. And that's where I qualified. And as soon as I'd finished my articles, I married.'

'Was your husband in the same line?'

'No. He worked in the family pottery firm. He'd been to university and had then started working his way up from the bottom. That was his father's idea.'

'And not a good one?'

'There was a good living there. I knew that. I audited the firm's accounts. But Geoff's father was a pain in the neck. He's dead now, thank God.' She laughed. 'My husband and I split up five years ago, and we've been divorced two. But I wouldn't wish his father back on him. An opinionated man, but nasty with it. If you opposed him in any way, however sensible, you'd pay for it. Ugh.' She screwed her face round the sound of disgust.

They talked for an hour. She had seized a chance to take over the Beechnall office of the firm, with explicit instructions to expand. She had bought this house as all she could afford until she managed to sell the large villa in Stoke, part of the divorce settlement, but she'd move as soon as she had the money. That wouldn't be too long, since there seemed to be a firm buyer in line for the other place. She'd been here just over a year, and it was soon after her arrival that her mother had been taken ill, and moved from the coast to the University Hospital for treatment.

'Is this the first time you've lived here for any length of time?' Henry asked.

'Yes. But my mother always talked about Beechnall, and we used to visit my grandparents. Not often. They're dead now. So it's part of my mythology.'

'And how do you like it?'

'Fine. Of course I've been hard at work in the office.'

'Is that going well?'

'Very. I've had one or two strokes of luck, and have promoted a very hard-working man who'd been kept down by an idiot, my predecessor. Yes. And then my mother was with me, or in hospital. I've hardly had time to live. But it suited me. I haven't, or I hadn't, quite got over the divorce, or the fact that Geoff and I just didn't hit it off.' She smiled broadly. 'It all started so well, and then, ten

71

years later ...' She puffed out her lips, and waved her arms histrionically, comically, about.

She laid a hand on his coat sleeve as she showed him to the door. The gesture reminded him of her mother. She thanked him, and told him she'd ring about the funeral as soon as the arrangements had been concluded.

'It's tricky at holiday time,' she conceded, perhaps blaming her mother again. 'It'll only be a small affair. Not many round here will have known her. She spent nearly thirteen years in America with Edward Ball, the second husband.'

They kissed, and she walked with him out on to the foggy front path. She shuddered so that he ordered her back but she stayed under the lintel until his sharp footsteps died out far along the street.

CHAPTER SIX

Henry Shelton attended Marion Meeks's funeral in the first days of the New Year. The fog had gone, but cold rain made the Northern Cemetery miserably bleak. Perhaps fifteen people, a relative or two, a few neighbours from the east coast, a friend from the past, attended, a larger turn-out than Helena expected, but all subdued. The vicar read with

72

force, but the one hymn he had suggested proved a catastrophe, a badly played organ solo as the congregation stared in embarrassed silence at their books. Henry joined some dozen people at Helena's house afterwards; he ferried two old aunts in his own car, the widows of Marion's much older half-brothers, both in their seventies, who never stopped talking about prices, aches and pains, crime and the faults of the young, making no attempt to include him in the conversation. They did not thank him on arrival, but scuttled indoors out of the rain. Two hours later he drove them to the station in the same style, though this time they commented unfavourably on the day's arrangements, Helena's house, Helena herself and her hospitality. Henry, glad to be rid of these harpies, went straight home.

Soon after six he telephoned Helena to see if she had been left on her own, but found she still entertained, unwillingly, two or three grieving comforters, whom she hoped would leave inside the next hour. He invited her to ring him if she found herself in need of company. She failed to do so.

On the first evening of the new term a smartly dressed man, in a British warm, check trousers, polished brogues, knocked heavily on Henry's front door, ignoring the bell. Double-glazing, football pools or old-time religion?

'Mr Shelton?' Something of a military bark. 'My name is Geoffrey Gough, Helena's ex-husband.' Henry invited him inside. Gough opened his coat, removed a canary-yellow scarf. 'I expect you're surprised to see me?'

'No.' The silly answer earned a hard stare, and a scowl.

'You'll wonder how I got hold of your name and address.' Henry deliberately did not answer. 'I had it from a cousin of Helena's I ran across in the way of business. I enquired how my wife was shaping. He mentioned your name. The author, he said. You'd appeared on TV. He found your address for me.'

Henry made non-committal noises. He'd already taken against the man.

'This cousin said you visited Helena when her mother lived with her.'

'Once. And again after her death.'

'And that you'd been with Helena to the hospital.'

'Again, once.'

'That you were at her mother's funeral.'

Henry nodded, sat with his eyes shut, eccentrically. He had offered no refreshment, had no intention of so doing.

'And I thought to myself that next time I was in Beechnall I would call on you.'

'Why?'

'The fact that we are no longer married does not mean I have lost all interest in Helena. After all, we were together a matter of twelve years. And this cousin and his wife had talked about you, named you as Helena's

74

next husband.'

'They hadn't informed me,' Henry said sarcastically.

'It was mere speculation on their part. Probably without foundation. I've no means of telling. But, as I say, I still maintain my interest in Helena, and decided to follow it up. You may ask, "For what reason?" Mere curiosity. Idle curiosity. I admit that. As well as some concern for Helena.'

'If you're so considerate about that, wouldn't it have been better to write to Helena and make your enquiries that way?'

'I'm not so sure that she would have welcomed my intrusion. She could quite well have misconstrued it.'

'What makes you think I would receive it any more willingly?'

'I'd no idea how you'd *receive* it.' He emphasised Henry's verb sourly. 'But I don't mind taking a risk. I'll just call in, I thought, come on him unprepared...'

'Waste his time...'

'Yes. All of that. But now I've seen you, weighed you up to some extent...'

'Favourably?'

'On the whole, yes. I don't think I'd much like it if somebody barged in on me with a series of personal questions. It would catch me on the hop. I might be likely to give something away.'

'I'm more likely to clam up,' Henry said.

'Yes, I see that. Yes. But that in itself

75

says something.'

'Says what?'

'In your case, I don't know yet. But later it may offer a clue of some sort. Is there any connection between you and Helena?'

Gough sat back, smiled, winningly spread his arms, as if about to yawn. Henry began coolly.

'Apparently when Mrs Ball first came down to the hospital here, and then to recuperate in Helena's house, she mentioned me. I don't know why, because we hardly knew each other. Years ago when we were both young.'

'You're nothing like her age.'

'Fifty-nine.'

'You don't look it. I wouldn't have thought you were any older than me.'

'And you are?' Henry spread rudeness.

'Forty-seven.' No offence taken.

'Helena made contact with me. I visited them for an hour. It didn't seem very successful, but I invited them back. They didn't come, because—at least this is my presumption—of Marion's ill-health. Helena took me to the hospital. Her mother was desperately sick by then, and apparently grew rapidly worse. I attended the funeral. It seemed proper.'

'Of course, of course. Yes, I see. Helena's a very attractive woman.'

'She is.'

'But you have no interest in her?' Gough was

76

left without answer. 'Is that so?'

'One thing I've learnt,' Henry said, 'is not to believe what people say about themselves on questions of sex and money.'

'So you're saying nothing.'

'Exactly, and you're drawing conclusions.' Henry held up a hand to stop the next impertinent question. 'If you and Helena were still married, and you suspected that there was something between us, I could well understand that a visit here might well be one option you'd address. But as it is, two visits to her mother in her company, and some lubricious tittle tattle from a cousin and his wife, put me into your books for investigation. Mr Gough, it doesn't add up.'

'What do you mean?'

'I'm not saying you should show no interest in your ex-wife, but to come round does seem unusual, let's say, or exaggerated behaviour. I begin to wonder, to tell you the truth, what's wrong with you.'

As he spoke Henry wondered if he'd be as aggressive if Gough were three inches taller and broader across the shoulders. He was glad that he put his questions gently, without vocal heat.

'I was in this part of the world. I'm in ceramics. Yesterday I had lunch with George Meeks and his wife. They mentioned you, seemed very interested in you, and as they had kept contact, I understood, with their aunt,

77

Marion Ball, I concluded that there was good reason for their interest. They knew your name, looked you up for me in the telephone directory, and since I was forced to spend this evening in Beechnall, I thought I'd call in on you, off the cuff, y'know. It would have been politer to phone first, but I'd time to waste, and even if you'd turned me away from the door, at least I'd have seen you.'

'Why was this so important?'

'It wasn't, in any sense you'd recognise. I am curious, inquisitive. That's my nature. I like to poke into affairs that appear, however, casually, in front of my eyes. That may seem out-of-the-way, exaggerated behaviour to you. They were your words, I believe. You're probably right, but *chacun à son goût*. I have called.'

'And seen? And conquered?'

'I've come to no conclusions.'

'Would I make a suitable successor as Helena's husband?'

'I might be nosy, Mr Shelton. But you're a sarcastic sod. So I'd say no.'

Gough sat waiting, as if prepared for a physical assault. Henry looked him up and down.

'Is that all?' Henry asked, at length.

Gough rose, carefully, and with the aid of a wall-mirror, resumed his yellow scarf. He buttoned his coat.

'Thank you for your time,' he said. 'And my

apologies for the intrusion.' Henry remained silent. 'I think we could be friends.'

With this unexpected conclusion, mildly propounded, he made for the door. He waited in the front passage for his host to show him out. They parted without answer, word or hand-clasp.

Henry sat down smiling, hardly believing what he'd seen. The next visitor would be Satan or Father Christmas. He rang Helena after a short consideration, to find out what she thought of this because he, like Geoff, was inquisitive.

She showed interest in his account.

'What did you think of him?' she asked.

'A bit Rotary Club, Freemasonic for me, but decent enough. What do you make of it?'

'He must have been at a loose end. And sooner than sit about in a hotel bar he decided to call on you.'

'And what about his alleged interest in your welfare?'

'It's non-existent. Our settlement was all tidied up by the lawyers, and if I never saw him again I wouldn't regret it.'

'But his interest in you?'

'He hasn't one. And in any case if he wanted to know about me he could always ask George Meeks. He and Pauline used to visit my mother here. He was at the funeral. A tall, thin man with an Adam's apple.'

'Are they decent people?'

'As far as I know. Dull. Home-birds. He works in the Council House.'

'I don't know whether I should tell you this, but according to Geoffrey, George and his wife have me marked down as your next husband.'

She laughed briefly.

'People of taste,' she said.

Helena did not prolong the conversation, seemed eager to ring off, saying she had an hour or two's work to complete before she went to bed. Two or three days later she phoned again to inform him that she had ticked off George Meeks and his wife for their speculations about a prospective husband for her. They denied that they had ever voiced such views.

'And whom d'you believe?' he asked. The use of the accusative comforted him.

'Geoff, of course. They must have said something, though God knows what.'

Again, having made her point, she rang off, recalling her mother's brusqueness. He saw her a week or two later in the foyer of the Theatre Royal where he had gone to see *The Tempest*; they waved, exchanged distant, mouthed enquiries about health. She seemed to be in the company of two other women, of her age, but unknown to him. Henry had taken Jennifer Speed, who occupied the interval seriously criticising the company and nibbling at a grotesquely large ice-cream. She had recovered from her pre-Christmas shock.

'She's a very attractive woman,' she said of Helena. 'Too young for you, though.'

'She's older than you are.'

'She doesn't look it.'

Jennifer made a few enquiries there and then, almost out of politeness, and returned to her strictures on *The Tempest*, claiming that the producer was more interested in the brilliancy of lights than in the speaking of the verse.

'Why is that?'

'He doesn't think the play is dramatic enough. The storm's fine except it's next door to impossible to mount, and Prospero's account of his deposition and his sea-sorrow are just words to this generation; steam radio not television,' she put it sarcastically.

'Thank you, Grandma,' he said. He agreed with her, but liked to mock her earnestness.

'I tell you what,' she argued. 'They try to make Shakespeare fit the small screen so that people don't feel too far from home. Once they've decided to come out. But Shakespeare's mainly words, the most awe-inspiring ever written, the work of a supreme genius. And all this twat can give us are strobe-lights and thunder-claps and spots directed straight at the audience.'

'Hear, hear,' said a passing old fogey. Jennifer blushed, not realising she had spoken so loudly.

'But is the producer right? Is, let's say,

81

Ariel's account sufficient for our depraved ears and flat imaginations?'

'If they aren't depraved, they soon will be.'

'But Shakespeare was quite interested in masques and would have used lights and revolving stages and flying characters given half a chance.'

'The language. His language. We're losing it, allowing it to decay.' She walked away to rid herself of her ice-cream carton. 'And you're doing nothing about it.' She pointed a finger at his chest on her return.

'I love to cope him in these sullen fits,
    For then he's full of matter.'

She did not appear to recognise his quotation, and they returned to their seats, both subdued and delighted. Over a cup of coffee in her flat she seemed quiet.

'We could do with a few Prosperos in my neck of the woods,' she said. ' "Rough magic" is about all that would touch them.'

Jennifer had been dealing that week with a problem family. The mother had been rushed into hospital, and was unlikely to recover. The unemployed father, out of shock or idleness, refused to take care of his children, three boys all under ten. The youngsters themselves were out of control, disruptive in school, bullies, already picked up for shoplifting, living off their wits.

'What's their house like?' he asked.

'Filthy. It stank even when the mother was up and about. It's in a ghetto of a council estate where they put the defaulters on rent. It's quite a decent house really, but hopeless. Nothing's ever cleaned. The garden, quite big both back and front, is neglected and overgrown. If they don't want anything any longer, they just drop it and there it stays. The council has had to move in at least once to clean and disinfect the house.'

'And the father?'

'Weak, a bit free with his fists, but it's all too much for him. Drinks if he can find the money.'

'What will happen?'

'They'll take the children into care. But they're lost already. They're little Calibans. I don't think anything will set them to rights now.'

'Would you blame heredity? As in Caliban's case? Or is it environment?'

'Both, I suspect. But we haven't time to find out.'

'What will the father do once his wife dies?'

'God knows. He'll have to come out of his house. He'll take up with some other woman.'

'Is he capable of holding a job down?'

'I doubt it, now. They're all lost. It'll be prison, or the streets. If the boys are fostered out to decent people they'll still go wrong. I doubt if anyone or thing can save them.'

'Whose fault is it?' he queried.

'Are you asking me about original sin? I don't know. If I were in the shoes of those children, I'd be a delinquent.'

'But if they had had your upbringing and opportunities, would they still be criminals?'

'I don't know. Probably they would, but that's not fair to them. I mustn't work on that assumption.'

'Mustn't?'

'Never mind your philosophy, my man. "Won't", if you like, or "can't".'

She laughed, suddenly cheerful, came across and kissed him. He rested his head on her breasts as she stroked his face. They did not make love, and he was back at home and in bed by half-past eleven.

CHAPTER SEVEN

Henry went away for the three days half-term holiday which Kinglake granted to his staff and pupils. He spent them in a hotel in York, walking by day, reading and soberly drinking at night. Jennifer, who had been too busy to accompany him, received a postcard of the Minster informing her that the weather was nothing like good even for February. On one day it snowed as he drove into Scarborough; the place froze cold in the North Sea wind, and as flakes flew, the lights in shops and hotels

84

welcomed nobody. He had spent a holiday there as a boy, and it had seemed expensive without vulgarity, a place for decent Englishmen and women to rest for a week without riotous company, to enjoy entertainment but with the sharpness from the sea to remind them that holiday life with bands and theatre and pierrots and roast beef every day had its drawbacks.

'This is what made England great,' he said to the man sheltering with him from the snow.

'Ay. Keen,' the man answered, clearing phlegm from his throat.

'Is it always like this? At this time of year?'

'You get used to it. It's bracing.'

'I like it. I wouldn't mind living here.'

'It's not so bad. Gets crowded in the summer. But that's where our prosperity comes from. And people are coming back to it again. Getting fed up with Spanish sunshine and topless women and skin cancers.' The man enquired about Henry's origins, and described his own life. He had retired a year ago as a foreman joiner for a big firm, and now spent nearly as much time working at his old trade as indulging himself in retirement. 'One thing people don't understand about recession is that those who are employed, or have money are better off than they would be if full employment was the regular thing. Of course, those in work are terrified that they might lose their jobs, because they've seen it happen, in

85

safe, gilt-edged companies. But those who have the cash spend it on improvements, and they call on old-fashioned workmen like me to fit new, properly made doors, windows, pelmets, wall-panels. I feel a bit of a traitor going into some of these houses, though I'm what you'd call a Conservative voter.'

The man delighted in talking. He stood with his feet apart, solidly, poking his close-shaved moustache with a fingernail. It seemed odd to Henry to hear this lecture delivered under the fancy awning of a pastry-cook's while the snowflakes whirled in front of them.

'I'm sixty-seven next,' the man said, 'and I eat as heartily as I've ever done. My wife's cooking is excellent, and I do justice to it. I've a bit of arthritis,' he held up a slightly warped hand, 'but I can still walk and work. I've more money than I want. I keep saying to my wife, "Let's go on a cruise," but she says, "What for? You don't want parties and dances and late dinners." I tell her I've never tried them, that I might acquire the taste, but she says, "Acquire it on your own then, that's all I can say." And she's right. I don't want this high living and traipsing round foreign parts.'

'Aren't they worth a try?' Henry asked.

'That's what I put to myself.'

'With no result?'

'I think we're here only once, and that's it. It's up to us to make ourselves as comfortable as we can.'

'Comfortable?'

'That's the wrong word perhaps. Do our thing's more like it. I get satisfaction out of completing my jobs. I don't want to boast but I put a spiral staircase in a year or two ago, and I often go and look at it and think that when I'm gone that'll still be there solid as ever. And I have my pleasure that way. I don't want six-course dinners or fancy, undressed women or foreign parts. I've seen 'em. I did my National Service in the Navy.'

The snowstorm had blown itself out, leaving the roads wet now and shining.

'Didn't last long,' the man said. 'And I'd better get myself home. Or the wife'll think I've walked under a bus.'

'Or gone on a cruise.'

Henry watched the carpenter stump up the road. He would have liked to talk longer. The man's sense and steadiness cheered him. How the joiner would fare when it came to his turn to die, Henry didn't know, but while he enjoyed his health, his wife's meals, the work of his hands, he seemed admirable. He'd accepted the universe.

The wind whipped the coat-tails of the few pedestrians so that Henry Shelton walked as fiercely as he could to keep warm. The grey sea threatened, and out towards the horizon he followed the dark bundle of a shower. He turned into a shop and ordered coffee. A young woman served him over the counter so that he carried his cup and a heavy currant bun, thick with icing, to one of the tables. Both coffee and cake were delicious, properly made. When he finished he returned his crockery to the counter, and bought two more buns in a white paper bag.

'Not many people about,' he said to the girl. In fact at least four women had been in for bread or confectionery while he sat at his table.

'What do you expect', she answered, 'in February?' She had a foreign accent. 'I wouldn't go out unless I had to.'

'What would you do, then?' he asked, smiling.

'I've plenty to occupy me, don't you fret.'

'These buns were superb,' he said. She seemed to bridle at the word. 'Do you make them here?'

'Just up the road.'

The door clinked open, and a woman with a basket sidled in. She spoke to the girl behind the counter, and was answered, in some Slavonic language. Henry wished them good-morning; both replied in English. The tables and chairs were well polished; he had left a crumb or two for somebody to clean up. In the summer, young women in black frocks and tights and white frilly aprons would scuttle round serving and clearing. He looked at the name on the window. Braithwaite. As he quietly closed the door, the two inside were thoroughly engaged in swift, incomprehensible

88

dialogue. He examined watches and clocks in the windows of jewellers, bought a *Yorkshire Post*, and hurried back to the car-park as another snowy squall caught the streets. He read, ate a second bun, which filled him, though he told himself that what he really needed was a large basinful of mutton broth. Henry, scratching his face, struggling with his newspaper, wondered why he had thought of this. He'd not had mutton broth for twenty-odd years, and before that very infrequently as both Joanna and he found it too fatty for their liking.

Now he turned his hand to the crossword until the snow blew over. He told himself he should get up out of the car and take another stroll round. This seemed not altogether sensible as the skies threatened, but he tied his scarf, buttoned his raincoat and set off. This time he passed hotels, with brass plates and printed menus, and signs that even on a morning like this the steps had been thoroughly cleaned. A postman, lugging a red and blue bag exchanged greetings with him. They did not delay on a windy corner. Henry wished he had remembered to bring his camera so that he could have taken pictures of these deserted streets, delivery vans, the dark puddles in the road. A silver-haired man looked out from one of the front windows, his hands clasped behind his back, his red face Napoleonically forward. Henry raised fingers in salute, but received no acknowledgement as the man stared seawards.

This was no way to spend a holiday, he concluded. Wind and water. He stood, holding the top of wrought-iron railings, scrutinising a small public garden, access now barred. The ground was dark, with pockets of shallow snow, the shrubs damp and dully shining. In a sheltered corner, a bed of winter pansies, yellow and blue, struggled against the weather. He thought back to the silver-haired ancient in the hotel window. What would he do all this capricious day? Stride or stumble from armchair to armchair, from newspaper to television screen, from lounge to bedroom and back, certain of warmth, but not venturing out? This was an afternoon for bridge, seated with similar escapers from life, looking out, as early evening blackened, at the surly sea, the foam-flecks, the uncheering street-lights, the wet roads. Henry thought he had done better than they. At least he had gone out into the fresh air, and seen cliffs, and had felt, however antagonistically, the snow on his face. He wished Jennifer were here; she would talk and cheer him and make fun of the expedition, but she had refused to come, pleading pressure of work. She would have pointed out something worth seeing in this Viking land, would have looked forward to dinner and wine, and have given promise of her warm body in bed. This place, with its hints of summer welcome,

90

boarded-up booths, broad empty pavements, unpainted centres of refreshment, entertainment and rest, lacked people. He, Henry Shelton, needed company. As he hurried back to the car-park, throwing a wary eye round the sky, threatening again, he wished good-afternoon to a middle-aged woman with a terrier. She made no reply but waddled on, mouth set in a thin line. He had joined the suspicious characters, the oddities wandering singly about the town seeking victims, voyeurism or sexual interference their aims. He unlocked his car and sat tapping the steering wheel, willing time to pass. The morning after tomorrow he'd be sitting in a warm classroom, instructing his young ladies in the lyrics of Catullus. He repeated out loud, tapping the metre:

'*Ille mi par esse deo videtur,*
Ille, si fas est, superare divos,'

and smiling to himself. He would make sure that his young ladies could translate this, name principal parts of verbs, or more usual forms of '*mi*' or '*suopte*', those grammatical bits and pieces which examiners frequently delighted to enquire about in his youth and might occasionally parade for elucidation even these days, but what of Catullus the lover? Was a teacher required to ask whether these lines demonstrated something akin to the girls' own

91

feelings for those friends their brothers brought home, those paragons met at the school's termly disco? He supposed not. Nor did the students themselves raise the matter. The editors offered a verse translation or two in their introduction, and Sappho's original Greek in the appendices, but, but ... He'd tried once to make his pupils learn, '*Lugete, O Veneres*' by heart, but this had brought down a few letters of parental complaint about his head. His editors quoted Macaulay: 'there are chords of my mind which he touches as nobody else does.' Was this true of himself? He doubted it. Catullus was just above half his age when he died. Here was young man's poetry, suitable for your Shelleys, not for schoolmasters trapped by late middle-age and sleeting showers in a Yorkshire car-park. He'd make for his hotel, home in exile, he decided, and *quidquid est domi cachinnorum*. Precious few home-bred laughs for him; that's why he went off out, from the warmth and comfort of a York hotel to the cold ankle-biting winds of Scarborough streets.

The shower blew itself out.

He stepped up from his car again, and made for the urinals. He stretched his legs, endured a last look at the sea, the small, cantankerous foam, the enmity of sky and leaden waves. A lungful of air reviving him, he skipped over the chain of a fence, and back, before he squinted about him to see if his antics had been observed. It appeared not. He found his way sedately back to his car, and began the journey to York.

As soon as he was settled on the return, he recalled that he'd nothing much to read. Scarborough was the sort of place that might well have had a good bookshop, but he'd made no attempt to find out. Those in York might still be open when he arrived and had parked his car back at the hotel and if he felt like venturing out again in the dark. Henry smiled grimly; he was incapable even of catering for his own small pleasures.

Back at the hotel he decided against going out again, made himself a pot of tea in his rooms, and read *The Times* he had ordered that morning, played with at breakfast and forgotten to take with him, another sign of his holiday, slap-happy preparations as opposed to the forethought in everyday life. He ate his third bun, poured another cup, read a leading article on the training of the long-term unemployed, and an account of a murder trial, before taking a bath. That seemed the pinnacle of luxury, to be wallowing at five in the afternoon. A man of habit, he could see the sense of a morning shower or an early or late evening soak, but this time was inappropriate. In his dressing gown he listened to the ITN news at five-forty and followed this by half an hour of the BBC, starting at six. He dozed during the latter, lulled by gloom. The forecasters promised no better weather for the morrow. He thanked God he had a job; in this wet chill, he was better off drilling his pupils than wandering about the world not knowing how to occupy himself. He dressed, went down to dinner at seven.

The meal over—he had indulged himself with lamb, sprinkling mint sauce liberally over potatoes, peas, bright carrots—Henry made his way out to the lounge, which was almost deserted. He trudged upstairs, and after hesitation telephoned Jennifer Speed.

She sounded inordinately cheerful.

The weekend and the last two days had driven her nearly wild. She furnished him with a local case or two; parents who refused to testify about the savage injuries to their children; an old man who had fathered offspring in his time on both his daughter and granddaughter; an elderly spinster murdered by two youths for thirty pounds. His complaints about the inclement weather on the Yorkshire coast seemed insignificant. He delivered them, nevertheless. Jennifer sounded genuinely sorry for him.

'When are you coming home?'

'Tomorrow.'

'What time?'

'Immediately after breakfast.'

'Tell you what. I have the day off. Come in for lunch. I'll spend the morning slaving over the cooking stove for you.'

94

'I'll take you out for a meal.'

'Oh, no, you won't. I shan't rise very early, and I'll combine cooking with a bit of cleaning. I fancy gammon. Baked. Will that do?'

'Marvellous.'

'I'll take it out tonight.'

Henry, much cheered, took his *Times* down to the bar, drank whisky, read Philip Howard on the rapacious nature of the English language, helping itself to foreign vocabulary, right and wrong. Few people came into the room: a married couple, three businessmen or commercial travellers, a highly scented middle-aged woman displaying her legs. He could not hear what they said, but watched the men working up, in a Rossini crescendo, to a cackling burst of laughter. Each delighted in the company of the others.

He questioned the barman about entertainment. A smart, young fellow, he described a nightclub or two, but outlined their drawbacks. It was late now for films, concerts, theatres. After a search a pamphlet was produced. The man was friendly, genuinely attentive, but clearly could not understand what Henry sought.

'It will have to be telly, by the look of it,' Henry said.

'It always is.'

'You don't sound very impressed.'

'Let's put it like this. I'm in here most evenings, and I'm not missing much.'

Henry bought the barman a drink on philosophical consideration, finished his own second glass of Scotch, and dragged himself upstairs. The lounge was no fuller; he heard no revelry inside or out. Upstairs he prepared for his early morning departure, not a long job. There was room to spare in his cases.

Someone knocked violently on his door.

He opened to the middle-aged woman with the legs.

'He's collapsed. In my corridor.'

'Who?' He asked his ridiculous question, then followed her into her room, which, quite different from his, had a small corridor, an atavision. In this small space a man lay, face down.

'Have you rung for an ambulance?'

'No.' She fluttered.

'Do so. Nine-nine-nine. Ambulance. Then the hotel desk. Quickly as you can.'

She slipped into her room.

Henry knelt by the body, tried the pulse, which seemed non-existent in the warm flesh. He turned the man gently over, without difficulty, laid him on his back, opened the mouth. He could observe no superficial wounds or bruises. He loosened the collar and tie. The man seemed to be breathing. Again Henry felt for the pulse. Not much life there. Henry made sure that the head was comfortably back, that there were signs of breath, heaved up the left leg, laid the right hand back, and rolled the body on to its side. The eyes remained closed.

Henry stood to his feet, and looked down helplessly. Dropping again to his knees he fumbled under a pullover, into a shirt and vest for a heart-beat. With relief. He straightened the clothes, stood awkwardly up again. He seemed to sway on his feet.

After a time, the woman re-emerged. He had heard her voice as he tried to apply his bits and pieces of first aid.

'Did you get them?' he asked.

'Yes.' Barely breathed.

'And the desk?'

'Yes. They're sending somebody up.' She looked down at the body. 'Is he alive?'

'I think so. Who is he?'

She stepped back, and answered with hesitation, small hand in front of her mouth. 'My brother.'

'Does he suffer from heart trouble?'

'I don't know.'

A man in the hotel uniform appeared. 'Was he like this?' he asked. 'Did you move him?'

'I turned him over, in case he's sick.'

'Has he said anything?'

'No. Hasn't opened his eyes.'

The porter knelt down beside the body, but did not touch. A further official in evening dress appeared, did and said nothing important, asked how long since they had rung for the ambulance and enquired if Henry were

97

a doctor. 'Ah, I see. I don't think we've a doctor staying tonight. That's unusual.' He sighed, made a sad, expressive face. 'I'll institute enquiries. Not that anybody can do much here. Still, the ambulance shouldn't be many minutes.'

He spoke to the woman, checked names again, and left.

Henry, the sister, the porter stood around. It seemed long enough. Once the invalid breathed heavily, a rough snort which startled them. The porter leaned over, then straightened, said he'd go outside to guide the paramedics upstairs.

'Has he been ill?' Henry asked the woman.

'On and off. He's not very robust.'

'Will it be his heart?'

She shrugged, dismissively, attempted another sentence about his health, but broke off, unwilling to waste time. It seemed long minutes before the ambulancemen clattered in with a stretcher. They bent to their knees, slightly moving the body, efficiently, in no hurry.

'What's his name?' they asked Henry.

'Harold Oakes,' the woman answered.

'Harold, can you hear me, Harold?'

The eyelids fluttered. They nodded, satisfied, continued their examination, informing the patient in matter-of-fact voices that he was all right now. In the end, they lifted him to the stretcher, adjusted straps and blankets.

'Are you his wife?' they asked the woman.

'His sister.'

'Are you coming with us to the hospital?'

'I will if you want me to. I can get a taxi back.'

She shot into her room, and reappeared in outdoor clothes equally quickly.

'Shall I lock up?' the porter asked.

'Yes, please. And thank you, all of you.' Her equanimity surprised Henry.

The hospital party made its steady way out. A small group of spectators had gathered in the corridor, mainly elderly people, one man in dressing-gown, to watch the departure. The porter locked the door, moved towards Henry.

'What's the trouble?' one of the bystanders.

'Heart,' the porter answered loftily.

'Cardiac arrest?'

'No, sir.' He stood by Henry's door, and whispered. 'Some of these bloody people. They know it all. You coming downstairs, sir? A drink might do you no harm.' Henry said he'd had enough for one night. The porter blamed the cold weather for these troubles. 'Had one last week. An old gent. Ninety-odd, they say. He died, mark you. Went out like a light.'

They parted politely, with reciprocal thanks.

At breakfast next morning Henry saw neither the sister, nor the porter. When he settled his bill at the desk, he enquired after Harold Oakes. The receptionist knew nothing, but rang somewhere in enquiry, found nothing out, expressed regret.

'The night staff might know,' she said.

'I shan't be here tonight. To ask.'

'No, sir. Pleasant journey. The forecast's better.' She looked up brightly. 'You could ring us later about Mr Oakes. I'll make enquiries.'

CHAPTER EIGHT

Henry enjoyed his lunch with Jennifer.

She was cheerful, pulling his leg about arctic excursions to Scarborough, but looked at her most dishevelled. She sweated in the kitchen, dress rumpled, her pinafore creased, and her hair, though short, needed combing.

'Stout people, like me, need quiet,' she said, loudly slapping her belly. 'Luxury, order, calm, to be at our best.' She was right, and dismissed herself to the bathroom after lunch while he was ordered to wash the crockery. She had cleaned as she cooked so he was not occupied long. He took off his jacket, used too much liquid so that suds dropped over the sides of the bowl. Finished, he settled to a coal fire in the sitting room and watched the windows. The day outside stretched colourlessly cold, without rain or snow.

Jennifer reappeared at her best, wearing an enormous silk dress in autumn colours, green tights and shoes; her hair was now immaculate, face made up.

'Worth waiting for,' he declared.

'Nothing too good for you. Did you ring that hotel? About your man? I meant to ask you, but I forgot.'

'Yes. He was being kept in hospital. But was making good progress.'

'The hotel remembered you?'

'They did. My name. His name. His sister's name. The lot.'

'You must have made an impression on them.'

'Of course.'

'You're not thinking of taking a walk, are you?' Jennifer asked.

'I can see you're not. Dressed like that.'

She laughed, preening herself, standing like a piece of classical statuary, one hand behind her head, one delicately at her waist. He constantly amazed himself by his admiration of this plump figure. She was large, oversized, but elegant. Her weight did not encumber her; she could move swiftly if it was necessary, was strong of arm and leg to match her quick thinking. The Department of Social Services, if that was the organisation she worked for, had found a winner.

Henry recalled his first meeting with her.

He had been sitting disconsolately at a party at the Cosgroves' house. They were both doctors, and he had coached their sons for

101

'O'-level English and Latin. Both boys, by dint of his drilling, had passed and the grateful parents occasionally invited him to functions at their house. He invariably went, but rarely enjoyed himself since the guests were mainly medicos who talked of symptoms and money and golf and holidays. This evening he had been introduced to Jennifer Speed, who had recently joined the staff of the hospital where Hugh Cosgrove worked. She sat next to Henry Shelton, casually drew him out about his work, gave him some notion of her own niche in what she called the 'hierarchy of healing and saving'. She had the plummy voice of a plump woman, but was sharp-witted, mildly funny.

In an interval away from her (he had gone to procure drinks), Fiona Cosgrove had button-holed him.

'I see you're sitting with Mrs Speed?' This surprised him, as Jennifer wore no ring. 'Getting on well?'

'Yes. She's very pleasant.'

'And interesting?'

'Yes. I suppose. Rather quiet.'

'Good. I'm glad. She needs company.'

He thought Dr Cosgrove was about to turn away, when she swung round, edged him and his two glasses into a corner.

'A tragic case,' she said.

That was the last word he would have applied to this fattish girl in her flowing, gorgeous dress. Eyes seemed large, exotically

102

attractive, so that she reminded him of some oriental woman in a *chaddar*, where beauty depended solely on the movement of the eyes. There had, however, been nothing of the mysterious about her; she talked openly, fluently, yes, prettily to him.

'Why's that?' he asked Dr Cosgrove.

'She hasn't said anything to you?'

'No.'

'You've never met her before this evening?'

'No.' Get on with it, woman.

'Her first husband was tragically killed.'

'Accidentally?'

'Yes. In a crash at an air-show. He was watching a plane land when it blew up. He was killed. About twenty people were injured. He was the only fatality. It was some way from the main runway or there would have been more deaths. They'd been married less than two years.'

'How long ago is this?'

'Three years, perhaps. Her husband was keen on aeroplanes. He loved air-shows. She didn't go with him. She took it well, poor girl. They were ideally suited, people said. He was a very lively man, a civil engineer. Very good at it.'

'How old is she?' he asked.

'Jennifer? Now? Thirty-ish. She took it stoically. I don't know if that's good. They doted on each other. Did many things together, but not everything. She moved her house. Kept on with her job. That's where I'd met her. Tremendous worker.' Dr Cosgrove looked over her glasses. 'A year or so later, she began to see another man. It surprised us. We thought it was serious. And we were delighted about it. And then he left her. Just like that.' She snapped her fingers.

'How long ago is this?'

'Since he left her? Oh, two, three months. They'd been going round seriously together for six months before that.'

'And why did he leave her?' Henry asked.

'God knows. He seemed a decent man. Lectured in art history.'

'Did he go away. From the district?'

'No. But he was due to go. Plymouth, I think. He just dropped her. By letter. She showed it to me. She couldn't eat, sleep. She came to me at the surgery. I went up to her house, later, and spent time with her. I think highly of her. It was then she showed me this note of dismissal. Quite absolutely callous. No future for them. Some men. I don't know.'

'What did she say?'

'Not much. She seemed too overcome to talk.'

'And that's two months ago?' he asked.

'Thereabouts. I was surprised to see her tonight. I've been pressing her to turn up, but I didn't think she would. How does she seem?'

'Pleasant. I couldn't have deduced any of this from her behaviour.' He smiled, putting the doctor in the wrong. 'She'll wonder where I've got to.'

When he returned Jennifer Speed was sitting quietly as before, staring ahead, the expression on her face unstrained.

'Sorry I've been so long,' he began. 'Our hostess grabbed me.'

'Hostess?' Jennifer's mind was elsewhere.

'Fiona Cosgrove. She's a very nice woman. And a good doctor, I believe.'

'She's my GP.'

Jennifer seemed not to have noticed how long he had been away from her. She had lost something of the easy speech she had before he'd disappeared for the drinks, but he wondered if that was his fault. Perhaps he now read into her diffidence hints of the troubles Dr Cosgrove had described. She sipped her wine, and allowed herself gradually to be drawn back into social conversation, a large, shy, solemn young woman, content to sit by him, and listen, and sometimes question him, as he talked about the defects of present-day education. She asked about the use of Latin, and seemed to agree with him that there was something to be said for the retention of these academic, 'difficult', subjects in days of astrology, pop videos, non-verbal entertainment. He argued that there was nothing intrinsically difficult about Latin except in its higher reaches, which barely concerned him; students had to learn rules in a systematic way, and apply them, and they'd achieve success. This would not make linguists of them any more than learning the properties of a chemical would make scientists, but it qualified them at their first public examination.

'So apart from a bit of paper, there's no other advantage?'

'It teaches grammatical terms, and makes you interested, if the teacher's any good...'

'And you are?'

'Oh, yes. It makes them interested in etymology, where words truly come from, and why they mean what they do now.'

'So, somebody like me, who didn't do Latin, is at a disadvantage?'

'In a sense. In the same sense as if you didn't learn chemistry or geography. You'll be lacking something, somewhere.'

In these exchanges she grew more animated, and once grabbed him by the forearm with both hands. They could laugh, each, at the earnestness of the other.

When they discovered that they lived not ten minutes' stroll apart, they decided to walk home together. Both had left cars behind so that they could drink. Both had taken alcohol in moderation, and it seemed somehow a small victory for common sense that they'd save money on taxi fares, though the journey would take them nearly three-quarters of an hour. They set off early, soon after ten, replete with Cosgrove comestibles, and Henry quickly learnt that Jennifer, in spite of her size, could match him in speed and length of stride. She had, he noticed, changed her high-heeled party shoes for something more sensible. Had she expected to walk home, or did she feel so uncomfortable in party-wear that she'd slip off patent leather as soon as she took her taxi?

Fiona Cosgrove made a point of seeing them to the door. She seemed delighted, shaking hands effusively, warning them to be careful.

'I'm never anything else,' Henry had said.

They had met again, cautiously, during the next month, going to the theatre to see an amateur *Electra* and once to the music club to hear the Takárcs quartet. Jennifer made an excellent companion, but talked of herself only in the context of her work. She spoke freely of that, and it was nearly a year later, when both had drunk more than usual, that she mentioned, very briefly, the cause of her husband's death. She gave no detail, but implied that she and her associates attracted bad luck.

Now on this dull holiday with winter rampant they sprawled in front of her fire, and once again he proposed marriage. She answered with a beauty of politeness that must have reassured the sick and the needy in her office, refusing his offer as she invariably did. This time he pressed her.

'Is it my age?' There were twenty-four hard years between them.

'You know it isn't.' Snappily. He waited. 'You don't look anything like fifty-nine, and even if you did that wouldn't matter.'

'Why then?'

'I've told you, but you won't listen. Superstition. I'm convinced that marriage is not for me. Barry died when we'd had less than two years. Standing there. Innocently enjoying himself.'

'Joanna died.'

'That's different. What I mean is you had, at least, some sort of warning. You knew for months that she wouldn't recover.'

'Does that make a difference?' he asked.

'Yes, but I can't exactly say why. You could prepare yourself.' She took his hand. 'I'm very grateful to you for your offer. It builds my ego. But it worries me.'

'So you say. It's not reasonable.'

'Nevertheless, it's true. You do me a power of good. When I was upset by that old man's death, I just walked past your door to help me out. Fortunately you saw me and dragged me inside. And when we go to a concert, or the theatre, or on a day's outing, or', she giggled, 'have a night in bed it steadies me. But', she held up a finger to prevent his interrupting, 'I fear what will happen if we took on each other permanently. At present, we've just about got it right. The perfect balance. And that's good enough reason for me to leave things alone. I'm pessimistic. If I try, however reasonably, to

108

change good into better, then nemesis follows.'
'Things may well change of their own accord. And a steady relationship, legal or sacramental, might keep us in good order.' He sounded pompous, even to himself.
'Don't stop asking,' she said. 'I like it.'
'This isn't a game,' he grumbled.
'I know that.' She leapt up, threw her arms round him, nearly toppling him from his chair to the ground. 'I wouldn't want to live in a world where a Henry Shelton doesn't exist.'
'I feel important.'
'What's Latin for that.'
'I don't know. *Gravis*, perhaps. *Magni momenti*.'
'What's Latin for "impatience"?'
'Same word. *Impatientia*.'
'Henry. Will you teach me Latin?'
'I beg your pardon.' He showed his surprise.
'What I said. Will you teach me Latin?'
'Yes.' He spoke hesitantly. 'If that's what you want. But it entails work. There's quite a bit of dull rote-learning. And you don't ever have the chance to use the language. Even literary people don't know it now, so you come across fewer tags.' He laughed, clasped her hands. 'Go on. Convince me. *Convinco-convincĕre-convīci-convictum*.'
There followed his explanation of principal parts, though he warned that she wouldn't be on to those for a bit.
'They try to make it interesting nowadays.

The books are all about Roman life. Plenty to read. In my day it was just learning grammatical rules, and then applying them in daft sentences.'

'Principal parts,' she enthused. 'It sounds sexy. How often shall I need a lesson?'

'Twice a week. It depends how hard you work. With youngsters a lesson a day is best, but we'll see how serious you are.'

'You don't believe I want to learn it, do you?'

'I'm an old cynic,' Henry said. 'There are all sorts of things we'd like to know, but we can't be bothered to put in the time and effort to learn. If you're interested you'll do all right.'

They fixed the first lesson on the next Saturday at noon. He would provide a textbook. She seemed excited, questioned him about Roman poets.

'I wish I had started before,' she said. 'I don't know what I'm doing with life.'

'Do you want a family?'

'I don't think so. We weren't trying when Barry was alive. I deal with problem children amongst others. I know the snags even in the best-regulated homes. I don't feel any great mothering instinct. Barry didn't need me in that way. He wanted a wife, an equal, a partner. But don't you ever question yourself about what you've done with your life? And come up with some pretty dusty answers?'

'Yes. Often.'

'And are you satisfied? What about when you die?'

'I'm not leaving behind any great masterpieces. Of art or social change or anything else. But I've taught my pupils English and Latin—on the whole clever, well-intentioned children, I admit—pretty well according to my modest abilities.

'Could you have done better?'

'I doubt it. My life has suited itself to my personality. No great ambition. No irresistible desire to plaster my name all over the hoardings or the front pages or the telly screens. One of the quiet lives.'

'The salt of the earth,' she said.

'Probably.'

They sat to watch television like an old married couple, ate an ample tea with the six o'clock news, and Henry left soon after seven. Both claimed to have work to prepare for the next day. In his case this was not so, but he felt pleased to leave, as if the last hour or so had been spent in prison, pleasantly, but with most options restricted.

He garaged his car, had a stroll round the house, outside and in, and put on his slippers, took up a library book. So comfortable was his armchair and so warm the house with thick curtains drawn that he nodded off. The ringing of the front doorbell woke him, leaving him disoriented, clutching the arms of his chair. The bell pealed again. He rose, not without pain, and shuffled out of the room. He expected nobody; this would be a charitable appeal, though he could remember no envelopes being left, or an attempt to sell him double-glazing or convert him to some apocalyptic religious sect. He switched on the hall light. The air outside swept coldly in as he opened the door.

'I wasn't sure . . .' a woman's voice, 'I ought to come round like this without notice.'

He recognised the voice as that of Helena Gough.

Henry invited her in. His eyes felt heavy. He took her coat, hung it on the hat-stand, thinking here was another like her ex-husband trying to catch him out.

'It's beautifully warm in here,' she said.

He led her to the small sitting room he had been occupying, and, kneeling, mended the coke fire in the grate. As he straightened up he offered her coffee or alcohol.

'You sit down,' she ordered, rather ungraciously, 'and rest your legs. I oughtn't to come round here bothering you. Especially for nothing.'

'It's a cold night to venture out for nothing.'

He scrabbled in his mind to remember when he had seen her last. The *Tempest* evening in the theatre.

'That's what I've done. If my ex-husband can burst in on him unannounced, so can I. At least, that's what I thought, if anything so

112

vague and shapeless can be called thought.'

'He had a purpose, or so he said.'

'I haven't.'

Her mother, all those years ago, would snap back at him like that, for no good reason, except to establish in her mind a superiority over her lover. It had seemed graceless, then, especially from one otherwise so free of herself with him. He could not understand it.

He made no answer.

Helena looked well dressed, her hair groomed, her perfume attractive. She had not walked out of her house on impulse; she had prepared herself.

'How are things with you?' he asked, relenting.

'Fine. Pretty hectic at work, but I suppose I ought to be pleased about that.'

'Plenty on?'

'Yes. We're doing well.' She put her hands together. 'There is something I want to ask you about, that's if you don't mind. Though whether it's worth bothering about, I don't know. No, I don't think I'll trouble you.'

'Please yourself.' He disliked this uncharacteristic hesitation on her part.

'Oh, all right.' She slapped her thigh, almost as if by chance. He raised a finger.

'Just before the confidences start, shall I get you a drink?'

'No, thank you. Perhaps afterwards. I don't know. I might want to run off. It's only a small

113

matter. Nothing world-shattering.' Henry waited. 'You'll perhaps remember that I mentioned a man in the office who'd been kept down by my predecessor. This man—his name is Eric Moore—is very efficient, and I've promoted him.'

'So far so good,' he said as she paused.

'He's very grateful. He's worked for years for the firm. In a very subordinate position.'

'Is he qualified?'

'No. But he's just as good in his field as a qualified man. Of course he can't sign this, that or the other. But he's quick, knows local conditions, sees snags, doesn't panic...'

'Why doesn't he qualify then?'

'He's too old. He's in his fifties. Late fifties, I guess.'

'Like me.'

'He looks a lot older than you.'

Again they sat unspeaking. Helena seemed in no way embarrassed, merely taking her time.

'As I say, he's very grateful. In fact he's more than useful to me. He's ideally what I want. I've seen to it that he's paid, and paid decently. Within six months of my arrival we had reorganised the whole place. He worked like a dog. He was very suspicious for a start, expecting to be slapped down, but he came to trust me. I guess for the first time in his life he'd been given anything like real responsibility. He was always very cautious, but he realised before too long that I was listening to what he

114

was saying, and often doing something about it. All to the good, you say, but where's the snag?' She paused.

'Let me guess,' Henry said, sharply.

'Go on, then.' She showed her surprise at his intervention.

'He's now so confident that he's stepping out of line, trying all sorts of schemes you don't want.'

'No.' The voice stopped him, again with the roughness of her young mother. 'If that was the length and breadth of it, I'd soon make an end. I reckon I could stop that with a blistering ten minutes, restore the status quo.' Helena moved in her chair, uncrossing her legs, putting her feet together. 'No. I've said he was grateful, and that's not surprising. But now he's obsessed with me.'

'In what way?'

'Sexually.' Again she paused.

'You mean he's making passes at you, harassing you, touching you.'

'It's not exactly like that. I see I haven't made our Mr Moore exactly plain to you. He's a shy man, been put upon, all his life, at home and at work. Nor does he rate himself very high as an attractive male. So he's not likely to shove his hand up my skirts. It might perhaps be better if he did.'

'Would you mind?' Henry asked, to embarrass her.

'He's utterly unattractive to me. Again I

think I'm capable of giving him the brush-off. No. He follows me everywhere with his eyes. He's always opened doors for me, that sort of thing, but now he's everlastingly hovering round. If I stay to do an extra hour or two, so does he. He'd decorated a page of notes with sketches of me. They were just recognisable. He's no talent in that direction.'

'Clothed or naked?'

'Head and neck. I found a note, a love-letter he'd written to me. Whether he'd left it where I could find it, or not, I can't make up my mind. It expressed his admiration, said he could not live without me, praised me for changing his life.'

'Passionate?'

'For him, I suppose, yes. Nothing Mrs Whitehouse could object to.'

'And is this', Henry put the question slowly, 'in any way affecting the efficiency of his work?'

'No, not as far as I can tell.'

'So.' She mockingly imitated his word, before he continued, 'Why not give him your blast on the subject?'

'I don't want to hurt the man. He's been very useful to me. He still is. He's a decent fellow, having a bit of success, and I don't want to spoil it.'

'I see.' Henry touched his chin. 'As a teacher I used to find great advantage in having my female pupils in love with me. Got more out of

116

them. I'm a bit past it now.'

Helena smiled bleakly.

'The other evening I happened to look out of my upstairs front room. It would be nine o'clock. Thereabouts. And there on the other side of the road, he stood, just staring at my house. I watched him, but he didn't do anything.'

'Was his car about?'

'Presumably. There are so many parked, he couldn't get close.'

'How long was he there for?'

'Well, I finished off my upstairs jobs in about twenty-five minutes and he was still there. I looked again at ten o'clock and he'd gone.'

'He didn't push anything through the letter-box? Or chalk a message on the wall?'

'No. He lives some distance away. Six or seven miles.'

'It was just the once?'

'That's the only time I've seen him. I don't deliberately go upstairs to spy on him.'

'I think I would. I'm deuced curious.'

'I'm not interested enough in him. Personally. But there's no good reason for him to be in the street. Is there anything I can do? Or not do?'

'If I were in your place I'd do nothing. Just leave him to grow out of it. Obviously work's important to him. Keep your eye on that side of it, and let the rest sort itself out.'

'As it will?' She asked, business-like.

'I've no idea. I can't give you guarantees. But these things usually do. He has a wife and family, I take it. They ought to provide distractions of their own. We don't much like getting nowhere.'

Helena thought about this, lengthily keeping quiet.

'Thanks for listening, anyway. It's probably me. I'm getting lonely. I've been working hard. I've finished with my mother's estate now. And I've another diversion on the cards.'

'What's that?'

'Moving house.'

'You've hardly been in your present house ten minutes.'

'Eighteen months. But it wasn't ideal. I bought it because I could raise that amount of cash at that time. Now Geoffrey and I have divided ourselves legally, I'm better off, and it looks as if I shall stay in Beechnall at least for a time.'

'What's wrong with your present house?'

'Wrong part of town. Rather noisy. Not much garden. Always needs money spending on it.'

'List its advantages.' Henry spoke like a schoolmaster.

'Handy for the office, but not too close. Plenty of room. Warm. Low council tax.'

'Snobbery on your part?' he queried. 'Your move?'

'Something in it. Also I like to have a few

118

obstacles in view. And I've cracked the snags at work. Don't you ever feel like that? An idea that there's something unsatisfactory about your life?'

'Not so much now. No.' He spoke quite firmly. 'No. I shuffle along from one little crisis to the next, quite pleased to be left alone. On the whole. I have my bad days, as you might guess.'

'Women?' she said with a mischievous rise in her voice.

'I love 'em.'

Neither laughed; both frowned.

'Isn't the house too big for you?' she asked.

'Yes. But I don't mind that. I like elbow room. I can afford it. I've nobody I can leave my money to, so I might as well spend it on myself.'

'You go in for pricey holidays?'

'Certainly I go away twice or three times a year. But nowhere very expensive, to some warm place, with something to look at. Scenery, museums, architecture.'

'And you go on your own?'

'Yes. Mostly. I don't mind that. I quite like my own company.'

'Lucky you.'

Again he offered Helena a drink; again she refused.

'No, thanks. Sit still,' she said. 'I think you're doing me some good just by answering my questions. I don't make head or tail of you.

119

But that adds to the attraction. Don't you have a regular woman friend?'

'I'm getting old, you know.'

'Do you?'

'Yes, then. I suppose I do.'

'You only suppose. Don't you know? Do you not think of marrying her?'

'She'd have some say in that.'

'Has it been discussed?'

'Yes. I think we could say so. Yes.' He sounded amused.

'Is it the woman I saw you with at the theatre?'

He stared hard at her so that she dropped her eyes.

'I know I've no right to ask you these things?' she faltered.

'No. But I don't mind answering. Yes. It is.'

'Would you tell me her name?' Helena's voice trembled.

'Jennifer. Jennifer Speed.'

'Um.' Helena made a long, humming sound, then smiled, beatifically, and stood gracefully up. 'Thanks very much. I've wasted enough of your time.' She waved down his disclaimers. 'I'd like to meet your Miss Speed some time.'

'Mrs Speed,' he corrected. 'Why?'

'She looked interesting.'

'When you saw her she was giving me a lecture on Shakespeare.'

CHAPTER NINE

On the following Saturday the two women met at Henry's house for lunch.

He had refused help from both with the preparation of the meal, and had sat them down in his sitting room with glasses of sherry, dry for Helena, sweet for Jennifer. They had arrived within a minute of the appointed seven o'clock, seconds apart so that they were already exchanging introductions on the drive when he opened the door. This did not altogether please him, for he had been preparing initial words all day, and now these were wasted, but he appreciated punctuality in his visitors. He retired to his kitchen, and could hear their voices. Though he had no idea what the two were talking about, they did not lack fluency, and when he carried in the hot plates and ordered his guests to the table, they were laughing together like old friends.

Helena congratulated him on his cooking of the roast beef and Yorkshire puddings.

'Didn't you expect him to be any good, then?' Jennifer asked.

'Yes, I did. But in a different way. Beef, roast potatoes such as these you have to prepare yourself. I expected a delicious meal, but cooked mainly from packets.'

'Have you any objection', Jennifer asked, 'to

cooking from packets?'

'Not at all. I often do it myself. Saves time.'

'Not money,' Henry said.

'Henry's your good, old-fashioned craftsman.' Jennifer spoke sweetly.

'Who taught you to cook?' Helena asked.

'My mother. I was an only child. And then Joanna, my wife, thought I ought to do my share of the household chores, including the preparation of meals. After all, she was out working when we were first married. In fact, she continued right up to the beginning of her last illness.'

'Wasn't there competition between you? To see who cooked better?' Helena.

'No.'

'He's crafty. He watched it that he wasn't too outstanding.' Jennifer.

'How do you know that?' Helena asked.

'I don't. I deduce it from present knowledge.'

'I take it you had no family.'

'No. Three miscarriages. Then we gave it up.' Henry seemed to answer nonchalantly.

'We're a barren lot,' Jennifer said. 'Not a child between us. That's so, isn't it?' She stared at Helena.

'Will that be a cause of regret, do you think?'

'Probably. I've never felt much of the mothering instinct, but when I'm old and lonely perhaps I'll miss them.'

'Isn't the best of children to be had when

122

they're young?' Henry intervened.

'No idea.' Helena dismissed the suggestion. She spoke ungraciously. Jennifer intervened, as if they encroached on dangerous ground, to ask how she enjoyed living in Beechnall.

'Henry and I have spent most of our lives here, and we don't see things straight. Is the place attractive to a stranger?' Henry leaned back for the answer.

'Yes, I like it. Plenty of work for me. That's the first consideration. It's no use living somewhere these days if there isn't a living to be made.'

The other two looked at her hard.

'Have I said something wrong?' They gently shook their heads. 'No town is any good if there isn't a roof over your head. I found an excellent variety of housing that's cheaper than London and the West Midlands. There's entertainment of all sorts if you know where to look for it. Not that I've a great deal of time so far. Yes, I approve of the place.'

'That sounds slightly grudging.' Jennifer.

'That's my fault, not the town's. I intend to get about more. I'll ask your advice.'

They talked easily, edging away from any awkwardness that they stumbled on. Henry had cooked a large rice pudding.

'We had this on wash-days,' he said, 'when I was a boy. It was awful. I've now decided how good and rich it can be.' Nevertheless he insisted they load their helpings with ice-cream and black cherry jam.

At the end of the meal he refused to allow them to wash-up, but put them together in the sitting room to 'get to know each other'. He left them whisky and water to speed the process, closed the door tight shut.

'He's young for his age,' Helena began.

'Fifty-nine? Yes. Could be. He's teaching me Latin.'

'Why?'

'Because I asked him to.'

'Are you dong well at it?'

'He makes it all very clear. And so I bother myself to learn what he's taught me.'

'People are remarkable,' Helena croaked. 'Why Latin and not Greek? Why not a modern language you can use?'

'Henry teaches Latin. He's likely to be up-to-date.'

'In a dead language. Fair enough.' Helena laughed croakingly. 'Don't they always say that you should never ask your husband to teach you anything, to drive a car, for instance?'

'Henry's not my husband. Secondly, most husbands haven't had much experience of instructing anybody. And a car? Well, that's a macho thing. Not for women, in the eyes of many men.'

'Did your husband teach you?'

'No, I could drive before I met him.'

They talked easily, without inhibition, not

124

confessing much, not probing. Henry returned from the kitchen with a brandy bottle, and three glasses. They had not touched the whisky.

'Let's finish in style,' he said.

'It's very comfortable here,' Helena answered. 'Too much of that and I might well drop off.'

'You've been talking nineteen to the dozen,' he said, pouring the liquor and handing out glasses. 'Somebody or something has suffered.'

'Not you,' Helena answered.

'Is this a wine, or a spirit?' Jennifer asked, lifting her glass.

'It's a spirit distilled from wine.' He leapt from his seat, to pull a dictionary from the shelves. ' "An ardent spirit distilled from wine. Formerly brand-wine. From the Dutch. To burn, to distil and wine." '

'Ardent,' Helena said, wetting her lips.

'It's strong,' Jennifer replied. 'I didn't know you went in for this sort of thing.'

'Only for distinguished guests.'

'That's you, then,' Jennifer said to Helena. 'He's never produced it for me.'

They waved their glasses in the direction of their companions. Suddenly from the street they heard and felt a heavy bang that shook the walls. They put their glasses safely down.

'What the hell's that?' Henry jumped from his chair, made for the front door. The women, each glancing at the other for a lead, rose and followed. In the hall Helena, going first, said, 'Coat weather,' and slipped hers on. Jennifer followed her example.

The front gate hung open. They could see nothing of Henry. They moved out on to the pavement.

Ten yards down the road a knot of people gathered round two cars which had collided head-on. The accident was hidden at first from the two women by the parked lines of cars on either side of the road. Both drivers must have taken the narrow lane in the middle of the vehicles and resolutely refused to give way. A diamond heap of headlamp glass littered the road; brown water dripped from one punctured radiator; behind the windscreen, hands still on the wheel, a man in a trilby hat sat with his wife by his side. He had half-wound down his window. A young man with fair hair dragged straight back and fastened in a foot-long pony-tail explained the predicament in a loud voice.

'He just come on and on. Nothing would stop him. I hadn't time to reverse. Or do any bloody thing before he nobbled me.'

'You were stationary?' Henry, in his schoolmaster's voice.

'Yes. I'd stopped. He didn't brake nor nothing.'

'You was coming pretty sharp down the street.' Voice of a spectator to the young man.

'Not so fast I couldn't stop.

126

Jennifer had rounded the cars, and had tapped on the driver's window. Obediently he wound the side-window right down.

'Are you all right?' she asked.

'Yes. I think so.' The driver was much older than she had expected. She helped him gently from his seat. He tottered to the front of the car to examine the damage. He shook his head, bemused.

The other driver and the hostile witness were still at it.

'You come down that street like a lunatic.'

'I bloody stopped.'

'Where do you live?' Jennifer asked the old man. 'Is it far?'

'On this road. I'd only just set off.'

Willing hands rolled the old man's car into a space some yards down the street. The young man reversed away. Now he strutted to where the old people were standing on the pavement. Advice flew. 'You have to report it.' 'Get the AA. They'll see to you.' 'Are you Relay?' Addresses were exchanged. Witnesses offered their services. Jennifer acted as secretary to the old man. The younger man returned to his point, vehemently. 'I was stopped when you hit me.'

The old man did not answer. Jennifer took his wife's arm.

'Was it important?' she asked. 'Where you were going? We can always call a taxi. Would you like to go inside for a bit? Or come into Mr

127

Shelton's house?' The woman, thick-set with iron-grey hair, refused to leave her husband's side. The old man said hardly a word, but again the young driver began to storm.

'You could 'ave stopped, but you didn't. You came right on into me. You could'a stopped. Easy. But you didn't.'

Henry Shelton took charge.

'Look,' he said, not without authority, 'it's no use starting an altercation in the street.'

'It was 'is bloody fault.'

'Let the police, or the insurance companies, or the courts decide that. I take it you're insured?'

'Of course I bloody am.'

'Good.'

Henry took the old man by the arm.

'You're a bit shaken. Take him inside, Jen, and sit him down with a cup of tea. Then he can phone the police and the AA. Time of accident?' He glanced at his watch which read twenty-five to four. 'Let's say 3.20 p.m. Is that right?' To the young man.

'Roughly.'

'Yes. Take them in.'

They had collected a small, but constantly changing crowd, largely children. Jennifer left with the old people. Helena followed them indoors.

As the door closed behind them, the young man turned again to, or on, Henry.

'It were 'is fault.'

'It's no use arguing the case with me. I didn't see it. But you have the names and addresses of witnesses. Inform the police. They'll tell you what to do.'

'He just come on. I couldn't believe my eyes.'

'Go and check the state of your car. The police won't be long. They'll breathalise you.'

'O'd boggers like him. They didn't ought to be allowed on the road. They aren't capable.'

Henry turned his back on the driver, took a step towards the old man's front door, but was jerked to a sudden stop by a hand on his shoulder.

'Do you hear me? What I'm telling you?'

Henry pointed a finger at the hand gripping the cloth of his jacket.

'I can hear you. I can also see that you've laid your hands on me. Assaulting me is not doing you or your case any good. In front of witnesses.'

The young man let go, his face red with anger or embarrassment. The crowd fell silent. Henry stepped off again, the spectators parting obsequiously to let him through. He rapped on the door. Helena showed him in.

'How are they?' he asked.

They spent an hour with the old people, sorting out their story once they had settled them down. The telephone calls to the police and the AA were made; the man seemed almost calm, had his account straight, expressed his gratitude in a steady voice.

129

'Whose fault was it?' Helena asked.

'Probably the old chap's. He sees the car approaching head-on at a fair speed and is so surprised he fails to stop. The other driver couldn't have been going all that fast or there would have been more damage.'

'Do you think he had stopped?'

'How do we know? That's his story. And it's quite likely.'

'Unless he's on drugs,' Jennifer suggested. 'Or drink.'

'He didn't seem like it. Aggressive, yes. But that's probably his usual line.'

Helena, back in Henry's kitchen, casually questioned Jennifer about drug addiction locally. A friend of Helena's had had his legs kicked from under him in broad daylight by a young man high on drugs.

'Where was that? London?'

'No. Not a mile from here, and not a month ago. The victim was the son of one of the secretaries at work. He's a grown man, not a schoolboy. It frightened the life out of him.'

'Did he report it?'

'Yes, I think so. But it was all too late.'

Helena listened carefully because she had been impressed by the way Jennifer and Henry had commanded the situation in the street. Jokingly she congratulated them.

'I'm a bossy-boots,' Jennifer answered. 'Always have been. Poking my nose in. That's why I have the job I have.'

130

'Don't you have to stand back, be uninvolved?'

'To some extent. But you have to be interested in other people and their affairs. Curious.'

'And that's growing more dangerous,' Henry said. 'You're likely to be dealing with people who are notably free with their fists, or boots, knives nowadays, have recourse to violence at the beginning not the end. And, of course, if you fail to intervene and some child gets killed or maltreated, then the press mauls you.'

'I'm a bit better off,' Jennifer admitted, 'being attached to a hospital.'

'And you?' Helena enquired of Henry.

'Teachers are always organising something. It's part of the job. You get into the habit.'

'So watch out,' Jennifer warned.

In the evening the two women walked partway home together, and arranged to attend a concert. They discussed Henry.

'He's never recovered from his wife's death,' Jennifer said.

'But he's energetic, and looks years younger than his age. He's very attractive, don't you think?'

'Oh, yes. But he's modest. Doesn't see how handsome he can be. And when I tell him he thinks I'm pulling his leg.'

Three weeks later, well into March, as Jennifer had just finished her Saturday

131

morning Latin lesson, Henry asked if she had seen Helena.

'Yes, we've been to two concerts and she came to my house one evening for a Chinese meal.'

'Do you like her?'

'Yes. She's good company. I guess she could be awkward if she's crossed. She's on the defensive. Perhaps that's because she works in a man's world. Or something else. I think she's attracted to you, Henry.'

'Oh, yes.'

'You could do worse. She might take you out of yourself. In ways I can't.'

'Ways you can't? What on earth are you talking about, woman?'

'Oh, come, just look at it straight. You need a wife.'

'Who says so?'

'You do. Or why do you keep asking me to marry you?'

'I think I need you as a wife. That's not quite the same thing as needing a wife.'

'I'm not so sure.'

Her conversation was without guile or malice. He screwed up his eyes.

'You are not by any chance trying to get rid of me, are you?' he asked.

'No,' Jennifer answered. 'To tell you the truth I don't know what I'm doing. I'd like to see you happily and comfortably settled. But if you were I'd be jealous.'

'Why mention it, then?'

'To find out how you stand, I suppose.'

'You wouldn't like it personally if I married?'

'I don't think I would. But I'm so awkward; it's my fault.'

They left it there, but met again the same evening to make love. After that they could sit quietly, side by side, she leaning against him.

'I've ordered three tickets, for you, me and Helena, to a recital next Thursday. I only saw an advert this morning. A string orchestra. Are you free?'

'Is Helena?'

'She is. I've checked.'

They wrangled about payment for the tickets; she enjoyed yielding in the end, and stayed the night, complaining she wouldn't get her Latin homework done.

On Thursday, Henry picked both women up from Jennifer's house. The day had been sunny, and the air still struck warm, more like June than April. Jennifer smiled a welcome, dressed almost jazzily in a jigsaw frock of bright small pieces. Helena, more soberly but elegantly garbed, stood back from them and their badinage, a glass of sherry in her hand, tall and strikingly handsome.

'Have you brought a coat?' Jennifer asked, like the mother of a feckless urchin.

'I think it's in the car.'

'I hope it is. You know what it's like in these

churches. And it's only April.' She spoke with a velvet voice, a high summer of content, her hand on his forearm.

'Where is it?' Helena asked.

'St Jude's. It's outside the city, the other side of the Trent. Victorian gothic, biggish, no architectural interest,' Henry answered.

'Snooty,' said Jennifer. 'Who was Saint Jude?'

'Wasn't he one of the early Christians? A brother of Jesus? I think he wrote or was supposed to have written one of the books in the Bible. Next to the last book. An epistle.'

'About what?'

'Don't ask me. I'd have looked it up if I had known you were so interested.'

'You're the nearest thing to a scholar I meet.'

'Are you two always on like this?'

'In a way,' Henry answered. 'Jen has come to realise how ignorant I am, and she enjoys rubbing it in.'

They set off in high spirits. Jennifer had arranged a parking place for them in a woodyard not five minutes' walk from the church.

'How do you come to know about this place?' Helena asked.

'Inside information. I helped a daughter out, once. They were grateful.'

'I audit their accounts, but they don't offer me places to park.'

'I know.' Jennifer, in the front seat, turned

expansively. 'It's the difference between our jobs. Yours can be properly rewarded with money. Mine has tips, in gratuities in kindness.'

'Oo-er.' Henry, exaggerating. She slapped his thigh, quite hard. 'You'll have us off the road.'

Early, they found themselves decent seats, and settled down to watch the audience arriving. The men on the whole wore suits and ties, were middle-aged or elderly. Parted silver hair suggested decorum. The women brightened the Gothic darknesses, with bright dresses, handsome coats, and now and again a hat. Conversation was insistent, but low-key. Officials bustled about on unimportant errands. The chairs and stands for the orchestral players were in place and already starkly lit. The three consulted their programmes. They began with the Bach Suite No. 2 in D.

'A typical cultural event,' Henry complained.

'Expound,' said Jennifer, loudly, grinning to herself.

'Where are your young people? Your artisans? Your unemployed?'

'Where would you find such people together?' Helena reasoned. 'It wouldn't be at a pop concert, would it? The prices are too high there.'

'You'd be surprised,' Jennifer answered.

135

'How many without jobs, how many schoolchildren scrape the money together for these big pop events.'

'Why?'

'Hype on the TV they watch, the radio programmes they listen to, in the magazines where they believe what they read. Why, even your quality Sundays have damn great columns on pop releases these days.'

'God help them,' Henry said.

They had their heads together for this, and Henry, still observing the audience, felt more pleased than he had the right to. Or so he told himself. Was it the company of these ladies, or anticipation of Bach, Dvořák, and Tchaikovsky? He did not know, but drew his companions' attention to the fact that out of the eighteen players on the programme only two were women.

'Why is that?' he asked, faux-naïf.

Both turned forefingers at him, from either side. The movement and the mock fury on their faces might well have been rehearsed, so synchronised and severe was the performance.

'Old-boy network,' Jennifer said.

'Do you know either of the two favoured females?' he asked.

'No.'

'They're traitors to the cause. And allowed in for that reason only.' Helena.

'Just to be blamed for any wrong notes?'

They laughed, so strongly that the man in

front, face as red as a pork-butcher's, turned right about.

The double basses appeared first, picked up their instruments. Now the rest of the players occupied their seats without delay. The leader marched in, to scattered applause. The conductor, perfect in tails, received a less perfunctory welcome. He bowed, stared at one or two latecomers looking for seats. He polished his baton between the thumb and first finger of his right hand.

The string orchestra, almost professional, played the Bach string suite with vigour and, slightly less at home, enjoyed the Dvořák serenade. As they rose for the interval, the man on the row in front with his red face and double double-chin, pronounced the G-string air the best tune ever written. Henry and his party slipped along their row to the aisle, Jennifer with grace in spite of her size. They stood together, deciding against coffee or wine. Jennifer waved to, then ducked away towards, a group near the orchestra seats.

'I must speak to that little lot. You keep Helena amused, will you?'

'She's full of energy,' Helena commented, watching Jennifer bulldoze her way down the aisle.

'Oh, yes. Are you enjoying the concert?'

'Very much. More than I thought I should. I'm out of practice.'

'Do you play any instrument?'

137

'The piano, a bit. Does Jennifer?'

'The clarinet. She used to play round local orchestras a lot before she got too busy. Gilbert and Sullivan, that sort of thing.'

'Was that while her husband was alive?'

'Yes. And before. Has she mentioned him to you?'

'Yes,' Helena answered. 'Once or twice. I gathered it was some sort of tragedy.'

Henry briefly outlined the circumstances of Barry Speed's death. It seemed not amiss to do so with people edging past and a buzz of conversation and greeting shielding his low-voiced account.

'How old was he?' she asked.

'Late twenties, I think.'

'Her sort of age?'

'As far as I know. A bit older perhaps. She's thirty-five now.'

'You shouldn't tell me such things,' Helena said coarsely. 'How long ago was all this?'

'Eight years.'

'She was working for the social services then?'

'Yes. A different department.'

'Was she stout, then? As she is now?'

'I didn't know her. She's been as she is as long as I've known her. And that's four or five years.'

'She's attractive,' Helena suggested.

'In spite of,' he answered, rudely. She stared back at him. 'Are you sure you don't want a

138

glass of wine? Or cup of coffee?'

'Certain. She looks happy enough now.'

Jennifer was standing at the front by the orchestral players' seats with a small, laughing, shifting circle of six people, a family perhaps. She had linked arms with a tall young man who had the casual look of a student. The group moved considerably in the enjoyment of their conversation, though over the same small area, but Jennifer still remained anchored to the boy.

'Yes,' Henry agreed. 'She's learning to come to terms with it.'

'That wasn't always so.'

'No.'

Helena watched the exhilarated cluster again.

'Who's the boy?' she asked. 'She doesn't seem very willing to let go of him.'

'I've no idea. Jen's fingers are in more pies than I can guess. And one set touches or impinges on another. She knows dozens upon dozens of people.'

'She's a bit of a marvel, isn't she? In your view?'

'Never mind my view. I hear people all over the place praising her. Consultants at her hospital to petty criminals. She puts a great deal of her spare time into it.'

'Is that the secret?' Helena asked.

'To some extent. As you should know from your own case. Single people who haven't families or aged relatives to look after, and who are prepared to spend their time, can make an enormous difference. Especially when like Jen they're expert at the job. And you, I'd guess.' He checked her disclaimer. 'Now, I'm my own man, but I only put in at the school where I teach the effort they pay me for.'

'Why is that?'

'I'm efficient. I have it all worked out. I don't think I'd make my teaching of Latin any better if I gave it another three or four hours a day.'

'You're teaching Jennifer Latin, aren't you?'

'I am.'

'Is she doing well?'

'Yes, she is. I test her in the same way as I test my younger pupils so that we can see what progress is being made.'

'Is she good at it? Talented?'

'She's intelligent, and conscientious, and well organised. So she doesn't make too many errors. But she's not one of these gifted individuals you hear about who can read a list of foreign words once and know them for ever. I do my best. I try to correct the Latin she learns with the English we use.'

'Is that why she wanted to learn it?'

'I don't know. I think she wanted to learn a subject that she just might have learnt at her school, but didn't, and that isn't much taught these days. There was a feeling among some people, not many, that subjects like Latin trained the mind.'

'Does it?'

'Learning Latin trains the mind to learn Latin. Just as doing crossword puzzles teaches you to do crosswords. You learn the setter's conventions or codes, you learn to search your vocabulary in curious ways, you learn to use dictionaries and works of reference. And if you enjoy it, well and good. And if you feel superior to those who don't know it or can't do it, well, we're all, or some of us, competitive.'

'You wouldn't advise me to take up Latin, then?'

'You'd have to make that decision. I take it you didn't do it at school?'

'No.'

'You were more of a mathematician?'

'I suppose so.'

'And when you hear that Jen is learning Latin, are you envious? At all?'

'Not a whit. I don't mean to be rude. I'm pragmatic. I think I couldn't use it in any shape or form. And it has no mystery about it. But that's my fault. Is it worthwhile learning Latin?'

'Not for you, I'd guess.'

They talked about the music, and he noticed, suddenly, that Helena's attention seemed fixed on Jennifer's group. He glanced that way himself. Jen and the young man were no longer arm-in-arm, but now held hands. They swung the locked hands backwards and forwards, gently, with embarrassment, as if to excuse their overt affection by a childish game.

A pang of jealousy tore through him. He caught his breath.

Immediately he settled his mind: Jennifer Speed was a responsible, level-headed woman and if she held hands with a young man there'd be a respectable reason for the action. She was perhaps encouraging him to some decent, self-enhancing activity he felt too diffident to embark on without the expressed confidence, and she, clutching his arm, taking his hand, thus encouraged him while the group talked of some quite different subject. She knew her way round, did Jennifer.

The cassocked verger clanged a brass school handbell to signal the end of the interval.

'Time we moved,' Helena said. She had not noticed his concern over Jennifer. He moved along the row to his seat. She followed. Before he sat down he looked again towards Jennifer's group which was beginning to break up. The young man, standing close, was stroking her left buttock. He moved his hand openly, without any attempt at concealment; she did not draw away. Both laughed, he looking down on her. A minute later Jennifer slipped into the end seat next to Helena.

'You seemed to be enjoying yourselves,' Helena said, gesturing towards the place where the group had stood.

'Yes. They're really lively people.'

'A family?' Helena put Henry's questions

for him.

'Yes. And no. A mother, father and a daughter. She's playing the viola. And one or two people I've met at work.'

The reassembled orchestra, joined now by a soloist, opened the Bach Suite in B Minor for flute and strings. Henry's turmoil was stilled, and he could smile involuntarily at the dazzling speed, the wit and intricate joy of the final badinerie.

'What do you think of that, then?' Jennifer asked him, across Helena, when the applause had died down.

'Superb.'

'Local girl.'

'The soloist?'

'Yes. From Wollaton. She's making a considerable professional career for herself.'

'Is it possible?' Helena asked.

'It's not easy, but she's doing it.'

Jennifer talked about the soloist's family and career. Her voice was matter-of-fact, ordinary. She knew something, and passed on the information. This was the level-headed, knowledgeable, social Jen he knew, at ease, everybody's friend and mentor.

On the final item of the programme, the Tchaikovsky serenade, the orchestra performed with panache, long bows flashing, every player a virtuoso. Emotion spilled, caught listeners by the throat, blatant yet ordered, demonstrative, plangent,

143

magnificent. The orchestra excelled itself so that large sound bounced from the walls. Many of the audience stood to applaud.

'I liked that best,' Helena said outside.

'Don't tell Henry,' Jennifer said dramatically.

'Why not?'

'There is no God but Bach, and Henry is his prophet.'

They laughed, Henry loudest. He offered them a drink either at his house or at the Goat and Compasses, but Jennifer refused as she had work to complete before tomorrow.

'How long will you stay up?' Helena asked.

'Until it's finished.'

'And what time will that be? The small hours?'

'I hope not, but it depends.'

Helena, after he had dropped Jennifer, returned with him to his house, where they brewed coffee. He still felt uncomfortable, unaccommodated, displeased even with himself. Helena spoke excitedly about the concert, wishing she had spent more of her leisure on music. She had recently bought a CD player, and asked what she should listen to. She spoke with an enthusiasm that surprised him, as if she had undergone a religious conversion.

Her ex-husband had no interest in music, though he had learned to play the piano as a boy. They had not attended concerts, and had rarely listened to classical music on radio and television.

'Just before we started to quarrel really seriously, I went to a concert or two with a school friend. She was keen, and knowledgeable. Geoff didn't mind. He was perhaps pleased to get me from under his feet. Though he always took things, bad things, personally. I was very busy at work, but I could make time for concerts, but not for what he wanted to do. It wasn't important. Just a further last straw on the camel's back.'

'Were you glad to break up?'

'In the end, yes. He was determined on divorce, and, to tell you the truth, so was I before we'd done. It's an odd thing, divorce. You don't know—rather, I didn't know—what I'd done. With bereavement, which is worse, you have no choice. But with divorce you can't help thinking, because you remember what it was like when you first met.'

'You were in love?'

'In so far as I know what that means now, yes. He was good-looking, you've seen him— he's a bit blown these days—he was lively, well-to-do, likely to be richer. But he was ordinary. What used to be called a pipe-and-slippers man. He worked hard, but he needed coddling when he came home. He'd no idea that my work was just as testing and tiring as his. And he would have claimed that that was my fault. He earned quite sufficient to make

145

my work unnecessary. Or so he reasoned.' She grimaced. 'I could be a nuisance. I knew how to fight my corner. That was a phrase I learnt from him. I knew how to wound him. I felt sorry for him sometimes, but I kicked him just as hard. He deserved it. You don't like to hear this, do you?'

'It surprises me.'

'You don't think it's lady-like?'

'It sounds heartless as you tell it.'

They talked, neither sure of the other. His mind switched sorely to the memory of Jennifer hand-in-hand with her student. He changed topics.

'Are you having any more trouble with that man at work? The one who haunts your street?'

'No. He came back again; I saw him one night. And I put it to him.'

'You went out to him?'

'No. I challenged him with it in the office when I'd got him on his own.'

'And what had he to say for himself? Did he deny it?'

'No. I thought he would. So I faced him with it in what you'd call an unlady-like way. I said I'd seen him outside my house two or three times. He looked a bit sheepish, so I said, "Eric, what the fuck do you think you're up to?" That set him back. He doesn't like bad language.'

Helena stopped.

'And?' Henry pressed her.

'He drew himself together. On his chair. It was quite funny and odd to watch him doing it. And then he said, "Helena, I can't help it." I didn't answer. It wasn't my job to rescue him. And then he started: how grateful he was, how I'd altered his life, made a somebody of him, and all the rest of it. I let him go on and asked, "What has this to do with skulking about outside my house?" He answered in a simple sort of way. "It gives me tremendous pleasure," he said, "just to think that you're there behind that door or those curtains." I was cruel to him. "Do you tell your wife what you're doing?" I asked him.

'Did he?'

'Of course he didn't. He didn't seem able to help himself. He was like an adolescent, who's confined physically but with a mind running riot.'

'Wouldn't it have been better to leave him then to his little fantasies?' Henry asked, sternly.

'Why?'

'It did you no harm, and satisfied him.'

'If that's where it stopped. But there's no telling. He might have been exposing himself next, or being beaten up by roughs in the street. There have been one or two cases of queer-bashing recently. And he'd do as a gay. For them.'

'And what's the result, then?'

'Result?' Helena mocked him. 'There isn't

147

any result. He knows I know. He works hard for me, and all I hope is that this doesn't put a stop to that.'

'And if it does?'

'I shall sack him.'

She sat back as if satisfied. He, picking up her cup for a refill, bent quickly and kissed her cheek.

'You're a hard case,' he said.

'Don't you bloody well start.'

He began to talk about some essays of Primo Levi he had read.

'He was a really interesting man, and I suppose what I mean by that is he thinks as I do. Or as I would if I were as clever and level-headed as he is. And this is a Jew, who'd been in the concentration camps. And yet he writes, and I suppose these were short journalist pieces, as easily, as humanely and calmly, as acutely as if nothing worse than a long, fascinating education was all the trauma he had behind him.'

'Why are you telling me all this?'

'Because this highly intelligent man, with a head full of marvellous ideas, committed suicide in the end. It must all have proved too much for him. This clever essayist who convinced me must have covered a shivering individual incapable in the end of coping with life.'

'And does this apply to me?'

'I was thinking of your man, your Eric.'

148

'I doubt if his head's full of fascinating ideas. I don't see the connection, anyhow.'

'He can do his accountancy well, but he's baffled by life, by his emotions.'

'And what are you suggesting?' Helena laughed, quietly but with scorn. 'That I save him from suicide, by yielding to his lewd desires. If I did he'd be terrified, and much more likely to cut his throat.'

'Possible. But don't forget that under that middle-aged elderly, respectable appearance is this eighteen-year-old lover. Or loner.'

'Umh,' she said, 'and talking of that, did you see your Jennifer making up to some young man tonight? There he was, publicly stroking her bum as if it was his private property.'

'I did notice.'

'Who's the young man?'

'No idea.'

'Hasn't she mentioned him?'

'Not as far as I know. Not to draw my particular attention to him.'

Helena looked him over, her face troubled.

'I thought there was something between you and Jennifer. Some sort of understanding.'

He did not answer at once.

'We're lovers,' Henry said. 'We have sex. When we feel that way inclined.' Helena smiled at his expression. 'But I doubt if we're in love. Or rather, if she is.'

'Not like Eric.' She encouraged him.

'No. I have', he hesitated, 'offered to marry

her, but she won't countenance the idea.'

'I've seen her with this young man before. In the Central Library. They seemed fond of each other.'

'How long ago is this?'

'A week. Perhaps more.'

Neither took the conversation further. When half an hour later Helena said she must go or she'd never be up for 'her Sunday morning clean-around', he drove her home at once. She thanked him for the evening, but seemed as withdrawn as he felt.

CHAPTER TEN

At their next Latin lesson, Jennifer's homework was as well prepared as ever; she had learnt vocabulary and rules, handled them accurately. Her manner seemed friendly, humorous, keen, self-deprecating. When they had finished and he had set the next week's tasks, they drank a cup of coffee, and she, not unusually, left at once. She had not mentioned her young man; her behaviour was exactly as it had always been.

'Shall I be seeing anything of you this week?' he asked at the door.

'Probably not. I'm up to my neck in work.' That was quite likely the truth.

Henry examined his despondency. He had

not been wildly in love with, he repeated the phrase, in love with Jennifer, but she had, if there was any truth in his suspicions, upset the status quo. He had for the last year or so come to believe that she was always there, 'an ever-fixèd mark', and though when both were busy a week or so might pass without a meeting, he had come to rely upon her. She was a part of his life; more importantly it now seemed than he had understood at the time.

As soon as she was out of the house he wondered if he should have questioned her. That she would have given him straight answers he had no doubt. Yet she had not mentioned the 'young man'. The trouble was that he might not have liked Jennifer's answers.

That afternoon, quite by chance, he met the head of Jennifer's department as he was walking his dog in the park where Henry had chosen to stroll.

Frank Hempshill stopped, whistling his labrador back. Henry did not know him well, though he had met him at office parties. A man of perhaps sixty-four, near retirement, he dressed smartly, even off duty. Today he wore a raincoat, high-gloss brogues and carried a polished walking-stick. He looked both younger than his years, and taller than his height. He had touched the brim of his smart tweed hat with a gloved hand. Now he felt at his clipped grey moustache. He enquired after

151

Henry's health, and came immediately to the business that had caused him to interrupt his smart pace.

'Have you seen Jennifer Speed lately?' he asked.

'Yes, I saw her this morning. She came for a Latin lesson.'

'I beg your pardon.' Hempshill seemed affronted. His grey eyes chilled behind steely spectacles.

'She's learning Latin.'

'Oh, yes.' He relaxed.

'With ask, command, advise and strive
Use "ut" not the infinitive.'

That established his credentials. 'Did she seem well, cheerful, normal?'

'Yes. Why shouldn't she be?'

Hempshill lifted his chin heavenwards, as if making up his mind, not replying, watching his labrador, which circled energetically.

'This is confidential. I ought not to spread this. But I know I can trust your discretion, and I know you're a close associate of Jennifer's.'

He let this sink in. Henry said nothing.

'It concerns', Hempshill, clearing his throat, continued, 'a junior member of the department.' Again he coughed. 'You realise this is a private matter.'

Henry wondered if the member of the department was the 'young man', and whether

152

Jen's antics in love had in some way annoyed her superior, undermined his confidence in her. Two smartly dressed men, on the verge of old age, faced each other on an April afternoon of windy greenness and dull skies.

'One of the younger members of my department is concerned in a police case.'

'Man or woman?'

'A young, married woman.'

Henry felt relief, cancelled it. Perhaps this was the young man's wife.

'This young woman, I shall give no names, young woman, is concerned in a police prosecution of one of her clients for murder. Three murders, in fact. I shall give you no details, though, if you read the local papers, you might easily put two and two together. Now it would seem that some blame attached itself to this young woman, who fell short, it appears, of her duties. She could well be named in the courts, questioned, and our department might attract unfavourable notice, publicity. And perhaps rightly.'

Hempshill traced a pattern in the sandy mud with the toe of his right shoe. Henry watched, but could make nothing of the resultant marks.

'The young woman concerned has been with us nearly two years, and has given every satisfaction. But in this case she on several occasions failed to make contact with her clients. Not that this is unusual. There are many who make sure they are out when we

153

arrive, or refuse to answer the door. But for reasons best known to herself this young woman not only failed to make contact, but filled in reports suggesting that she had interviewed the couple concerned and that matters were, if not satisfactory, at least not dangerous.'

'Why would she do that?' Henry asked.

'Ah, we're always asking that question in our department. People act out of character, and we do not know why. Perhaps, because she had been doing so well, she resented her failure to contact this couple. It reflected on her efficiency. It might even have been done in what I can call "good faith".'

'What's that?' Henry had begun to grow annoyed with Hempshill's stilted, hesitant speech.

'When we are looking after people, we not only see and question them, we take notice of other evidence. State of the house, for example, as seen through the window. But also information we receive from relatives and neighbours. You can see that here we are on dangerous ground. An experienced social worker will know how to evaluate this evidence. And in this case the young woman in question, not being able to contact the people she's looking after, may have put too much trust in these secondary sources. It's difficult. We have to make constant judgements about what to pursue and what to disregard.'

'Where does Jennifer come into this?'

'Not directly. She had no direct contact with the subjects. But in a case like this, when the police are making enquiries, we look to it that a solicitor is available to our officer, and always, this is my own institution, a senior colleague to advise both the girl, in this case, and the solicitor, who may know the law but not the circumstances under which we work. I asked Jennifer if she would act as "friend" in this case.'

'And?'

'Being what she is, she agreed. Now Jennifer is a gem. If everybody in my department worked as conscientiously, our rate of success would be much greater. But I don't need to expatiate to you on Jennifer's virtues.'

Henry glanced upward to the deaf-mute skies.

'The case has proved more serious than we anticipated, and I don't wish to overload Jennifer, willing horse as she is.'

'You mean you want to take her off the case?' Henry asked.

'No. I do not. She is not, as you should have gathered, officially connected with it at all. What I really wanted to check with you was that she was not overstretching herself. I am relieved to find you do not think so. She has not mentioned this particular affair to you?'

'No.'

'No. She would not. Yes. Well, thank you,

Mr Shelton. Keep your eye on her, will you? There are not too many Jennifer Speeds around.'

Hempshill touched the brim of his smart hat, brandished his stick and set out, his dog dashing forward. Henry watched the retreating, slim back, troubled.

That evening he rang Jennifer twice, but failed to make contact. He left no message on her answer-phone. He tried again and failed on the next two days. On the following evening he walked round to ring her doorbell, without success. On Saturday she appeared, punctual as ever, for her Latin lesson.

'I've been trying to get hold of you all week,' he grumbled as he hung her coat up. He described his meeting with Hempshill.

'That's typical', she answered, 'of him. If he's done something he's unsure about, he confesses it to somebody who has a sympathetic face, always making sure that the story he tells shows him in a good light.'

'So there's nothing to worry about?'

'I wouldn't say that. The girl, her name's Clare Statham, is in pretty serious trouble. She was careless, and had already been warned by her immediate superior, Jo Pickford, to try to straighten this case out, well before the murders. The newspapers will be after us, I expect.'

'And is that what Hempshill fears?'

'He won't like it. He wants everybody to love

156

him. But he's within a year of retirement. It won't make much difference.'

'And you? You're not worrying yourself to death over the case?'

'No. I'm doing my best. Not that there's much I can do. And Clare resents my interference.'

'But you're all right?'

'I am.'

She tapped with her forefinger on the open book, with the unmarked exercises, which lay on the table, calling him back to duty. He wrenched the top off his red biro, and began to mark. Jennifer had done as well as ever. Tick followed tick. She, at last, began to smile.

Henry did not mention the 'young man'. To his observation, and he watched carefully, Jennifer was exactly as she always was, cheerful, smart, keen to learn, polite afterwards. He enjoyed teaching her.

Later in the week he learnt, piecemeal over three evenings, from the newspaper, that Clare Statham had committed suicide. She had rung her office, speaking in a normal voice, to announce that she would not be in that day, that she was off-colour. She had connected a pipe to the car exhaust and had killed herself in the closed garage. She had left notes. Her husband no longer lived with her. An inquisitive neighbour and the milkman had been suspicious, and had telephoned the police, her husband and then her office.

157

Henry, greatly uncertain, decided against contacting Jennifer. She was due, anyway, to appear on Saturday for a lesson.

He thought her face seemed, if not drawn, rigid, lacking expression, but she sat down as usual. He marked her exercises on the dative case. 'Large apples are suitable for kind girls.' She had done well. He began to explain the use of the ablative.

'I've never heard the word before,' she said.

'It's connected with removal, taking away, deterioration, weathering, from Latin *latum*, supine of *ferre*, to take, to carry, and *ab*, away.'

'Supine?' she queried.

'Verbal noun. But let's not go into that. I'll just tell you the principal parts of the verb. *Fero, ferre, tuli, latum*. How's that for a right irregularity?' He wrote it down for her.

'More than one root, I guess. Like "go" and "went" in English. And an inability to pronounce "tl".'

'Interesting,' she said. He believed her.

After the lesson, as they drank coffee, he asked if she felt well.

'So-so,' she answered.

'I read about your Clare Statham in the paper.'

'Yes.' She paused, shook her head, deciding not to continue.

'You didn't expect it?'

'No. But now it has happened I'm not surprised.'

'Why is that?'

Jennifer scratched her face, narrowed her eyes. 'She had a great many private troubles that I knew nothing about.'

'Such as?'

'You're a nosy devil.' He felt shock at her rudeness.

'Hadn't you noticed before?'

'She had', Jennifer continued without hurry in a steady voice, 'an unhappy childhood, father dying, mother remarrying, illness.'

'Abuse?'

'No. Not in that sense. Life knocked her about. Then there's been the break-up with her husband recently. She seemed to us a quiet, well-qualified, well-motivated girl, but whenever you looked more closely you found scars. She had a decent degree, but it came out she barely hung on to her course, almost decided to give it all up twice.'

'You couldn't deduce any of this from her behaviour?'

'I didn't. Not that I knew her very well. In this last week or two, when I was supposed to be looking after her, I found her unapproachable. She was quiet, but I half-expected that after the errors she had made. Some people bluster, but not Clare. She'd answer my questions, in what seemed a sensible way; she was invariably well dressed, hair attractively done, make-up tidy. There were no signs of deep nervous distress. I took

159

her to be a girl who had, for reasons I could not fathom, bad emotional history, pre- or post-menstrual tension, domestic trouble, money worries, lack of real interest, done her job in a slipshod way, and then tried to cover up. Both Arthur Schofield, the solicitor Frank Hempshill brings in, and I questioned her quite hard, together and apart, but we were both left with the impression that an ordinary girl had slipped up, tried to hide it, and was sorry for what she'd done.'

'She covered her tracks?' he asked.

'She seemed shy, not very willing to talk about herself except in a superficial way. Such people exist. Even in departments like ours. She didn't even seem to feel sorry for herself. You make a mistake, and before you know where you are you're involved in a really serious matter. Most of us would be complaining about that, but not Clare.'

'Hadn't her superior warned her?'

'Yes. Yes and no. Jo Pickford had told her to be careful on this case, that she was dealing with a rum lot. But we're pushed for time. We're worked to death. As soon as Clare died, it's amazing how much came out, mostly from her husband and her mother and stepfather, but before that here was an apparently well-balanced girl who'd made a mistake.'

'You didn't find other slip-ups she'd made?'

'Not as far as I know. Something may turn up, oh, months ahead.'

'You look into possibilities of error?'

'We do. We have to.'

Henry paused, sat back, breathed deeply. 'You don't in any way blame yourself, feel guilty about any of this?'

'No. Why should I?'

'I know you. You think you should have spotted something? You missed some clue, and now you feel bad about it?'

'No.'

Henry waited again.

'Are you all right, Jennifer?'

'Perfectly.'

'You don't seem yourself. You're taking a sensible line, when you say that nothing you could have done would have altered this case. But that's not very like you.'

'I'm not usually sensible?'

'Let me put it like this: I'd have expected you to be more disturbed in your mind than you appear to be. And I wonder why this is.'

'I'm using common sense and not showing symptoms of being disturbed? I see. Therefore you accuse me of not being myself.'

'You may try to joke your way out of it,' he said. 'You are not yourself.'

'Um.'

'If you don't want to talk about it, all well and good. Just say so, and I'll shut up.'

Jennifer examined her feet. She sat, hands on knees, occasionally lifting her head to look him straight in the eye, as if to decide how to deal

161

with some new misdemeanour he had committed. She seemed in no way troubled, merely applying her intellect to satisfy curiosity.

'There's something I ought to tell you,' she said at length, then stopped.

'Go on.'

'I've been meaning to do so for some little time now.' Again the straight stare, before she relaxed into the back of her chair. 'I've fallen in love, Henry.'

'With whom?' The oblique case established the rule of reason.

'You don't know him. Timothy Glover.'

Again the hiatus. Henry breathed heavily.

'Well, aren't you going to tell me about it?'

'I'm afraid you're going to laugh at me. Or be very angry. He's only nineteen.'

The young man. Henry's throat tightened.

'Go on, then,' he said gruffly. 'Let's hear the story.'

'We met earlier in the year at a party. We danced.' Like many stout women Jennifer was light on her feet. 'And we talked.'

'And that was it? The torch was lit?'

'I enjoyed his company. He made an effort to keep me amused. I didn't expect that. I'm no oil-painting, and I'm sixteen years older than he is.'

'Did you realise he was only nineteen?'

'Don't be daft. I hadn't gone out of my mind. I knew he was years younger than I was.'

162

'And?'

'I took him home. Still talking. Still laughing. We had sex. He stayed the night. And all the next day.'

'What's he do for a living? Is he a student?'

'He's an apprentice electrician with Clumber's. He did well at GCSE, but they couldn't persuade him to stay on for "A" levels.'

'Why was that?'

'No encouragement at home. Didn't get on with his step-father. Wanted money. Saw this job advertised, thought it had possibilities, applied, walked into it.'

'Does he like it?'

'Not altogether. Like all jobs it has its periods of tedium.'

'Good phrase. Second declension, neuter. So you're encouraging him to take up formal education again?'

'I'm doing no such thing. What I'm doing is, to my immense surprise,' she made him wait for her conclusion and repeated verb, 'is enjoying myself.' Jennifer seemed in no way on the defensive. 'I wake up every morning to a new world.' She laughed at herself.

'And will it last?'

'Will anything?' she answered. 'I haven't thought about it. I'm revelling in what I've got while I can.'

'Does he love you?' Henry asked.

'He says so. As far as I can see, it's true. It

163

may seem surprising to you, it seems so to me, but there it is. It's possible, isn't it?'

Henry failed to answer.

'Tell me about him.'

'What do you want to know?'

'Is he good company? Does he read a lot? Does he like music, go to concerts? Is he a pub type? Does he believe in God?' Sarcasm rang.

'Steady on,' Jennifer said in mock alarm. 'I've only known him a couple of months or so. *You'd* think he was ignorant, hadn't read a great deal, and I suppose that's true. But he's intelligent. He was on the science side at his school. He's quick to solve little mathematical problems.'

'Such as?'

'How much material I'd need for a pair of curtains or what it would cost to redecorate my rooms.'

'And is he shy?'

'He is that way inclined. Until you get to know him better.'

'Has he had many girl-friends?'

'I can't answer that. He mentions odd ones.'

'He wasn't living with one of them?'

'No.'

He raised the coffee pot in a mute question. She shook her head; she muttered that she'd had two already. Now she seemed to have lost her zest, perhaps regretting her confidences.

'I see,' he said, and sighed.

'What do you think?' She put the question,

slowly, quietly, and waited for the answer.

'I suppose you're doing the right thing in making the most of it. *Carpe diem*, eh?' She did not react. 'But it can have its dangers.'

'Such as?'

'If the age difference proves too large. So he leaves you, or you drop him under pressure.'

Jennifer lifted her head.

'You wanted to marry me, Henry, and the difference between our ages is twenty-four.'

'Yes. Our society, rightly or wrongly, is more inclined to accept that. Women, at least in men's view, seem to age more quickly than men, in appearance at least. I stress it's in the view of men. The television managers will accept wrinkled male newsreaders, but the women are much younger, and pretty.'

'So you think I'm foolish?' she asked.

'No. But I don't want you to get hurt. Life's knocked you about badly enough as it is.'

'Is that why you took up with me?'

'It is not. You were good company, interesting, intelligent. Your job opened up to me facets of life I'd never got near. I thought our physical relationship was good. You're lively but not flighty, or volatile; you're sensible, independent, reasonable. I enjoyed every different minute of you.'

'And now I've let you down?'

'No. This is obviously the end of our relationship, but I don't blame you. Why should I? You've chosen to do what suits you

165

best. Why shouldn't you?'

'I've hurt you, Henry.' She spoke gently.

'I'm disappointed. We are none of us so sure of ourselves that we can put up with rebuffs. You were there. We helped one another, had good times together. I loved you, Jennifer. In so far as somebody like me can, I loved you, and I thought you loved me.'

'I did, Henry.'

'But you found something better, more exciting, and you chose that.'

'It all happened so quickly. I could hardly help myself.'

'You didn't tell me immediately.'

'No. I ought to have done. I blame myself.' Her eyes were wet; a squeezed tear dribbled on to her cheek. 'I could hardly believe what had happened. And I was selfish enough not to want to break up what existed between us for something that might disappear in a few days. That was wrong. Wrong to Tim as well as you. I'm sorry. You've been good to me, and for me. And now I'm treating you like this. I'm rotten. The only thing I can say, Henry, is that I'm sorry.'

'You've told me now.' His voice drooped.

'Oh, Henry.'

She wept openly. Her tears angered him. They sat in his room, she sobbing aloud, he withdrawn, looking nowhere. In the end she poked at her eyes with a small, sodden, lace-edged handkerchief.

'I'd better go.' Her voice sounded quite changed.

'Yes.' He stood up. She scrambled upright. He saw that she wanted to make some suitable movement towards him, shake his hand, kiss him, hug him to her. He held himself stiffly out of her reach, signalling with his left arm her path to the door.

'This will be the end of Latin lessons, then?' she said, barely audible.

'We'll see.'

He hurried her out to the street, closing the door on her before she had taken three steps away from the house.

CHAPTER ELEVEN

Henry went glumly about his work.

For the first day or two Jennifer's defection was constantly in his mind, but he drove his classes hard in an attempt to expunge the pain. His success was limited; he'd set tests which needed hours to mark, but in the middle of the task he'd find his thoughts had drifted away, had become darkly depressed without specific reference to Jennifer. Deliberately he took more physical exercise, but this seemed against his will. At a concert, baroque music, he enjoyed standing amongst the people in the interval, but found himself on the watch for

Jennifer, half-dreading her appearance. His mind grew sluggish, unlit. He could not read, or listen, or watch television for long. In class his temper was short.

Twice he apologised for shouting at girls who had committed errors he expected them to make. His class looked on him with suspicion. Nobody laughed. He failed to make his little jokes. Once he found he could not recall the name of a girl he had taught for two years. He drilled his pupils as though he expected them not to learn. Tears were the rule in his classroom now. And yet they did as well, or badly, as ever. He pondered this, and grew more wretched.

As he ate his tea on Friday evening, Jennifer telephoned.

'I'm just checking whether you expect me for Latin tomorrow?' Her voice sounded plummy, balanced as always.

'Have you done your exercises?' he asked.

'Yes. All of them.'

'Usual time then.' Grim, gruff, unyielding.

'Are you all right?'

'Thank you, yes.'

She rang off after a hesitation. He did not help her out.

Jennifer arrived exactly on time. Outside it rained half-heartedly. She wore a neat two-piece and blouse.

'Any snags?' he asked.

'I don't think so.'

168

She had done well. When he explained her mistakes on the two or three occasions where she had gone wrong, she took the point immediately, and seemed mildly annoyed with herself. He noticed that she had completed more sentences than he had set, a childish attempt, he thought, to make things up to him. He completed the marking, tested her memory, made her read out loud in Latin the passage for translation.

The lesson had been successful, but different. Before, when she had made an error, she would shyly lay a hand on his, in apology, or perhaps to cheer him for his failure to make it all clear to her. Now they sat at a distance so that the exercise book had to be passed between them. Their shoulders never touched, nor their hands. They kept an unnatural yard apart. He felt pleased to maintain the distance. At the end of the lesson he said he would test her on all five declensions next. She nodded compliantly.

'Is that all right? Have you the time?' he asked.

'I'll make it. If you think it's necessary.'

She accepted his offer of a cup of coffee, but there was constraint between them. He ventured a few comments on the baroque concert; she had not been there. She came out with a sentence or two on the Clare Statham business, but rather unwillingly as if it was no concern of his. As soon as she had finished her coffee, she rose to leave. He made no attempt to detain her.

Down in the mouth, he prepared his lunch. He had shopped earlier, to give himself time to spend with Jennifer. It had not been needed. He sat to listen to the one-o'clock news. Almost immediately, and to his surprise, he fell asleep, but uncomfortably, his rest being disturbed by broken, unpleasant dreams. These did not touch his loss; he found himself deserted and wanting in desperate situations. He had failed to set an important examination paper. In another lurid episode he found himself in a desert surrounded by oyster shells, which he twice tried to count, and failed. He woke with a violent start, he was falling. He sat still, controlling himself, steadying his mind. His bones ached; he lacked energy. On the radio cheerful voices discussed the funding and reorganisation of hospitals. Speakers called political opponents by Christian names; all seemed convinced of their ease, sincere, but rehearsed, forceful but without spontaneity, as if they had heard both sides of the argument so often that nothing could surprise them. He was faintly taken aback that the anti-government case received louder applause. The audience had made up its mind already.

His telephone rang. He dragged himself to his feet.

Helena Gough announced she needed to pay a visit near him, and asked if she could call.

'Still at work on Saturday afternoon?' he asked on her arrival, glad to see her.

'Not really. I had to drop a card through a letter-box in Clement Street. I wanted the man to have it by Monday morning.' They chatted for some minutes, and she drew herself up. 'I'd better be quite honest with you, Henry.'

He pulled a wry face.

'To tell you the truth Jennifer asked me to look in on you.'

'She was here this morning,' he answered, 'for a Latin lesson.'

'Was she? When she spoke to me she wasn't sure whether that arrangement still stood.'

'When was that?'

'Wednesday, no, Thursday. She dropped into my office for coffee. We sometimes can arrange it.' The odd placing of the adverb indicated her unease.

Henry looked at the carpet, wishing he had a cup and saucer or glass to play with, but she had refused his offer. His eyes felt sore, bunged up with sleep.

'She told you about this Timothy boy, then?' he asked, sounding angry to himself.

'Yes.'

'She told *me*.'

'You weren't surprised, were you? We saw them at that concert in St Jude's.'

'Not altogether.' He closed his eyes, like a martyr. 'What do you make of it?'

'Make of it?' Helena asked. 'She just came

171

plainly out with it. Said she was in love, that she was really happy.'

'And what did you say?'

'What could I say?'

'Think, then.' He sounded irritable. 'What did you think?'

'I suppose you mean about the difference in their ages. It's not uncommon. They could have a first-rate sexual relationship. He'd be full of libido. It could be very good for her.'

'So you think she's wise?' he said.

'I don't know that wisdom comes into it. They fell into her bed. She liked it. And that was that. They were away.'

'Will it last?'

'Shouldn't think so.' Her answer dismissed both his sincerity and naïvety. 'But you never know.'

'Were you surprised?'

'Certainly Jennifer seems a very level-headed woman, and so I wouldn't have thought she'd have gone in for cradle-snatching. But I'm a bit of a cynic about social workers. Those I've known, and I admit there aren't too many, have had a background of deprivation or ill-fortune, and it's as if they're determined to make up to themselves by keeping others out of the traps and tragedies. It can't be true for all of them, for sure. And it might well be that their own troubles have been relatively minor. But it set them in the way to putting the world to rights.' She paused. 'I

172

don't know anything about Jen's childhood, but she lost her husband, shockingly, and then when she was just beginning to pick the pieces up, this bastard she was living with dropped her.'

'She's clever.'

'I agree.'

'So when she . . .?' he broke off, unwilling to formulate his question precisely.

'So when she falls for this boy, it may be the most sensible thing she's ever done. He loves her, he says. There's a riot of marvellous sex just at the time when she thought it was downhill all the way, when she feared she had no sexual attraction left, that she was a fat, wobbling middle-aged do-gooder. And here's her Timothy, stripping slim as a wand, rousing her again. Just think. Use your imagination, man.'

'You sound excited about it yourself.'

'So I am.'

'Has it happened to you, then?'

'No,' she answered. 'But it happened to my mother. With you.'

Henry thought that over, shocked.

'That's not the way it appeared to me.'

'You weren't excited?' she asked.

'Yes. More than you know. It was unexpected. In 1950, in spite of the war. I did not expect Marion to snatch me up like that. But I don't think I expected it to last. And she was very much in charge.' He smiled at the

173

feebleness of the phrase.

'Jennifer wanted me to come and see you, to check up. She cares for you. Even when her life's been turned upside down.'

He grimaced.

'And what do you suggest I do?' he demanded.

'Put up with it, for a start.' The blunt sentence reminded him of Helena's mother. 'And continue with her Latin lessons.'

'Why?'

'Because, for whatever daft reasons, she wants to learn the language, and so far, she says, she enjoys getting it right. And Latin doesn't change.'

'What do you mean?'

'It's a dead language. The words, the grammar, don't alter. There they are fixed. To be mastered in a time of rapid, wild newness, if there is such a word. She's an interesting woman. She's worth persevering with. You ought to have married her, Henry.'

'I asked her often enough, but she refused. I used to think it was because of the terrible end of her marriage to Barry, but perhaps it was because she was, consciously or otherwise, waiting for this fling with her Timothy.'

'That's not likely,' Helena said.

'No, perhaps not.'

Helena did not stay a great deal longer. She enquired about his work, and briefly described hers. As they stood in the hall on her way out,

174

she said, 'This must be pretty bloody for you.'

'Do you think it could have happened if we had been married?' he asked her.

'Oh, yes. It could have happened. There's no doubt about that. Whether she would have allowed it to develop is another matter. I just don't know.'

Helena clapped him on the shoulder, and bent to kiss him, not on the cheek, but on the lips. She drew rapidly away, promising to call before too long.

Henry felt the worse for her visit.

In the next Saturday morning's post he found a letter from Helena, asking if he'd like a drive round in her car. 'I had thought', she wrote, 'of looking at the place where my mother lived. That sort of thing. And you'd be the ideal guide. I shall be in my office from 9 to 12 on Saturday morning when you receive this. Just give me a tinkle, one way or the other.' He rang and accepted her offer before Jennifer arrived for her lesson. They agreed to meet at 1.15 p.m.

They drove to the suburb where Marion and he had lived forty years before. Helena parked her car, and they strolled inquisitively about. There had been some pedestrianisation, and, in the middle of what had been the main street, trees had been planted in brick-built containers, and seats had been placed. Litter from the market-place spread, from tumbled bins, while weeds grew feebly in the soil round the trees. The paving blocks, fairly recently laid, were already out of line, off level and in some places badly cracked. People, darkly dressed, hurried about in the April sunshine.

'Has it changed much?' she asked.

'Yes. No. They've pulled whole shops down, and left others.'

'Are those listed?' She waved at Dutch gables.

'I shouldn't think so. They'd be built at the end of the century, from the Eighties onward. There's a sort of dignity, or pomposity, perhaps, about them. People were beginning to earn a bit of money, and build big stone chapels, and they needed these emporia to match.'

'You love this place, don't you?'

'That's the wrong word. I see there's nothing much to be said aesthetically in its favour, and it's noisy and dirty, but it's where the exciting things happened when I was a boy, where the trolley-buses ran, and people I knew went about their business.'

'Do you know anybody now?'

Henry looked about him, at the single figures, the groups, the chatterers, the silent, the beggar in rags, the chidden children.

'Not a soul.'

They turned into a short side-street, a cul-de-sac, of faded, brick, terraced houses with small front gardens, a yard or two only in depth, behind Bulwell-stone walls and small wrought-

176

iron gates. A wall covered with ivy cut off two-thirds of the end of the street, where palings staggered across the rest. An enormous willow drooped, towering skywards.

'What's behind that?' Helena asked.

'The river, if it's not in a culvert now. The river, I'm sure. And a supermarket car-park.'

'What was it in your day?'

'Fields.'

A woman stood at her front door, eyeing them. As they paused for the moment, a young couple, with a push-chair laden with a child and groceries, angled past and turned down an entry.

'Don't be so bleddy mardy,' the mother had instructed her child. 'I don't know what's wrong wi' 'im, moaning all the time.'

'Did you talk like that?' Helena asked.

'I imagine so. Though my parents didn't come from this part of the world. That's your mother's house, if I remember rightly. Number eleven.'

'It looks respectable, but a bit small for big families.'

'You were used to cramped spaces. And oddly they made it worse by never using the front room. If you called in on somebody you knew, you invariably went round to the back. You never knocked at the front door.' He pointed out the beauty of the hand-made bricks with their thin, straight lines of mortar. 'It's a different world.'

'What sort of people lived here?'

'Decent working-class families who could pay their rent. Some stayed for years, though there'd be changes. Widows, the unemployed, those on part-time, would have a struggle. This was in the Thirties, when I was a child. We had an economic depression then.'

'Don't boast. Did no people buy their houses?'

'Hardly at all. Those who were socially mobile, or restless, could get a new rented council-house if they wanted it, with biggish gardens back and front, and a bathroom.'

'It hasn't changed much, has it? In appearance, I mean. This street must have looked much as it does now, when my mother was a girl.'

'Basically. The paintwork on doors and windows would have been less bright, more standardised brown.' He pointed to a thin strip of incongruous stone-cladding in the middle of a terrace and several flush or fancy-glassed doors. 'There'd be none of that. And most would have had a neat bit of privet hedge behind the wall.'

'And aspidistras in the front window?'

'My parents had one, certainly.'

'It's a curious word. Does it mean anything?'

'I don't think they know, really. Some connect it with the Greek word for a shield.'

She looked impressed at his modest learning, and, turning, said, 'What does it feel like to stand here again after all this time?'

'It's hard to say. I remember some of the people best. One family in particular. But this wasn't anywhere near where I lived.'

'Did you ever go into that house?'

'A time or two with your mother.'

'So you met my grandparents?'

'No. Never. They were out.'

'That was the idea, was it?' she asked, forcefully shy.

He shuddered.

'And while things were happening in Worcester, in America and elsewhere to my mother, and to all the rest of the world,' she said quietly, 'these houses still stood here. Continuity.' She tacked on the word, with hesitation.

'They've tarmacked the cobbled road,' he answered.

The pair returned by a circuitous route to the car, and he took pains on the way to point out where a line of cottages, or an over-high chapel, a police-station, and here and there whole streets had been pulled down. He found it difficult to recall the old locations exactly. The wind seemed chillier here; the patches of blue smaller between clouds.

'Did you go out together? Walking?'

'Yes. But never to public places. Your mother would order me to meet her somewhere. Usually it was on a Thursday night. She visited a girl-friend, and I walked

179

her home.'

'Was it dangerous?'

'No. As far as I remember there was hardly anybody about.'

'Will you show me?'

'I expect it's all changed. It'll be a mile and a half away.'

He gave directions, not very clearly, and they parked finally in an estate of decent detached and semi-detached private houses built inside the last thirty years. Henry looked round, recognising nothing. They wandered about the streets, commenting on front gardens, but made no progress in their research.

'You'll have to ask,' she chided.

He followed her advice, and explained about the farmhouse to a middle-aged man who was cleaning his car. The man listened, scratching his nose, appearing to view their request for information suspiciously, and then pointed.

'It's that direction. Mind you, it'll take you all of twenty minutes to get there. It's on Belton Road. And then I don't know if it's the right one.'

'Are there a lot of farms about here, then?' Helena asked sarcastically.

'It was all farming land here when I was a boy.' He turned his back on Helena, and gave exact details of the itinerary to Henry. These he then repeated as if checking his own accuracy.

'It was called Sprake's Farm,' Henry said,

thanking him.

'I don't know about that.' He shook his head. They set off before he gave them his third version.

On the way they passed their car. 'Mustn't lose sight of that,' she said cheerfully. They followed their instructions and finally reached Belton Road. There was nothing rural or agricultural about the place. The street seemed slightly more up-market than the rest, with well kept detached houses, wide drives, rose-bushes, panelled garage doors. There were trees in the gardens, but nothing above twenty-five years old.

'This is the name,' he muttered uncertainly. 'Belton. He said it was along here. Five or ten minutes' walk.'

'Let's make tracks.'

They stepped it rapidly out along the slightly curving road without much hope. Helena complaining.

'It was your idea,' he said, mildly.

'Will you remember it? If we get there?'

'I doubt it.'

The front gardens gave way round a curve to the windowless rural wall of a barn, and then to the entrance to the farmyard and, beyond, the two-storey end of the house. The yard stretched wide, surrounded by unmatching buildings. A huge lime tree leaned slightly towards the centre from the barn-side. Half a dozen cars had been parked very squarely in the corner furthest from the house.

'Has it changed much?'

He tried to make up his mind.

'This barn was here, and the house. I think there was a wooden gate, a five-barred affair, across the entrance. I didn't often come up as far as this. I used to wait further down for Marion.'

'Was the road made up then?'

'No. Not really. And nothing like as wide as it is now, though you could get a small lorry or a tractor along it. Just about.'

'And what was on that side?'

'A hedge. Fields. A few trees.' He pointed. A lime tree, equivalent in height and girth to the one in the farmyard, stood incongruously on the edge of one of the front gardens, leaning slightly over the road. 'That must have been there. And there was a garden that side of the house.' They took the few necessary steps. A hawthorn hedge straggled beside the pavement. As far as they could make out, the land behind was still a garden, untidily kept, strong with shrubs.

'Who lived here?'

'A girl called Olive Rempstone. She was at school with your mother. And on Thursdays Marion would come up here for her tea after work.'

'And meet you at?'

'Eight. Half-past. It varied. It didn't happen often. Just over a few months in winter. It was dark out here. There was a wood about a half-mile down the road.' He waved a vague direction.

'I wonder who lives here now. Do you think it's privately owned?'

'It might be a business by the look of all those cars.'

The number was roughly painted in white on a brick in the blank wall of the house. Two hundred and forty-three.

'It makes a decent house,' she said. 'What date would it be?'

'Early eighteen hundreds, I guess.'

Helena was laying a flat hand on the bricks of the barn.

'My mother must have seen these, and yet in completely different surroundings.'

'It seemed very out of the way, miles from anywhere.'

Helena set off, rather sedately, back along the route by which they had come. She stopped after a few yards, pointed to the ground.

'And this must be roughly where you waited?'

He grinned. 'Roughly.' He looked back at the barn wall. The house behind him had a name-plate: 'St Ives'. The next, No. 227, was called 'Avalon', then 'The Hollies'. He could not read the names of those over the street.

'And you'd walk along in the direction of this road?' They now did so.

'Yes. I guess so.'

183

'Where did it come out?'

'Somewhere in the park, and then on to the Hucknall Road.' He waved his hands about him. 'There was a wood here, a copse.' Not a tree stump remained.

'And you'd dally there?'

'You could say so.' He grinned at her word.

They gave up on the road, turned, made for the car. As they opened the door she said, 'Let's go back to the farm. You drive so I can look round.'

They did so, and stared again at the barn, the end wall of the house, the yard, the garden hedge, the lime tree, making little of them.

'I wonder what sort of business they run?' she asked.

'Breeding pedigree dogs? Or it may be an office for accountants.'

'They'd surely have a plate.'

'You'd think so.'

He reversed the car into the entrance and, facing the other way, asked, 'Now where do we go?'

'It's over forty years ago, isn't it? I wish there had been a bit of your lovers' wood left.'

They sat in silence. Helena spoke first. 'Will you drive down this road to see if there's anything you recognise?'

He did as she ordered, and in no time the road had turned at a right-angle, and he guessed from the look of the trees that this was the end of the estate and that they were skirting the park. He said as much.

'You walked through the park?'

'We did.'

'See if we can get in. There must be a gate somewhere.'

They met a main road and after a hundred yards turned off this into the park. Notices instructed him to drive at no more than 10 m.p.h.

'We'd be coming the other way,' he said.

'Do you remember this?'

'I think so.'

'Stop here, then.'

They strolled round for some time, but he was unable to identify the gate where he and Marion had entered on those dark nights.

'There was a bandstand,' he recalled. 'Not a glass-sided, roofed-in affair. A wooden platform three or four feet off the ground.'

They searched in the grass for traces, but nothing remained.

'Did you ever hear a band?' she asked.

'No. Kids used it for their games.'

'Did you and Marion?'

'No. Ours were quiet.' He remembered her squeals.

They walked in a wood, then under an avenue of trees, then on to the cricket field, where he noticed they had cut down the elms and moved the pavilion from one corner to the far side. Houses had been built right up to the edge of the ground, and a pub brassily replaced

185

the farmhouse. They returned to her car. This time she took the wheel.

'Would you join me for a cup of tea?' she asked. 'If you're not busy?'

'What about you?'

'I could do with a break.'

Back in her house, they sat formally at a table covered with a cloth. She cut sandwiches, and fetched out chocolate éclairs and cream shells. He found himself hungry.

'This is quite a spread.' He felt awkward.

'I have to reward you for your conducted tour. Did you enjoy it?'

'Yes.'

'Do you go back often?'

'No, never.' This was not strictly true. 'The houses, the streets, have little appeal, since the people have changed.' Not, he thought, that the population in his boyhood had been any more interesting than today's, but they were known to him, subjects of exchanges between his father and mother, neighbours, parents of schoolmates. Not strangers.

'Do you seem a different man? To yourself?'

'Yes. Of course. And yet my patterns of considering and observing are pretty well what they always were. Sometimes I think exactly like that seventeen-year-old again.'

'In love?' she queried, awkwardly.

'No. Not that. My experience is greater. If I've learnt from it. Your mother's incursion into my life knocked it topsy-turvy. I couldn't see for the life of me why she wanted anything from me.' He tried to keep the tone light.

'And have you in your mature wisdom sorted that one out?'

'I think it was because I was educated, that I was preparing to go to university. I could talk to her about books and music. There must have been some physical attraction. Though that's difficult. Her fiancé, and she always wore his ring, seemed to have everything. He was strong, a good athlete, handsome, his father owned a big shop, a very thriving concern, had money, and...'

'She had to have you? As well? That's Marion. She must have her own way. She made big demands on everybody. She threw out your man, and married my father. When she'd wrung him dry, she dropped him, and married again. Did it upset you when she suddenly went away?'

'Yes. Though I knew our relationship could only be temporary. And we did write for a short time.'

'What were her letters like? Have you kept any of them?'

'No. She had small, neat handwriting of the sort I wouldn't expect. But her letters were rather flat. What she did at work. How she spent Saturday night at the church-hall disco. What she saw or bought in the shops, or saw at the cinema.'

'Nothing about my father?'

'Not that I remember. Though it must have been much at this time that she met him, and gave Stephen Slater his marching orders.'

'Did she ever come back to see him?'

'Not that I heard. I don't even know if she visited her parents.'

'She wouldn't bother,' Helena said. 'Not unless she wanted something.'

'You don't speak very highly of her?'

'Oh, we hit it off, on the whole. My father must have been a bit like you, a big reader. A quiet man. Had interests. He gave in to her. And in the end she dropped him.'

'Can you remember it?'

'Easily. I was fourteen, all ears. She was complaining at my father most of the time, though he had a good job, and we lived comfortably.'

'Did she go out to work?'

'When the fit took her. There was no need. But it put my father in his place. We lived in a flat. Two years later she married the second husband, Edward Ball. By this time I was making my own way, though I was still at school. I lived with an aunt, my dad's sister.'

'And that was satisfactory?'

'What can be satisfactory to a girl of that age? They were all right but old. They gave me a room where I could do my homework. I did reasonably well at "A" levels but I wasn't staying on. I joined my present firm at eighteen. Mr Telford-Jones was a friend of my father's. When I'd qualified they moved me down to the Potteries, where I met Geoffrey.'

'And your mother?'

'Her husband had a job that took him to the States and Canada. She had to live out there part of the time.'

'So you didn't see much of your mother?'

'Hardly anything. Nor did we write or phone. She did turn up at my wedding, but it surprised me. I think they were back in England then. But we had very little to do with each other, even when Edward Ball was terminally ill. He died the same year as my father.'

'Unexpectedly?'

'My dad? No. He'd had heart trouble. And his waterworks. My mother had gone to live on the east coast, at Sutton, and we began to get in touch again.'

'Did she go to your father's funeral?'

'She did not.'

Helena spoke easily of the family history. Her words implied criticism of her mother, but her tone of voice never carped. She briefly described the break-up of her own marriage, her transfer to Beechnall, her mother's time in the hospital and at her home. Helena crossed elegant hands, interlocked fingers.

'When I talk to somebody like this, it makes me wonder what family life's all about. You have children, and then you don't know what to do with them.'

189

'Most parents stagger on from day to day, and hope that their school will set the children to a worthwhile career or life. My parents were prepared to spend money on me to keep me at grammar school and university provided I did well enough. But it baffled them. They had reared a monster. Somebody who thought quite unlike them, whose interests were different, who spoke differently, who married a woman who seemed alien. And they'd sacrificed all sorts of little comforts that they would have enjoyed to bring this about.'

'Weren't they proud of you?'

'When I passed exams, or got jobs. But I guess they sometimes regretted it. They'd educated me, and though I won scholarships it cost money, and the result was I went off to London, and Malvern, and Hereford, and rarely came home. They would have argued that they'd started me on my career, and it was to be expected that I'd pursue it elsewhere.'

'And when you did meet them did you get on with them?'

'Well enough. We all made compromises. And glad to. I answered questions about my work as a teacher. My mother was specially interested. She loved talk about education. I was the only child. They were well up their thirties when I arrived. My father, a cabinet-maker, was a man who liked his own company. Nothing very sociable about him. His garden, his home, were sufficient outside his workshop.

He didn't need pubs, clubs, churches, outings, even holidays. Life, everyday life, provided sufficient variety.'

'Is that, was that, unusual?'

'I don't know. I was born in the depression, so people hadn't money to throw about. Things became easier during the war, and afterwards. By the time I'd done National Service and university they were well up their fifties, and in their sixties by the time I came to marry Joanna.'

'Did you enjoy staying with them?'

'For short periods only. Little and often, like firing the Flying Scotsman. They were in no way in awe of me, but I feared they couldn't entertain me in the manner I expected. Big meals. Snippets from the *Mirror*. I took them out in the car. To Chatsworth and Haddon and Rufford and Belvoir and Belton.' The name snagged at his remembrance of the afternoon. 'They walked round very staid, as if they were trying to do themselves good. I suppose my father might have been interested in some of the furniture he saw, but he said very little. If I questioned him he'd talk very knowledgeably. He was intelligent, would have profited from an academic training.'

'They're not still alive, are they?'

'No. My dad retired at sixty-five and died within a year.'

'Lost without his work?'

'I don't think so. He caught a chest infection,

did nothing about it, and when the doctors got at him it was too late.'

'And your mother?'

'She'd always been delicate. And suffered from cancer from her fifties onward. She died during an operation six months after Dad. Perhaps it was as well. The cancer was too far gone for her to have had much of a life had she survived. Not that she was exactly gregarious. They were people who kept themselves to themselves.'

'Was it a good home to be brought up in?'

'Well, yes, or yes and no. In the sense that they had no social graces. I had to find my own way in that field. But yes in that they supported me, and encouraged me in an ignorant fashion. When I became a teacher in grammar schools there were dozens of the pupils who were, like me, firsts in this kind of education. The parents had not the slightest idea what was required of them or of the child. Even those, like my parents, who cared and wanted their offspring to do well.'

'So they made you to some extent what you are now?' she asked.

'They must have done.'

'When you describe your father,' she said, 'I can't help seeing you. A puritan, afraid to enjoy yourself, independent.'

'I'm not so sure about that. For my father and mother—and their parents, I expect—life was too chancy, money too short, for

192

independence. If you practised that, it was up on the allotment, where you made your own mind up about which vegetable to grow, or about this flower rather than that. You could be as bolshy as you liked up there, that was your prerogative, your place. But not at work. Not there.'

'But surely some people stood up for the rights?' she queried.

'Yes. But the scales were weighted too strongly on the employer's side. Things did change, were changing. Two wars, for a start, with only twenty years between them. Dreadful.'

'When you think about it now, were you lucky?'

'Yes. I had the right sort of head for the work, and I was prepared to do as I was told. When I came to teach in a grammar school, the ethos was exactly the same. You did as sir instructed you, or it was wrong. We drilled people to pass pretty exigent examinations, and in some ways this was good. If you're going to make a contribution to a subject, even if you're just going to put it to good general use, you have to learn a large number of facts and techniques for a start. Some youngsters didn't see the sense. "Go home and learn Pythagoras's proof, or the imperfect tense of *parler* or *amo* or *luo*, or the properties of sulphuric acid, or the capes and bays of the United Kingdom." They didn't want to learn, and couldn't see the occasion arising when such knowledge would be of value to them. On the whole I suppose they were right, but at least we taught them how to study, to acquire new knowledge.' He stopped.

'Go on,' she said.

'Well, there was another, opposite line of argument, too, in my day.'

'Which was?'

'Its proponents claimed that it tore people away from their roots, and that these roots were valuable. People like me changed our accents and flaunted our knowledge, and were the worse off for it.'

'And is that true?'

'Yes and no. My usual answer. Is listening to a Mozart symphony better than watching a football match? Or is it mere personal preference? And people of my father's age saw little opportunity to change their life-style. Some did win their way to high schools and colleges but, on the whole, people of his class paddled up and down their usual bit of backwater most of their lives. Some used libraries or debating clubs or argued politics at work or at home. A few were religious. Or sporty. But if I were to answer you honestly, I'd sooner live my life than my father's. I wouldn't claim any moral advantage for myself. I might claim that reading great works of literature broadened my imagination, but I'm not sure of that. Did I love, in all its senses, more

194

strongly or even sensitively than my father? I can't be certain. We lack a sense of neighbourliness, for sure, but that was the result of economic circumstances. I can only say I much prefer my way of life to my father's or grandfather's.'

They talked on but, when about nine o'clock Henry said he must go, Helena made no attempt to stop him. She kissed him full on the mouth, and said she understood why her mother liked his company so much.

'I hate the dark nights,' he said.

'It'll soon be spring proper, and then hot summer.'

'Thanks.'

She did not stand at the door.

CHAPTER TWELVE

The local newspaper splashed Clare Statham's suicide. The coroner spoke sympathetically and at length about the difficulties of social workers, who carried the responsibility of an uncaring society on their slender shoulders. Arthur Kinglake, the headmaster of Henry's school, observed cynically that the coroner must have had one or two that morning. Verdict: suicide while the balance of the mind...

On Saturday, Jennifer Speed did not turn up

for her Latin lesson. She had sent no message of excuse, and this surprised him because she had always been punctilious about such matters. 'I work on the principle that other people's time is more valuable than mine.' When he was convinced that she was not coming he rang the house and received no reply. Even her answer-phone was turned off. Perhaps she and Timothy had gone out on a jaunt, determined on uninterrupted pleasure.

He rang Helena, but she knew nothing.

'It's not like her,' she said. 'I'll make a few enquiries.'

Henry telephoned Frank Hempshill, her boss, who knew nothing, but agreed it was not Jennifer's usual way to miss an appointment without making proper excuses.

'You don't think it's this Clare Statham business?' Henry asked.

'I wouldn't think so. God knows that was bad enough. The office has been troubled, I can tell you. It seemed so unexpected. The coroner was sympathetic, though. Joe Royal's an old friend of mine. A doctor.'

Just as he was about to sit down to lunch, Helena rang back to say she had made no progress in her enquiries. Jennifer had seemed so normal at work on Friday and had not spoken of going away.

'Shall we go round to her house?' she asked.

'Will it do any good?'

'I'll feel better in my mind.'

At two-thirty she called in, and they decided to walk.

'Put your car into the drive,' he advised. 'It looks rather large and fast. The local joy-riders might well take a fancy to it.'

Jennifer lived perhaps ten minutes' walk away. Her house, a semi-detached built early in the century, was freshly decorated. The large front windows shone.

No one answered three peals on the doorbell. They peered through the windows; the room appeared in apple-pie order as if Jennifer had cleaned it not half an hour before.

'Can we get round the back?' Helena asked. They tried the gate leading to the rear of the house and found it bolted.

'I could get over that,' Henry said. He scrambled up on to the dividing wall, a narrow brick-width structure with blue coping tiles. From there it was possible to put a leg over the gate, and a foot on the middle supporting board, and thence drop to the ground. It was not difficult, but he found himself badly out of breath when he'd finished, and he had grazed his hand. He unfastened the bolts—there was fortunately no lock—top and bottom to let Helena through. He carefully closed the gate.

The small garden seemed deserted. It was neat, sparingly spread with late spring flowers. They stared down its short-length in silence, then moved to the window. Once his eyes were used to the light, Henry saw that the place

197

was empty.

'She's in there,' Helena said.

'I can't see anything.'

'I caught a glimpse of her through the kitchen window.'

Helena was hammering with her fist on the back door.

'Jennifer, it's Helena. And Henry. Let us in.'

A neighbour, an elderly man, had appeared at his back door, disturbed by the noise.

'We're looking for Mrs Speed,' Henry said by way of excuse.

'I haven't seen much of her this last week or two.' He coughed himself back to coherence. 'I thought I saw her car in the street this morning.'

'Did she look all right?' Helena asked.

'As far as I could tell.'

'Knock again, Henry. Loud.'

He did so, and the three waited. Nothing happened.

'Who shall I tell her called?' the neighbour asked. 'If I see her.'

'Henry and Helena,' Helena answered. The man repeated the names, rather stupidly, and went inside 'to write them down before I forget'. As soon as he had closed his door, Jennifer's opened. They slipped inside.

Jennifer faced them silently in the kitchen. She stood, back to the table, her skin pale and unwholesome. She had dressed neatly enough, and the kitchen showed no disorder, sink and draining-boards clear, plates and saucers stacked, saucepans shelved. Yet about her was an air of loss, of inhumanity. Her flesh lacked life, bloom, was white, heavy, corpselike, adipocere.

'We thought we'd come and see you,' Helena said.

'We were a bit concerned.' Henry.

Jennifer looked from one to the other as if they spoke some language she did not understand. She moved her hands on the surface of the table, smally, inconsequentially. No invitation was offered to go elsewhere. Jennifer regarded them both with dull suspicion.

Helena took two steps across and gently threaded her wrist under Jennifer's arm. It was allowed.

'What's wrong, Jen?'

She might as well have kept silence.

'We wondered what had happened.'

'You didn't come for your Latin lesson, and you didn't let me know.'

'Latin.' This was the first word Jennifer spoke.

'You're usually meticulous about such matters, and so I thought something must have happened to you. Helena hadn't heard, either.'

'I'm sorry.' Jennifer forced the words out, letting her hands dangle. Helena still held her by the loose crook of her arm.

'What is it?' Helena asked, then more

sharply, 'Can't we sit down somewhere?'

Jennifer nodded woodenly towards the dining-room door. Helena led her forward, guided her to an armchair, encouraged her to subside. Her body seemed enormous, melting. Before, Jen's vigour and colour had made her size part of her charm, a source of energy, large but strong. Now she sagged. She held up her left hand to shade her eyes from the north light of the window.

'Have you had anything to eat this morning?' Helena asked. Jen lifted a listless head, lips open. 'Come on, have you, now?'

Jennifer shook her head, and groaned weakly.

'I thought as much. Henry, come and sit by her. I'll see what we can do.'

'No,' Jennifer said.

'Toast. You can manage toast. Now, move, Henry. Get hold of her hand, man.'

He did as bidden, found her flesh clammy.

'You must keep on eating,' he said. Immediately he was aware that he'd tripped into error. A week or two on a starvation diet might well improve some matters. 'You must let me know, and Helena, if there's anything we can do.'

Jennifer looked away, not bearing to meet his eyes.

'When you didn't turn up I wondered what was happening. You've been doing so well.'

She glanced at him, a quick jerk of the head,

then away. He stroked her left hand with the fingers of his right. She did not notice.

'You must let us know if anything goes wrong. You can't carry all the world on your shoulders. God knows, your job's stressful enough.' He spoke the sentences with pauses between, wishing Helena would return. He could hear her clattering, outside in the kitchen. 'You'll let us know, won't you? Promise. It often does you good just to tell somebody all about it even if they can't help solve the problem. You'll promise, now. In the future. Give us a call.' He remembered her walking past his house in the cold of winter, hoping to catch a glimpse of him. He leaned over to kiss her squarely on her cheek. The gesture had as little effect as his words. He did not give up. 'We're very fond of you, Jen. You know that. We'll do anything we can. You've only to ask. But you mustn't stay here all on your own, suffering.' He seemed to himself to be making sounds for the sake of it, or talking to a child as yet without language.

They sat in silence.

Helena burst back into the room with a tray.

'I think I found everything, and made it all work.' She comically indicated a cup of coffee, and two slices of toast. 'Do you take sugar? And milk?' She forced the murmur of an answer out of Jennifer. 'Anything on your toast?' Helena moved Henry to the other side of the hearth.

201

Jennifer picked up the coffee, tested it, put it down at once.

'Too hot?' Helena asked. 'Let's give it more milk.'

As they waited, Helena kept up a quick, but natural, flow of talk about weather, about a shopping expedition, about a holiday in Normandy she had half-decided to take. Jennifer disregarded her as she ignored the toast, concentrating solely on lifting the coffee cup, sipping at it, replacing it. Helena suddenly turned, faced an unframed picture above the mantelpiece.

'What's this?' she asked. 'Is it French?'

Henry stood up to see better. While they discussed the picture, it gave Jennifer the chance to eat and drink. He edged closer.

The picture, a not very large print of an oil-painting, showed a wide Parisian street between tall, six- and eight-storeyed houses with a jungle of crooked chimney-pots projecting into the sky. The boulevard below was spacious, with trees, and kiosks, and each broad pavement thronged with people, darkly dressed. The roadway accommodated horses and carriages, three and four abreast, so thick that one could easily imagine the jangle of harness, the rattle of tall wheels. The painter had spread over the whole scene a kind of rust-brown sunshine, from clouds to the leaves of the trees, from chimney-stacks to carriage-wheels, to horses' flanks. What would one call

202

these vehicles, Henry wondered? *Cabriolets?*
Fiacres? The effect of the picture was both of
movement and stillness. People walked and
talked, horses neighed, hooves clopped. The
place, overrun with life between the high
buildings and balconies, yet caught for ever the
same painted stasis. All human life is here, and
doing nothing or everything.

'The Boulevard Montmartre in Paris',
Helena read from a thin strip of print pasted
below. 'Who painted that?' she asked Henry.

'I don't know. It's marvellously good.'

'Why?'

'Because he's crammed so many
complications into one harmonious whole.'

'I reckon that's right,' Helena said, 'but who
painted it? It's as though he's perched high up
on one of the trees, or in a balloon.'

'Or another high building,' said Henry.

'In the middle of the road?'

'Camille Pissarro,' Jennifer said, in a
whisper but distinctly.

That she answered surprised them. It
rationally demonstrated that she had listened,
understood, applied her knowledge. The silent
bulk had frightened them; these five foreign
syllables cheered.

'Didn't he do some painting in England?'
Helena asked. That went unanswered. 'Take a
bite of your toast,' she encouraged. 'That's
better.'

Jennifer finished with her cup, refused a

second. She had taken one small round bite at a corner of one of her slices.

'Is there anything we can do, now?' Henry asked.

'I'm all right, thank you.' That sounded stronger.

'Any shopping? Dusting?'

'Shall I run you a bath?' Helena asked, taking up.

'I shall be better now,' Jennifer answered. 'Thank you both for coming.'

'What about lunch?' Helena pressed. 'Will you come home with me?'

To their surprise, Jennifer accepted the invitation. Helena ordered Henry back to his house for her car to convey them to her place.

'I'll get her ready,' she whispered, handing over the keys, 'and perhaps get something out of her.'

He accomplished his errand without trouble, and the two women drove off, leaving him to walk home for a second time. He felt left out, though he saw the sense of Helena's actions. She clearly knew how to organise. He stood in the street outside his house in uncertainty. He would ring Helena that evening.

At about seven o'clock, when he had settled to read a Scott novel, *Old Mortality*, Helena telephoned him.

'Are you busy?' she asked. 'Can you come round?'

'Is Jen still there?'

'No. She went home about an hour ago.'

'How is she?'

'So-so. I'll tell you all about it. Walk round, and then I can ply you with information and alcohol.'

'Shall I need it?'

'Probably.'

He took a quick bath, changed his clothes from one set of casuals to another, and was at Helena's by eight. As he rang her doorbell, the council-house clock in the centre of town chimed the hour. A south wind.

Helena seemed square-jawed, determined, marching him quickly into her sitting room. She placed a large, iced gin and tonic at his elbow. He did not much like gin, but she had made no enquiries.

'How did she seem?' he asked, sipping.

'Depressed.' Helena waved her glass at him.

'Did you find out why?'

'I did. She and the young man. It's come, it's coming, to nothing. As I expected. As she did.' Helena drank. 'It's sad. She sees it all so clearly. He's young, and wild, wants to go out with his dirty drinking pals, with other girls, and she yearns to keep him cocooned in her company all night; if not all day. She knows she's being unreasonable, but it's how they lived in the first week or two. And that was unlike anything that had happened before. Now she sees this Tim Glover as he is. They haven't many interests in common. He's a bit ashamed of her, she said, as she's so fat, and physically old enough to be his mother.'

'And?'

'The worse thing, in my view, is that, in the middle of all this rejection and depression, she's kept her head, her social worker's poise. She knows how she'd advise some thirty-six-year-old, overweight woman in these circumstances. But that knowledge makes no difference.'

'She told you all this?'

'In time. And I got her to eat a bit. She's losing weight.'

'Deliberately?'

'No.' Helena answered grimly. 'I don't know if she's doing anything deliberately these days. She broke down once while we were talking, hugely, sobbing and screaming, cursing herself for being such a fool. But that was better than these long silences. I tried to convince her that she had a considerable place in the world, that she was highly regarded at work, that she helped dozens of people every week, that she had outside interests, concerts, and books, and learning Latin.'

'And what effect did that have?'

'None whatever. But that's what one would expect.'

They both drank deeply into their gin.

'She's so emotionally deranged that reason makes no impact. She said to me—she spoke utterly lucidly sometimes—"I know the psychiatrist I'd send anyone else to in a case like this, but I can't go. I'd lose my self-respect. And I know what her treatment would be." "But it might nevertheless cure you, or make you feel better," I told her.'

'What did she say to that?'

'Nothing. Gritted her teeth. Kept her mouth shut. I tried all sorts of approaches. Time, healing. Her intelligence. Her value to society. I even tried crudity. "All it boils down to," I said, "is that you want this gadabout young man to poke his dick into you all day and every day." "I know," she said, "but he made me feel loved, wanted." I argued that all sorts of people loved and valued her. "Henry Shelton would marry you any time you agreed." And she shook her head. "Not now, he won't. Not after this." It was hopeless. I kept trying, but I was wasting my time. I tell you what it felt like. Nine-tenths of her couldn't make out what I was saying, were emotionally paralysed, and the other tenth, when it appeared, the professional bit of her, judged and condemned my efforts to talk to her as pretty feeble.'

'Did she say as much?'

'No. I suppose that's me. I wasn't any use at this sort of thing. And it certainly hadn't any effect.'

'She insisted on going home?' Henry asked.

'In the end, yes. I wondered if it wasn't that she hoped her Tim would phone her or drop in.

No, she didn't say that. I took her back. She was quiet by this time. I saw to it that she was settled, offered to stay, but she wouldn't have it. I left her. I don't know if it was wise, but I told her I'd call in tomorrow morning.'

'That's good,' he commended her.

'I doubt it. I wasted my time.'

'But if it's love she lacks, she saw, surely, that you were putting yourself out, in your free time, to help her. To care for her.'

'Again I'm doubtful. What she wants is a roll on the bed with Timothy-boy. To have a further recital of his specious promises.' She emptied her glass, filled it, moved across and filled his. 'Here's my comfort.'

'Stephano.'

'What do you say?'

'Stephano. The drunken butler in *The Tempest*. "Well, here's my comfort."'

Helena stared as if she could not believe her ears, and then began to giggle.

'There are some people about,' she declared in the end. Henry was also laughing in his subdued way. 'Drink up. I feel so helpless. Is there anything I should have said that I didn't? You know her so much better than I do.'

He shook a bemused head. 'What would the best thing be to happen to her?' he asked.

'For Tim Glover to come back.'

'But he'd leave her again, wouldn't he?'

'Probably.'

'How did he let her know that it was all over?

Did he write or did they have a quarrel, or what?'

'Nothing like that. He just didn't turn up. Then she couldn't get him on the phone. She wrote. No answer. She called round. Nobody would say where he was.'

'That's bad,' Henry said.

'Bad? It's awful. But that's this Tim. Takes what he wants, and, when he's finished, drops it. He had two or three weeks of her, and that was that.'

They talked, not sensibly, more drunkenly. At one point Helena threw a cushion on the carpet by his feet, sat down and leaned back heavily on him. He stroked her hair. She cried suddenly, not at length and quite out of character. In the end they made love on the floor, not without satisfaction. When she went to make coffee he stood stiffly and looked with displeasure at his white, hairy legs and his feet still encased in purple and blue socks. He felt some gratification, complacency even, but snatched up underpants and trousers to blunder upstairs to the bathroom. When he returned properly buttoned up, hair wetted and combed, Helena waited to pour his coffee.

They sat apart. He wanted to hold her hand, but feared to get out of his chair. They kissed when he left, an hour later, but without passion. He stood subdued, she sober, in her hallway.

Halfheartedly they promised to meet again.

CHAPTER THIRTEEN

Within the next few days, Henry received a letter from Jennifer asking if she could postpone the Latin lessons for a week or two. She felt much better, she claimed, and very grateful to him and to Helena, who had called in to see her again. She would need a little time to sort herself out, and then with his permission they'd resume their lessons, which she had greatly enjoyed and profited from. The note was quite beautifully written in black ink. He rang Helena on three consecutive nights to report this, but she was not at home. On the Saturday morning, Helena telephoned him to ask if he'd accompany her to an office party given in honour of a secretary who was leaving the firm. Helena apologised that the notice was so short, but she'd had three days at the head office in Staffordshire. He asked how he was to dress.

'Oh, wear a suit and a collar and tie,' she instructed. 'It's your style. That charcoal-grey and a white shirt. I really fancy you in that.'

'Yes, m'lady.'

They exchanged news of Jennifer.

'Wouldn't it have been a good idea to ask Jennifer to this party?' he enquired.

'I did so, twice. But she said she was in no shape for the social round. So, you see, you're

210

second best.' There spoke her mother's awkwardness. 'I'll drive so that you can drink.' When she arrived to pick him up, he was impressed by her appearance. She wore an ankle-length dress, goldenly belted but smooth, and her hair, simply but beautifully coiffured, shone darkly. She congratulated him on his suit, matching tie, black shoes, trimmed hair.

Once they were inside her workplace, its spaciousness surprised him. From the street it had seemed narrow, cramped. They were shown into a wide room—rather, two, with a dividing glass partition drawn back—and introduced to the evening's guest of honour, a middle-aged woman about to retire.

'This is the main office,' Helena told him.

'It's amazing what a few balloons and trimmings can do,' the other woman said. The computers were hidden under covers near the walls, and chairs circled the room. In a corner by the door a makeshift bar shone with glass.

'Will you miss it all?' Henry asked the woman.

'I shall, I shall.'

'You can always change your mind.' Helena, generously.

'Oh, I can't now.'

Henry thought there would be tears, but Lilian drew herself together. Helena introduced him to other members of the staff. Hands were solemnly shaken; clearly they all regarded Helena with considerable respect. Though each employee seemed friendly, and relaxed, they knew who ran the place.

In a corner Henry found himself with a couple of about his age, an Eric and Audrey Moore. Helena had been called outside. If he remembered rightly, Moore was the second-in-command, who had haunted Helena's street at night. He said little, but his wife more than made up for his silences. Henry interrupted Audrey's flow to ask her husband about his work here and whether he was busy.

'Very,' he said. 'Up to the eyes.'

'Even in a recession?'

'Yes. Mrs Gough's made all the difference.'

'You can say that again. Since she arrived it's nothing like the same firm. She's turned the whole business upside down. Don't tell me that women aren't capable.' Audrey rattled on, leaning forward now. 'And I'll tell you why. She's not only efficient herself, she's not afraid to delegate.' She led off about her husband's lean years, when he was treated as a clerk, fit to stick stamps on envelopes and that was all. 'He's not qualified on paper, but he knows a lot more about it than these young qualified accountants who come in. They've the theory at their fingertips, no doubt, but Eric has the experience. I know who I'd sooner trust.' She repeated her ideas with force, as if he hadn't quite grasped the gist.

Henry again interrupted her to ask Moore

212

about Helena.

'Yes, she's a remarkable woman,' he said. 'She has turned this office into a thriving concern.'

For a few moments, Moore vied with his wife to praise his boss, but soon gave up the unequal struggle. Henry lugubriously looked into his half-pint of lager, but Moore supported his wife with a bright expression, an exposure of false teeth. Her words flushed over both men, separating their silences.

Again Henry made an effort, asking if they had made holiday arrangements yet. Moore said they were going to Llandudno, and Audrey immediately described the north Wales resorts and why they had chosen this one in particular, and the west side. Past holidays were described, and as a climax she said they hoped to hear a Welsh male-voice choir. They had heard one in Beechnall not three months ago, and it had been an evening to remember.

'Are you Welsh?' Henry asked.

'No. Neither of us. We're both local. But our neighbours are, Gareth and Glenys Evans, and they belong to the Beechnall Welsh Society, and they invited us. The concert was a marvel.'

'Are you a musician, then?' Henry did not include the husband.

'No. Not really. I had a few piano lessons. But you didn't need any great knowledge to hear how good these men were. They sang as

213

one. In rich harmony. And you should have seen their faces. It was as if they were putting their soul on show; every man was intense, giving his all. The faces were different, of course they were, but they shared this one expression. Gareth has a brother in the choir, and, when he told us they were performing in Llandudno in the first week in August, we chose that week. That'll be the highlight, if it rains every night and day of the rest.'

'What did they sing? "Myfanwy"? "Comrades in Arms"?'

'My favourite,' Moore slipped in.

'Our favourite was "Mine Eyes Have Seen the Glory". Oh, it was wonderful. And they sang one or two in Welsh, but the conductor told us what it meant. I shan't forget that night easily.'

'And yet you weren't keen to go,' Moore said, surprisingly.

'No. That's so. I admit. But thank God Glenys pressed me. And Eric, he'll go anywhere to hear singing. But I was caught up.'

'She's not stopped talking about it since,' Eric added drily.

'These were ordinary working men, miners, bakers, postmen, quarrymen. But they could sing. By God, they could. It's a kind of tradition. It may not be the London Philharmonic.'

'What about women?' Henry jibed.

'I expect there are such things as WI choirs.

But the men worked together down the mine, day after day. And they'd sing as they went down the pit shaft. I love it, Mr ... er, Mr ...'

'I hope you don't mind my asking,' Eric said, 'but are you a relative of Mrs Gough's?'

'No. I'm an old friend of her late mother's.'

'We're glad to see you here.'

'In the hive of industry?'

Eric Moore pulled a sour face. Helena returned to rescue Henry, to brighten Moore's expression, to enquire from Audrey how far she had progressed with the decoration of her best bedroom. She led Henry off to further introductions.

The two danced a waltz, and he found to his surprise that Helena had little knowledge of ballroom dancing. She moved lightly enough, could follow him through the basic steps but was soon lost if he tried any elaboration. On these occasions she laughed, if mirthlessly, at herself and asked whence his expertise came. He ascribed his skill to lessons in the sixth form of his grammar school.

'Do you still go to ballroom dances?'

'Yes. Occasionally. Jennifer was keen.'

They played quiz-games, trivial pursuits, from lists posted on the walls. Some of Henry's answers excited admiration. His account of Amphitryon amazed Helena.

'How do you know all that?' she asked.

'Chance, mere chance.'

'Carling Black Label,' said some wit,

obviously listening in.

Helena welcomed them all, and invited Moore to propose a toast to the departing member of the staff. He did so, and well; he had prepared and presented anecdotes from her life. He knew a great deal about Lilian and her husband. He was witty at their expense, but without malice. He made one brief reference to Helena's magic, and called upon her to present the carriage-clock.

Helena shook hands with and kissed both Lilian and her husband. They held up their trophy. On shouts of 'Speech' from two rather drunken escorts, Lilian thanked them all, said she would miss them, and burst into tears. She clung to her husband, who comforted her with pats to the ample back, and by the time the escorts had led the company through a loud and tuneless verse of 'For she's a jolly good fellow', she smiled again. On her way back to her seat, clutching her clock, she kissed both Helena and Henry, to applause.

Helena told Henry it was time to leave at about quarter to eleven. Moore was left in charge, and seemed grateful for his commission.

Helena delivered Henry straight home, and refused his offer of a nightcap. She stood under a street-lamp, rather thin-lipped, said she hated these parties, had no aptitude for playing lady of the manor, felt about a hundred and eight instead of thirty-eight. She presented her cheek on which he dobbed an awkward kiss before she ducked into her car. Henry was left on the pavement, suspecting that it was somehow his fault.

At school the headmaster, Arthur Kinglake, had asked Henry if he would take over the running of the school during the last week of term. The Kinglakes were visiting Australia, and hoped to attend the wedding of a relative. This had been moved forward some days, and that meant that the school would be without a leader during the last week of term.

'There's hardly anything to do. Term's as good as finished. The conscientious teachers are running over their exam papers, and the rest are playing games. There are no official functions.'

'Why do you need somebody to supervise nothing?'

'Somebody has to be here all day. It may just happen that some decision has to be taken, something moderately important. Most of my work is routine, but some matter might arise during that week which needs an instant decision. I talked it over with my wife, and we agreed, not always the case, that you were the man. It means that you'll have to be on the premises from eight-thirty to four-thirty, that you will have to conduct assembly and be on call in the evening. You'll be adequately remunerated. You'll find Miss Cooper a tower of strength and a mine of information.' He smiled at the clichés about his secretary.

'Put her in charge, then.'

'Mr Shelton, Mr Shelton. She wouldn't want it or expect it.'

The conversation occupied a further twenty minutes, before Henry agreed. Kinglake handed over a list of duties, and Henry was invited to call in to his office at any time to observe or enquire in preparation for the second week in July. Henry thought himself a fool, attended an assembly or two—he had never done so before—and heard his name announced at the post-examinational staff meeting. He could not tell whether his colleagues were surprised, or pleased, or annoyed, that an outsider should be so easily promoted over their heads.

He gave Helena a comical account of his new responsibilities when she rang to report on Jennifer. She questioned him, closely and cleverly, on his duties, as if to make sure he knew what he was about.

'Suppose a large bill is incurred or sent in during your week? How will you pay it?'

'I shan't. I've no authority to sign cheques or raid the petty cash.'

'So what will you do?'

'Nothing. If he's overlooked something, then it's his fault, and his creditors will have to wait, whatever the consequences. But I can see that he must have a representative there all day, to talk to casual callers, to parents, or children, or their teachers, to settle their problems; both staff and pupils are worn-out and fractious by the end of term. What puzzles me is why he wanted me for his stand-in?'

'Has he not got a deputy?'

'Not officially, no. There's one man who sees himself in the position, takes the assembly on the rare occasions when Kinglake's not there, acts like an elder statesman...'

'Then why', Helena asked, 'did Kinglake not ask him? Especially as you say nothing's likely to happen. Is he giving the man the brush-off?'

'Not as far as I know.'

'Is the man any good?'

'Coulson's all right. Conscientious. He's in charge of geography, and does some maths teaching. A bit pompous.'

'How old is he?'

'Not as old as I am. Early fifties, I guess. Had most of his experience in state comprehensive schools. I don't know him very well. He's been there a lot longer than I have.'

'Full-time?'

'Yes. And his wife does a bit of junior maths.'

'Is he annoyed with you?'

Henry considered the question.

'I suppose he is. He's not said as much, but he'll consider me as a part-timer, a bit player in the large concerns of the school.'

'Then why did Kinglake appoint you?'

'It's not a permanent post. It's one week

219

when the serious work's over and done with. He may have been telling Coulson something, though I've not heard of disagreements between them. But then I wouldn't. I'm not there long enough. It may be malicious mischief on Kinglake's part. I wouldn't think so.'

'What's the answer?'

'He's trying to get me to work full-time, and this may be a bait. But I'd guess I'm an outsider, the oldest man he employs, reasonably dressed, dull, decently spoken, and not having any fish of my own to fry.'

'It seems silly to risk trouble for one insignificant week. You don't want the job, and Coulson does.'

'Kinglake's like other bosses. He enjoys power. He'll often throw his weight about just to show what's what. You ought to know.' Henry grinned to himself. She invited him round for a drink on the next day, saying she had her own equivalent little problem.

On his arrival Helena seemed in no hurry to discuss her problems but talked at length about Jennifer, and questioned him again about his week as headmaster. She spoke in a relaxed and cheerful way. In her opinion Jennifer's health had improved. She had lost a stone and a half but one couldn't see much difference on that score. Her skin was clearer, but her demeanour had altered for the worse. She sat mouselike, ghostlike, not speaking until spoken to, quite unlike her former confident manner.

'Has she started work again?' he asked.

'Just over a week ago.'

'How's she shaping?'

'She goes in. Work had piled up, but she's beginning to clear it. She'll manage, but that's about it, whereas before she was something of a genius at it.'

'Will working do her good?'

'I hope so. Living one day at a time is what she has to learn to do. Handling other people's problems, being constantly interrupted, will help her to manage that.'

'She can cope? With the frustrations and stupidities and....?'

'I think so.'

There followed another close examination of Kinglake's motives for leaving Henry in charge. This was rigorous, but now essentially frivolous. Neither could account for the headmaster's choice. Henry unseriously took the line that he was the obvious successor among the gaggle of mediocrities, his colleagues. Helena began to laugh a good deal at his mock-confidence.

'And what about you?' he asked in the end. 'You had some problem, hadn't you?'

'Of no importance.'

'But the reason for inviting me round.'

'Just an excuse. I want to talk to you. I enjoy it. You stimulate me.'

'Good God.'

She leaned back in her chair, clearly pleased with herself, creamily at ease, perfumed.

'It's not unconnected', she began, 'with the appointment of deputies. After the party I took you to, I asked Eric Moore to lock up. About half-twelve he judged it right to clear the decks. Most people had gone by that time. Being conscientious he walked round the whole place, upstairs and down (we let off the top two floors), and was surprised to hear noises, his word, from his room. His door was unlocked. He opened it, put the light on, and there on the floor was his secretary, pretty well naked, being screwed by some unknown young man. They jumped up, or rolled away or whatever, and Eric said, according to his account, "Please get dressed. I'm locking up." He went out to the corridor but didn't close the door. Very shortly afterwards the couple came out, a bit ruffled, and hurried downstairs, saying nothing. By the time he'd checked and closed everywhere and gone down to his wife, who was waiting for him, they had rushed out with not a word to Audrey. She had asked him what they had been up to and he had apparently replied, "No good." By the time he had turned the lights out and switched on the alarm, they had gone home.'

'And next morning he had told you all about it?'

'No,' Helena answered. 'I didn't come into

222

the office. I was doing an extra audit in Derby. I did it out of kindness to the husband of a friend. They paid me, of course, or they will eventually, but I couldn't easily send one of the young trainees out. Only the boss has enough free time to fit it in in a hurry. Don't forget that.'

'Did the secretary turn up next morning?'

'Apparently. Brazen, but subdued. But even when I came back Eric Moore didn't say anything. He "gave it a day", he said. Then he told me the story, but said he did so "on the grounds of security only". Ought we to review procedures? Miss Johnson had her own key, which had allowed her and a total stranger into his room. Was this wise?'

'And what was your line?' Henry asked.

'Non-committal. Entry into a room could be a nuisance, but no more. Anything important is left in the safe. I have a key to that, Eric has one, and that's it. I told him to forget all about it.'

'Had he spoken to the secretary?'

'Apparently not. According to him she's moderately efficient. I think he, or his wife, would prefer an older woman. But this girl is respectable enough. He likes to think he has something of a hold over his underlings. And it came as a shock to see her right on the carpet next to his desk with her knickers off and her legs open. He comes from a purer era.' She smirked at her phrase, repeated it. 'Purer era.'

'Like me,' he said.

'Yes,' she said. 'You speak for yourself.'

'And apart from this one interview with you, there's been no other mention?'

'No. We've been busy.'

'People can always find a minute or two to mention matters they're really interested in.'

'I suppose so.'

'Has he mentioned it to his wife?' Henry asked.

'I don't know. I never asked. He must have given her some story about rousting the couple out. Must have done so.'

'And you never said, "What does your wife think?" '

'No.'

She pursed her lips, mocking his prurience, eyes dancing. Henry had the sense to let the subject drop.

Later he asked if he should visit Jennifer. Again Helena seemed unduly amused.

'Not on the off chance,' she answered. 'Ring her first. Or, better, write. She's unsettled. Give her the chance to think things over on her own.'

'I will.'

'She's genuinely fond of you, Henry. You make a good pair, married or otherwise.'

'That's your advice, then?'

She held her head straight, every trace of humour wiped from her features.

'Some little time ago, we had sex. We were

224

both fairly drunk. But what I don't want you to do is to take that too seriously. I don't want you to do an Eric Moore with it. We enjoyed ourselves, briefly. It might even happen again. But. And that's the word. I was making no life-long commitment. Copulation is less important to me than to you. You'd express it all with some sentence such as "she yielded herself to me", which you wouldn't use if I allowed you to buy me a drink. We come from different generations. It's possible that morally I'm lightweight compared with you or the Old Moore. But don't read into the act what's not there. Is that blunt enough for you?'

'Oh, no,' he said, sarcastically.

It was. Disappointment drilled him. He did not know what he wanted from this woman, but it was not this curt dismissal of him as a lover. She was speaking again.

'The only time', she used an even tone, as if discussing some set of figures with a client, and inviting his closer attention, 'I thought in your way, or Eric Moore's,' that seemed unnecessary, 'was a day or two after, when it crossed my mind that I had had sex with a man my mother had seduced.'

'And?'

'I felt no obligation to you, nor guilt on that account. I guess it's not uncommon these days.'

They sat in uncomfortable, unfortunate silence, avoiding eye-contact.

'I'm twenty years older than you are,' he said. 'I deserve what I got.'

'You're taking it too seriously.'

'Did you think I was building on, on ... what happened?' he asked.

'It seemed possible.'

'Did I show it? Did I look like Moore skulking round your street?'

'No. You did not. But there was the possibility. If you see what I mean.'

She spoke without rancour, but coldly. He left the house perhaps half an hour later, but he had no idea what they talked about, or what he thought to himself, walking the streets on his forgotten journey home.

CHAPTER FOURTEEN

Henry wrote to, then telephoned, and finally visited, Jennifer. The process took more than a fortnight.

He found her at home on a Saturday afternoon, neat, but quiet, and claiming to be much improved in health. They talked, uneasily, drank a cup of strong tea. Jennifer described Helena's kindness. After half an hour he left, but arranged at the last minute to give her a run out in his car the following Wednesday. She declined to resume her Latin lessons as yet.

'Shall I need a coat?' she asked cheerfully when he called for her.

'It's not cold.'

They drove to Melton Hall, parked and, at Jennifer's insistence, began to walk.

'We mustn't go too far,' he said. 'There's a fair chance of showers.'

At five o'clock on a late June afternoon the sun warmed them as they strolled. Jennifer did not walk close.

'I don't know why you bother with me,' she said. 'I've made a complete fool of myself.'

'Look, Jennifer, there's no need to talk about it.'

'I want to. And even if I didn't I owe you an explanation.'

'No, you don't.'

'I dropped you. Inexcusably. Just because I was besotted by another man.'

'It happens,' he said.

'So does murder. I've thought about it ever since he pushed me out. It would be true to say that I've hardly thought of anything else. I acted unlike myself. I know most women of my age and weight would be flattered if a good-looking young man made a pass at them. But I misinterpreted it. This was different. It wasn't just causal sexual experimentation, it was for good, an eternal love.'

He said nothing, watched his feet as he trod a dusty path. Jennifer continued, her voice rather low, tuneless, without vigour.

'Why was I such an idiot?'

'We all need to be loved,' he answered.

'It was a combination of circumstances.' She had ignored his answer. 'I'd been working too hard. There seemed little purpose in life. That's perhaps why I took up Latin with you. It gave me something to aim at, and something a bit out of the ordinary. Moreover, I found I could do it. There were right answers, and that's not always the case with my work. Then there was this Clare Statham business. It wasn't my fault. I know that, but that doesn't take the guilt away. She wasn't suitable for social work, and she didn't want to confide in me. Why should she? But it all piled up on her, and she couldn't bear it. I don't think I could have saved her, but I didn't try hard enough. Even the edge of curiosity had gone. But what's the worst? I'll tell you. I was quite unable to help myself. When I fell for Tim, I wanted it. I knew all the snags. I even knew what sort of man he was. His friends queued up to tell me. But I didn't care. Which is the real Jen Speed? The one begging this fly-by-night to strip and fuck me, or the decent, careful, experienced middle-aged woman who'd seen plenty of obsessions, and their results?'

'Well ...' he began.

'Be frank,' she said. 'Tell me what you really think.'

'Checks and balances,' he said. It sounded comical. She glanced at him, then turned away

228

in apathy. 'I guess that we all have inside us potentialities for good and bad, and these are controlled by our beliefs, by economics, by society, by our state of health. Those of us who don't end up in the madhouse or prison have got it about right.'

'Why did I get it so wrong?' she asked.

'I don't know that you did. This Tim offered you something you couldn't get elsewhere, and which you wanted. It might even have worked out. Sixteen years' difference is not so great.'

'Not with somebody like him.'

'It's not for me to say, not knowing him.'

They walked on, exchanging ideas. Jennifer continued to blame herself, dully. He made excuses for her, but did not convince himself. The fresh air and exercise, he thought in desperation, would do her good.

'What if I'd become pregnant?' she asked.

'You'd have found a way round it.'

'I made him use condoms. I knew he was promiscuous. That makes him sound awful, but it's not so. Sex was pleasure to him, like alcohol or food; no more reprehensible than sitting in a comfy armchair. He didn't seem to consider the other partner. What she felt and thought wasn't his affair. Not essentially. Oh, he said some of the right things. He'd learnt them from other girls or the telly. They were part of the act. I had more money than he had; I was better educated than he was; I owned a house, and yet I hung on his every word or touch. I worshipped him. He liked that.' She paused. 'It made up for the rest of his unsatisfactory life.'

'Unsatisfactory?'

'He'd not much of a home, and was still working his apprenticeship when he discovered that women liked him. He can boast about this to his pals in the pubs. It helps make up for shortage of money, and unfashionable clothes. He wasn't a monster, Henry. I don't want you to think that. He was childish, and selfish. He was like somebody who has come into an unexpected fortune. He didn't quite know what was what. He hadn't any morals. Why should he? They'd only interfere with what bit of pleasure he did manage.'

'Yes.'

'I've been a fool, Henry.'

'Imagine he got in touch with you again—would you take him back?'

'No.' The voice was firm.

'Would you want to?'

'In some ways. But your checks and balances have swung the other way. I know how it would turn out now.'

'And so?' Henry would make her answer.

'I'd show him the door.'

They had reached the far end of the park and looked down into a small cleft, wooded, shrub-coated and bounded by a wall, beyond which stood a street of handsome, detached houses, with wide lawns, white outdoor furniture, silver birch trees, large shining greenhouses, conservatories.

'The true end of life,' he said, jovially pointing.

'What is?'

'Detached, four-bedroom houses with gardens fronting a park.'

'Thieves could break in,' she said.

'And moth and rust corrupt, but it is what most of us want.'

'Do you?'

'I've got a house. It costs money to keep up. But I'm satisfied. I don't want to change.'

'But, Henry, you offered to marry me.'

'I did.'

'That might have meant changing your house?'

'Yes. If you had convinced me that was what you wanted.'

'Would that have been hard?'

'No. Not at all.'

She looked at him in some surprise. That had been her prevailing expression all afternoon, as if she found the world different, baffling now.

They turned back and walked towards the car.

'Are you going away for a holiday this year?' she asked.

'I'm not thinking of it.'

'Why not?'

231

'I've kidded myself it's just as interesting here as anywhere else.'

'But it's not true, is it?'

'I don't suppose so. Are you going away?'

'I ought to. Once I've come to terms with my work, and straightened it out. And August is less likely to be busy.' She smiled wryly at this.

'What had you in mind?'

'Some out-of-the-way place. Devon, Cornwall, Pembroke.'

'Not Scotland?'

'I hadn't really considered it all that seriously.'

The subject died. He bought ice-cream cornets from a van, and they sat on a seat, licking, unspeaking. The sun warmed them. For some brief seconds, once he'd finished his ice-cream, Henry nodded off. When he awoke, Jennifer seemed to be watching him anxiously.

'I drifted off,' he explained. 'I often do these days.'

Inside the mansion, they looked at pictures, bewigged ancestors or stormy scenes at sea. Jennifer tried hard to interest herself in these, but it was clear to Henry that she had great difficulty. She stood in front of a family group, eighteenth-century, mother, father, three children, dogs and a pony, under the shade of an oak tree.

'I'm looking for the family face,' she said. 'There's not much evidence.'

She described a family she dealt with—she

knew three generations—and how alike they were.

'But not in their behaviour,' she concluded. 'I wouldn't mind doing some research on all this.'

'You'd do well to choose something easier.'

They enjoyed the afternoon's warmth and returned for late high tea at his home. Jennifer ate without appetite, to reward his preparation, but sat for an hour after the meal. To him she seemed unlike herself, as if the spirit had been knocked out of her, and as if she blamed him. This was guilt on his part, he thought, though that he should fault himself for her trouble was foolish. She had dragged herself back from two other emotional crises, he comforted himself, and she'd do so this time.

On the morning he took over the Mountjoy School for the last week of the term he received a postcard of a Norfolk mill from her: 'I am walking every day the weather permits. My shoes are filthy. Wish you were here. Jen.'

He opened the school, took assembly, explained where the headmaster was, said he hoped that they didn't think the learning process stopped because the term had advanced so near its end. They sang 'City of God, how broad and far' and he made them repeat the last two verses more heartily. He read some bland prayer chosen by the headmaster, listened to a notice or two read by members of the staff, and dismissed the children. He had hurried nothing, but his assembly was six minutes shorter than Kinglake's average. The teachers would not be pleased.

He had two Latin classes that morning, during which he continued to teach. His pupils did not seem to mind, so that he guessed they were bored by the games of 'cricket', hangman, noughts and crosses, battleships; Sega and Nintendo were banned; pencil and paper only. They had been expected to occupy themselves while their tutors completed end-of-term reports and everlasting lists of materials and text books. He filled the last part of his lesson by teaching them the limerick 'There was a young lady from Riga/Who went for a ride on a tiger' in Latin. He was rewarded later in the day when he overheard a girl repeating this, correctly, by heart to some younger scholars. Perhaps, he mused, he'd occupy a little of their time with the gender-rhymes at the back of Kennedy's *Primer*: Memorial Lines on the Gender of Latin Substantives. He was humming to himself,

Ēchō Feminine we name,
Caro, (*carnis*) is the same;
Aequor, *marmor*, *cor* decline
Neuter; *arbor* Feminine,

when he returned to the secretary, morning
234

coffee, and the mail. Nothing proved beyond him; Miss Cooper knew the answers to everything, but often put her knowledge to him in the form of a polite question. If she dealt with a parent's query, she told him how, and appeared to need his approval. He wondered if this was the case when Kinglake was in charge. He took a leaf from her book by searching out Coulson, his alleged rival, and asking him to conduct the Wednesday assembly, saying flatteringly that Kinglake had praised Coulson's handling of the children in the hall as well as his interesting addresses. This was a flat lie.

'I don't know how he can say that,' Coulson said grudgingly, 'since he's never seen nor heard me.'

'He's deep is our Kinglake,' Henry answered. 'He asks questions. He probes. He finds things out for himself.'

Coulson went away to complain to his cronies that Shelton was unloading his responsibilities on to other people's shoulder's, but without doubt he was pleased, made an effort, told the assembly some Korean moral tale, that drew 'ahs' from the older girls and shortened the first period by ten minutes. Henry, seated at the back, congratulated his colleague.

He spent the afternoon with the newspapers, as Kinglake had cleared his desk, left nothing to sign. He walked round the campus, both

235

houses, listening at doors, appearing not to look in at windows. At three he drank coffee again with Miss Cooper, who was already cheerfully typing material for the beginning of the autumn term. A quarter of an hour before dismissal an Indian lady in a superb sari demanded an interview. She wanted information about the GCSE examinations, the school's record, the possibilities opened up to her daughters. He explained clearly, had the figures of the school's performance to hand, promised he would interview the older daughter tomorrow. The mother, who looked affluent, did not speak English well, but seemed to understand him, went away comforted. He shook hands, not knowing if this was acceptable. Some bow, or graceful inclination of the head, seemed more decorous.

'Handing out the soft soap,' he told Miss Cooper.

'Yes. I heard you. I guess Mrs Desai was bullied by her husband into coming. He wants value for money. The two girls are very nice, no trouble, conscientious, doing well.'

'A credit to us,' he said.

'You could say so.'

The children were streaming out by this time and parents' cars thronged the streets. Kinglake had instructed him to give the place a quarter of an hour to clear and then to walk round to make sure that no one remained. Parents occasionally failed to turn up, and

Kinglake had more than once taken children home. He had left a street map of the city on his shelves. Today all was well; the caretakers were in and noisily cleaning with the help of the radio. Miss Cooper had locked her safe and filing cabinets, and had disappeared. Henry could see no further reason for his presence.

When he arrived home his tiredness surprised, even embarrassed him. He sat down in an armchair with a pot of tea, sipped and dozed. At six he began to watch the news on television, having knocked up a skimpy meal, which he ate from a plate on his knee. Finishing news and food together, he carried his crockery out, washed it, and telephoned Jennifer.

She, clearing her mouth to answer, was in the middle of a meal. Yes, she was keeping well, had coped with her work. He enquired if she would like to go out for a drink. She thanked him, but said she was too busy; she asked no questions about his new responsibilities at school. She spoke politely but wanted to get back to the dining table. Disappointed, and not relieved, he settled to house cleaning.

On the last day of term he was visited by one of the staff, a Mrs Huntley. She taught French and German and English, full-time, a thin spinsterish figure he had barely noticed. He thought, as others had already called in, she had come to wish him a good holiday.

She sat down, said she had a problem. 'I've
237

left it to the last day of term, because I did not know what to do, how to act. And with the headmaster's taking this last week off, it made it all more difficult. But I did not want to keep this to myself, in case something could be done.' Henry looked at the flat-chested figure in a dove-grey silk frock, hands winding together in her lap. 'Last night I mentioned it to my husband, and he said, "Tell the acting headmaster. Or at least discuss it with him."'

'Yes?' Henry stroked his chin.

'I have reason to believe that one of my pupils is being sexually abused by her father.'

Both waited for the other.

'Who is this?' he said, in the end.

She named an eleven-year-old, Samantha Falls. He racked his brains, but could not remember any contact with either the girl or her parents. Mrs Huntley described the child as quiet, conscientious, but not very bright. All through the year Samantha had seemed slightly withdrawn, tired as if she were not sleeping well, vaguely unhappy, not making friends. The teacher had kept an eye on her. She had done noticeably well in the summer examinations, much better than Mrs Huntley had expected. At the last parents' evening the teacher had questioned the Fallses to see if they could offer any explanation of Samantha's lack of energy or cheerfulness. They could not. Mrs Huntley, smiling with half-closed eyes at Henry, said that had she known that the child

238

was going to perform as well in the summer French and German she would not have mentioned this.

'Did the parents offer any explanation?'

'No. It was just her way, they said.'

'What sort of people were they?'

'Very ordinary.'

'Well educated?'

'No, not particularly. The mother did most of the talking.'

'And the father?'

'Small, dark man. You wouldn't look at him twice.'

'What does he do for a living?'

'I checked up on that. The school record says "company director". That can mean anything.'

Henry considered again.

'How did you find out about this abuse?'

'The girl told me. This week at the sports afternoon, Tuesday. I was walking round. I'm not very interested in athletics.' Mrs Huntley stared him out, defying him. Henry beamed at her, nodding safely. 'Samantha was skulking out of the way. She looked as if she'd been crying. I went and sat with her on a seat. Since she'd done well for me in the exams, I've talked to her, perhaps shown more interest. At least she'd listened to me and had taken in what I'd been trying to teach her, which is more than you can say of some of the others.' Again she looked with suspicion at Henry. 'Anyhow, I

239

asked her what was wrong. She didn't say much. I asked her if her parents were here for the sports. It was clear they weren't. She said she was glad, and then the truth came pouring out.'

'I see. The abuse was sexual, you say?'

'Yes. She spoke in a roundabout way sometimes. She didn't quite know how to put it to an adult.'

'But you were sufficiently convinced that something of the sort had happened?' he asked.

'Yes.'

'What did you tell her to do?'

Mrs Huntley paused, looked him over.

'I was in a quandary there. When I told my husband he said I had to be careful. If I went to the police, I'd only the child's word. He said I should report it to you, because that at least showed I was taking it seriously.'

'And what did you say to the girl?'

'I asked her if she had heard about Childline.'

'Has she?'

'Yes. And I have a friend who is a volunteer. I gave Samantha their number. I agonised about this, because I knew children told lies, but I said if it became too much to bear she could ring the number. I couldn't do much myself because we shall be on the Continent for most of August. I don't know whether I've acted properly in the sense that there might be more I could have done.'

Henry locked his fingers together and glowered down at his desk.

'I think', he began solemnly, 'that you've acted with great discretion. We clearly have to be careful, and yet we have a responsibility for the child. I have a friend who holds a senior post in social services and I'll make enquiries from her. I'll also pass at least a résumé of the information on to Mr Kinglake when he returns.'

The two talked on for a quarter of an hour, pleased with each other. When Mrs Huntley left, Henry consulted Samantha Falls's school record without learning over-much. He took his last tour of the school, talked to the caretakers, found nothing untoward.

That evening he consulted Jennifer by telephone and asked her advice. She listened carefully, asked sensible questions, but was not forthcoming with solutions. There was little he could do. If it was at the beginning of term he could keep his eye on the child, and she outlined the sort of symptoms he should be on the look-out for, but there was a seven-week holiday. Neither social services nor police would move a step until there was an official complaint, and one backed by evidence at that.

'So the girl has to suffer?'

'Yes. If it's the truth, and if the father is hauled before the courts and found guilty, she'll still suffer. If he's sent to prison, he'll not be able to work, so how does his family live? If

241

he's put on probation and consents to have psychiatric treatment the family will be in uproar.'

'Is it possible that the mother knows nothing about this?'

'Yes. You'd think it impossible, but I've known quite a few cases. You'd be surprised what people fail to see. Incest is something you read about in the papers. It doesn't happen in your street, let alone your house.'

Jennifer said she would talk to Mrs Huntley if he thought any good would come of it. He could hand on her telephone number. She'd speak to him again, but their hands were tied, all round.

'Have I, or Mrs Huntley, acted sensibly? Is there something else we could have done?'

'No. You did the right things. It depends, of course, how your Mrs Huntley talked to Samantha. I can't judge that. Perhaps when I've spoken to her I'll be in a better position to make my mind up.'

He asked how she was shaping, and was told that though she was nothing like a hundred per cent fit, she was able to do a moderate day's work. She became very tired, but went to bed early and started the day without a ruddy blush; her spoonerism comforted him. Was she still under the doctor? Yes, still taking the tablets. She laughed, coughed briefly. She'd be in touch before long.

The school secretary phoned him twice

242

before the month ended, and on the second occasion he called in. Miss Cooper seemed glad of his company; she had her instructions about papers to be typed or duplicated for the new term, and Mr Kinglake would be back in time for the GCSE results. He formed the impression that talks with the headmaster were frequent and she missed them. She was looking forward to a holiday in Pembroke, near St David's, where she had taken a cottage with a friend, a divorcee, who ran a post office. He enjoyed the hour, and completed the morning with a tour of the school. It was not part of his remit, but his mood was cheerful.

CHAPTER FIFTEEN

Henry took a three-day holiday on the east coast, in Suffolk. The weather blustered, but did not keep him cooped up. He walked the pebbles, examined Aldeburgh, spent a day in Ipswich, photographed the church at Blythburgh, talked with an elderly American couple at Southwold, watched a couple of artists at Walberswick. He ate an excellent meal each night in his hotel at Westleton, and wondered why he had confined himself to a mere three days.

On his return he found that an attempt had been made to break into his house. The burglar had not been successful, and had failed to force his way inside the building. He rang the police, and the detective who appeared said that there had been three robberies in the street in the last two days. He thought it possible that the criminals had been disturbed in his case.

'How would that be?'

'Car coming home late; somebody setting off early to work; a light switched on near by; a dog barking.'

'What would they be after?'

'Small, easily transportable objects. Videos, jewellery, bits of bric-à-brac. The sort of things you can dispose of without too much trouble in the pub or the car-boot sale.'

'Wouldn't it be difficult to make a living at that?'

'Well, it adds a few quid here and there. Makes your unemployment benefit go that bit further. And some of them do it for kicks.'

'I'd be terrified.'

'So you might be climbing rock-faces, but you'll find some doing it for pleasure.'

The policeman, a straight-browed, unsmiling young man, seemed in no hurry, edging observantly round the house, the garden.

'Block the back off from the front. And don't leave your wheelie bin where they can use it to clamber on. Make it as awkward for 'em as you can. And if you see or hear anything untoward give us a ring. More often than not it won't lead to arrests, but we'd sooner be told.'

'It's bad,' Henry said. 'Everybody you know has had a break-in.'

'Yes. It's our sort of society. And people aren't careful enough with their property. It tempts those with wrong ideas.'

'I've just been to the seaside. I'm considering retiring to the coast. It won't be as bad there, will it?'

'No idea. I don't know, but they'll get their share, I reckon.'

Henry had surprised himself by saying out loud that he'd move to the seaside. He had never before put the thought clearly into words. He'd enjoyed his jaunts to the coast, be it Scarborough in bad weather or Suffolk in a windy summer, but he'd never contemplated a permanent home there. Like many in Beechnall, which was as far from the sea as anywhere in England, he'd claimed vaguely that the ocean ran in his blood, that his ancestors were seafarers, Vikings, fishermen. His maternal grandfather had served in the Royal Navy. The old chap had many times told him the hoary joke about joining the fleet. 'Can you swim?' the interviewing officer had asked. 'Why?' he'd replied. 'Haven't you got any more ships?'

But now Henry had come out with this sea fantasy plainly to a stranger.

He smiled, amused by his own whim. Henry Shelton, teacher, epitome of the level-headed, had arrived at a decision without conscious thought and announced his conclusion publicly. It almost pleased him. He rang the largest house-agent in the city, and asked if they sold property on the east coast. They took his name, and mentioned local firms he could get in touch with. They recommended visits.

'May I ask', the man—he sounded young—at the house-agent's asked, 'if it's a matter of retirement or are you due to work out there? Or', afterthought, 'is it a second, holiday, home you want?'

'The first.'

'Retirement. Then I suggest you spend a bit of time at the places you have in mind. This is your own house here, is it? We'll give you a free valuation if you're considering selling.'

'Don't rush me.'

'Houses don't go very quickly these days, sir.'

'I'll have to consult the omens before I move.'

'You must please yourself, sir.'

The agent described the state of the market, issued advice, warned. He clearly wasn't very busy, but he made a good impression on Henry. This young man knew his way about, was prepared to spend time in search of work. Henry approved, fixed with himself the first day-trip to the coast.

On the day before this venture, he received a letter from a solicitor in London that considerably altered his mind. An uncle, a stockbroker, had left him over £400,000. The legacy did not come as a surprise, only the amount. He had attended the funeral some twelve or thirteen months ago, had been told that he had been willed a part of his uncle's estate, but until the complicated sale of assets had been completed, a long-drawn-out process, it was feared, he could not expect payment.

'We shall make all the haste we can,' the solicitor, a sharp young man, told Henry and a cousin who was to inherit a share equal to Henry's, 'but as you know, for example, the sale of a house these days is a far from easy process and less profitable than it was.'

'Can you guess what we shall get? Roughly?' the cousin asked.

'Well,' the young man replied, 'as long as you don't hold me to it.'

'Make a guess; intimate,' the cousin pressed. Henry disliked the word and the vulgar cousin.

'A hundred thousand. At least.'

'Each?'

'Each.'

The cousin had nudged Henry.

'Better than a poke in the eye with a sharp stick,' he'd said.

And now the amount had quadrupled. With what he'd already inherited from his parents, or earned, and this, he need work no longer. But there was no reason why he should give up his teaching. He enjoyed it; Latin was, on account of his efforts, now regarded at the Mount as a passable subject for assiduous girls. And he taught it keenly because he was certain, that was the word, that a knowledge of Latin and its grammar was good for students of the English language. If he withdrew, Latin would soon dwindle into embroidery, or cookery, and the world of Beechnall would be infinitesimally the worse for it. He stuck his chest out, an independent man, a man of means, strutted about his rooms.

His day at the seaside was packed with visits to three coastal towns, Mablethorpe-Sutton, Chapel St Leonards, Skegness, and one inland, Alford. The pile of advertisements from the house-agents, with smudged photographs and enticing, typed jargon, reached impressive proportions on the back seat, and twice spilled on to the floor of the car. He left his address for further information. He had no time for inspection of bricks and mortar, but took a turn along the front at Skegness to observe the antics of the holidaymakers. In the sunshine, not altogether warm, the world seemed a livelier place. He breathed fried onions, as he looked up to the great Lincolnshire skies. On the way back he made a stop at Horncastle, enquired after and found a piece of Roman wall. On the journey he had discovered from signposts that he was within a few miles of Somersby, Tennyson's birthplace, which he'd never bothered to visit. He remembered an old friend, a lecturer in education at the university, had told him that even these days the place seemed lost in the trees, neither here nor there, with an unusual Vanbrugh house next to the rectory. Henry, the new man, the *nouveau riche*, would find it, stir it. As he drove, he yodelled, sang Beethoven.

Henry worked his way through the brochures, putting selected items into a green folder headed 'The East Coast'. It took him a long morning, but he felt satisfied. He now knew the price of residences, two- and three-bedroom bungalows, Edwardian terraces, Thirties' semis, homes, boarding houses, a Victorian vicarage, a farmhouse with five bedrooms. Nobody would put anything over him; he could afford any of them, but that was no reason why he shouldn't get value for money.

What was he after? He did not know. A brick box where he could rush and live for a day or two in centrally heated comfort when he wanted a sniff of the North Sea? A larger place, spacious with an acre or more, where he could spend the long summer holidays, or even the rest of his life, filling it with pictures and furniture from the antique-shops of Lincolnshire? He did not know. That was the long and short of it. He needed advice.

He telephoned Jennifer.

'May I come to see you?' he asked. 'I have a little problem.'

'Not more child-abuse?' she asked.

'No, more self-abuse.'

'You sound pleased with yourself,' she warned. She sounded like the Jennifer of old. 'When do you want to come?'

They arranged for him to call immediately. He took it as a good omen, but when he arrived he was shocked by her appearance. Pale, thinner, drawn, her face seemed changed. She was still bonny, his mother's word, fat, but her flesh hung sloppily, without life, flabby.

He explained his problem after she had gloomily pronounced herself well.

Like the house-agent she enquired whether he wanted a place to live in for the rest of his active life, or a weekend *pied-à-terre*. He explained that it depended on the attractiveness of the new home and town.

'I see.' Her voice was drained of interest. 'It makes a considerable difference. If you keep your house here as well as the new place, you'll pay taxes and upkeep on both. That means that it's poor value, unless there's a really good reason for living there. You're not thinking of marrying Helena Gough, are you?'

'No. Why do you ask?' Caught out.

'Suppose you did, she'd need to stay here during the week, and one house, yours preferably or hers, would do. Have you asked her advice?'

'No. What makes you think I want to marry her?'

'You're not averse to the idea of marriage. She's attractive. You know her pretty intimately.' Had they talked? 'She'll also be quite well-to-do now. She'll want a move from her present house.'

'But why add marriage to it?'

'Don't know. People don't always act according to strict logic. She'd make you a decent wife. She'd be out of the house full five days a week. She can stand up for herself. She'd be prepared to put up with your unusual, old-fashioned little ways.'

'Such as?'

'Coming to ask another woman about buying another house.'

'Oh.' His monosyllable expressed genuine surprise. She smiled—for a second, something of the Jennifer he remembered. 'You think I'm odd, do you?'

'Not exactly. Except in one or two small corners, Latin and English grammar, string quartets, keeping warm in winter, pictures for your walls, you don't know what you want. You need guidance all the time. Like an adolescent. And, moreover, like an adolescent you resent the advice you need.'

'An unsatisfactory character?' he said, on the defensive.

'In many ways you're a very good man. People would come to you if they were in trouble. But you live on the margins of life. I don't mean by that, on the extremes. You're

251

completely the other way about. You're not likely to murder, or throw bombs. You don't feel strongly enough in the first place. You won't put yourself out. Perhaps it's explained by your circumstances. You've always been comfortably off. Your parents left you money. So did Joanna's. You've an interesting, pleasant, spacious house in the wrong district.'

'I bought it so I could look after Joanna properly. That wasn't an easy time.'

'No. It wasn't. I don't want you to get me wrong, but my impression is that you've always chosen the easy, peaceable, peaceful way. You've just had sufficient money to be able to do this. For instance, you could always have help in—private nursing, for example, for Joanna. You didn't have to throw in your job, or buckle down to a whole set of chores when you came home.'

'Little do you know.'

'I'm not saying you didn't do your best. Or that it was easy. But your energy is low for jobs you don't want to do. You get through them, but that's all.'

'In Joanna's case you know nothing about it.' He sounded petulant, even to himself.

'It's possible, I admit,' Jennifer spoke sternly, 'that you slaved so hard and it took such toll that you hadn't the strength or the will to offer such commitment again. You tiptoe round. You'll give a helping hand or a charitable pound or two, but that's the extent

252

of your interest. You are determined only to keep yourself out of trouble.'

In his disappointment and anger Henry wondered if she didn't describe her own case. A husband tragically killed, and two lovers who deserted her, had left her incapable of any fullness of life. She could react to the distress of others, but at second hand. Perhaps this made her better at her job, able to stand back from it, more equable in judgement, remote, objective. He did not know. And her rejection and loss burnt below, damped, tamped down, keeping her wish to assist, to straighten out, at manageable heat.

He said nothing. He chose, he told himself, the easy way. But he could not answer her criticisms; they seemed just in a rough sort of way.

'Go on,' he said. He had not realised that they had sat so long in silence. She looked at him apprehensively.

'It's no part of my intention', she began, slightly pompous on account of fear, 'to sit in judgement on you. I'm in no position to do so.'

'I value your opinion.'

'Even when I'm wrong?' she asked.

'What am I to do about this house business? Does it seem a good idea?'

'It seems unlike you. What do you see as the advantages?'

'I've been to the seaside twice this year. I like it. I would like to try living there before I'm too old.'

'Get on with it, then. What's the snag? Money?'

'No. Not at all.' He did not mention the legacy.

'What then?'

'I don't want to make a fool of myself.'

'Did Joanna choose your last house?'

'Yes.'

'And you want my help to choose the next. Do it for yourself. Make your own mistakes. Have your own little triumphs. You don't ask me, "Shall we learn the first declension or the third, first off?" Do you?'

'Somebody took that decision centuries ago.'

'Yes, but you know how to put it into practice.'

'Because I've done it so often.'

She laughed, unpleasantly, rapping the arm of her chair in mild derision. He felt overwhelmed.

'I didn't know you disliked me so much,' he said, at length.

'I don't.'

'Despised me, then.' He ground the words out.

'Don't be so ridiculous. I'm only telling you what you know quite well yourself. And if I do it too bluntly, then you can always put it down to my illness, my depression. I see the world as conspiring against me. I don't like it. And so I speak brutally, perhaps, if that's the word, to those I think need it, will benefit from it. You, Henry, love to be the man who can't make his mind up. It gives you an occupation, whirling round in mazes of your own making, and in the end doing nothing. I work all day on problems that are basically insoluble. You make your own up. Shall I buy a new house, a new suit? Shall I go abroad, or ask Helena out to the theatre? All to keep your interest astir, and your life pretty-coloured. You're a generous man, but you're careful with your money. You've got not real friends because you won't commit yourself. That Kinglake, you can see he wants to confide in you, thinks you know something about education. But not you. You back away. "I'm here to teach Latin. That and no more. If I yield an inch on that, put a bit of extra effort or thought in, it'll intrude on my precious time. Time I don't know what to do with in any case." You're a clever, well-read man, but you make yourself out as ignorant, dull, uninteresting.'

She sounded breathless. With exasperation, he thought.

'Given that all this is true, what do I do about purchasing a house?' He stressed his leaflet verb.

'Please yourself. Or, no. Don't do that or you won't even buy a coal-shed. Make yourself acquire something, right or wrong. You might choose wrongly. You might lose money. I

255

don't know. But do it.'

He nodded, and in measured tones told her about his legacy.

Jennifer put a podgy hand across her mouth, like a child surprised.

'Good God,' she said.

'Money no object,' he replied, jovially, master of the situation. 'Will you take a trip over with me, a day, a weekend, a few days and help me make the choice?'

She looked up and her eyes filled with tears, which slopped over on to her cheeks. Her face seemed unmoved under the wash of rolling drops. She sat, incapable of speech, as if the spilling of tears robbed her of all energy. Henry, amazed at her behaviour, looked away. Up to this moment, she had been troubled, had answered his questions unpleasantly but not without sense, had been critical, unflattering, but sufficiently in control of her feelings not to make an exhibition of herself. But the mention of £425,000 had punctured her reserve, broken the dam, brought the tears pouring.

He let her cry.

Now she seemed completely vulnerable, her face like a weeping doll's, swilled but little altered. She sat motionless, fairly straight, making no attempt to wipe her eyes.

Henry pulled himself up from his chair, stood by her, then took her left hand in his right. She returned his pressure. He knelt, still holding her hand, put his left arm awkwardly across her, round her waist. He heard the small noises issuing from her nose and mouth. Dropping his head he made murmurs of reassurance.

'What is it, Jen?' he whispered.

The crying moderated. He took a freshly ironed handkerchief from his pocket, and wiped her eyes. He returned his arm across her body. She seemed less agitated, but her breathing jerked from small inconsistency into climaxes of snatched roughness. For a time he did not repeat his question but laid his head on her breast and shoulder as if he needed the comfort.

They remained thus, until stiffness forced them to move.

'Your head's heavy,' she said. 'It hurts.'

Henry sat upward. She rolled slightly in the chair.

'That's better,' she said. She attacked her face with his handkerchief. 'I'm sorry.' She sniffed again. 'I'm sorry. I couldn't help it.'

'Will you come with me to the seaside?'

'Not next week. I'm too busy. But I can manage the week after. Let's say for three days.' She screwed up her eyes.

'That's good. I'm grateful.'

They talked, not easily. She seemed unwilling to mention his windfall. He talked to her about Virgil and Augustus, said it wouldn't be too long before they could begin on the *Aeneid*.

257

'It will be a struggle for a start, but it's worth it.'

'You like things to be a struggle,' she said. 'You're an old puritan.'

Once or twice she dabbed at her eyes.

CHAPTER SIXTEEN

Henry telephoned each evening after their meeting and he and Jennifer managed reasonable exchanges. Her work was heavy, but she took tablets, and by dint of early bed kept going. They discussed ideal houses; she consulted the magazines. He, at least, enjoyed it.

On Tuesday after one such conversation he rang Helena Gough.

'Hello, stranger,' she said. 'Where have you been?'

He gave some account of the way he spent the school holidays: the garden, a thorough 'spring clean', some decorating, small pieces of DIY.

'And I thought you'd be there reading Horace.'

'Why Horace?' he asked.

'It's the only name I could remember.'

He explained next about his legacy. When he told her the amount, she changed her tone, asked him how he was going to invest it. She

258

made a suggestion or two. He raised the question of his seaside house and said Jennifer had promised to spend three days searching with him.

'You think she's well enough?' she asked.

'I don't know. It might make a little break, a holiday for her.'

'I see.'

'Have you been visiting her regularly?' he enquired.

'I have. And she's been quite ill. Don't let her overdo it, will you? She's far from fit.' She spoke sternly about Jennifer, issued warnings. 'You're one of the few people who could do her good. But be careful.' When she next spoke, Helena's voice had changed. 'I've some news for you now. I'm going to get married.'

'You are?'

'I am. At the end of September.'

'And may I enquire to whom?'

'You may.' She giggled, keeping him waiting. 'Jeremy Sanderson.'

'Who's he when he's at home?' Joviality did nothing to erase incivility.

'He teaches at the new university, the old poly.'

'But what?'

'Economics. I know you don't think much of that. Though you might change your mind now you're one of the moneyed classes.'

She had met Professor Sanderson at a business dinner where he was speaking, and he

259

had invited her to two or three end-of-term functions at the college.

'Has he been married before?' he asked.

'Yes. He's divorced. He has a daughter who's seventeen. She lives with her mother in Wolverhampton.'

'Where will you live?'

'He's just bought a house in Woodthorpe. He's been living in a flat. We'll move in as soon as we're married. September twenty-sixth, Saturday. City Register Office. You're invited.'

'Congratulations.'

'We only fixed the date last week. We'll send our official invitations as soon as the printer's done them.'

'A big do?'

'Not really. Bigger than I'd really like, but ... It'll pass.'

'Arguing already?' he said. 'Are you happy?'

'At my age?' Helena asked. 'And knowing all the snags?' He could imagine her expression. 'Yes, I think you could say we are. Yes. No doubt. Haven't you got a Latin tag for us?'

He thought.

'Impossible, is it?' she asked.

' "*Omnia vincit amor: et nos cedamus amori.*" Love conquers all things: let us also yield to love.'

'That's good. Who said it? Write it on a bit of paper for me and I'll show it to Jerry.'

'Does he know Latin?'

'I shouldn't think so. Who is it?'

'Virgil. The *Eclogues.*'

'The whatters?'

'*Eclogues.* Short pastoral poems.'

'Put it on a postcard for me, will you?'

She spoke in a tone of triumph. My happiness is such I can demand all kinds of favours, and expect to gain them. She rang off, laughing, saying she was too busy by far to chunter her time away at the phone.

'"Chunter" means "grumble",' he said.

'I'm not grumbling.'

She put the phone down.

Henry walked away, saddened. His friend, Helena, was no longer a free spirit, but had put herself at the disposal of another man. Jennifer had asked him if he intended to marry Helena, and he had answered, properly, that he had no such intention. But the option had been there, and was so no longer. *Domus et placens uxor* was not a possibility. He was a nobody: *homo nullius coloris.* He had been rejected again, because he'd done, said, tried nothing. Helena had a sharp tongue, was a tartar. She wouldn't have suited him. His doddering between ancient languages and young children would not have recommended him in her eyes. The edge of his jacket sleeve was frayed; he touched it and was sorry for himself. He aimed a kick at a padded buffet, which skidded out of his way, but did not topple. Cursing, he sat down.

This was another of the moments when he took stock. It came as the result of a slight disappointment. If he thought hard he'd soon decide he did not want to marry Helena; she was too self-confident for him, too liable to speak an awkward mind. And yet. He needed a woman who would goad him. Fifty-nine, a part-time schoolmaster, cooking his own meals, cutting a dash nowhere; he ought to change. He waited, he considered, for a sign. If £425,000 wouldn't jolt him into activity, what would? From now on he would grow physically weaker, more apathetic, trudging the same streets, dull as they were. Could Helena have changed this? He doubted it. If she thought she could, and it had been worth her while, she would have made the effort. She had tested him sexually, and he had performed to satisfaction, so that it must have been life outside the bedroom where he fell short.

The telly, the radio, his books could not cheer him. He wondered despondently what Professor Sanderson looked like.

Next morning, Jennifer rang to say she had not been to work for two days. He said he would call round immediately, and soon talked down her tentative efforts to dissuade him.

She let him into her house, and crouched on the settee.

'What's wrong?' he asked.

It took some minutes to get the truth out of her. She had found her work more and more

262

burdensome, and had taken time off. She had not said anything of this when he had telephoned her. In the end she had dragged herself at the beginning of the week to the surgery, where the doctor, a sensible and sympathetic woman, had told her to take a fortnight's rest, had prescribed new anti-depressant tablets. These she had collected from the chemist's, had begun the treatment, against her better judgement, and felt, if anything, worse. She was useless, would never take up her work again, would be dependent on drugs for the rest of her life. By the time she had finished this recital of despair, she sobbed and groaned hysterically, quite out of character, so that he could barely make out what she was trying to convey to him.

'There's only one thing', he said, 'for you.' She now sat rigidly on the settee, the violence over. 'You must come and stay with me for a week or two until you're feeling better.'

'I can't, I can't.' Her voice sounded sepulchral.

'You can and you will.' Henry spoke firmly, grimly, though he had no idea whether or not he acted sensibly. She did not argue long. He suggested that she spent the first day or two at his house in bed. He would immediately go and make the bed up while she was to collect her belongings together. If she felt incapable of that, then—he handed her paper and pencil—she was to make a list and he'd see to it when he

263

returned. He'd be back in under the hour.

On his return he found her with a pile of clothes on the table. She had slumped back and sobbed that she couldn't desert her cat.

'You've a cat-door. I saw it. I'll make sure he's fed twice a day.'

'The milk. The papers. Any day now the gas board will read the meter.'

'Yes,' he said. 'I'll deal with them in due course.'

He fetched down her travelling cases, filled two. He checked that she had her medicine and nightgowns.

'If anything's missing, I can come back.'

'It's not fair on you. You've enough to do,' she wailed.

'Twaddle.'

Once inside his house, Jennifer seemed quieter, listless or puzzled into mute dependence. He had, he said, fixed a television set and a radio in her bedroom and she was to retire there at once. He carted her luggage upstairs, and she asked if she could have a bath. It seemed a hopeful sign. He laid out towels, flannels, a sponge, a new block of soap. She staggered on his arm so that they twice hit the wall as they walked the passage to the bathroom. She said she was capable of running the bath.

Downstairs he decided what they would eat, and began to prepare. After half an hour he made coffee, and shouted upstairs to see if she was ready. She feebly called his name.

'Yes?' he queried, outside the bathroom door.

'Henry,' she said.

'What is it?'

Again a groan. He pushed open the unlocked door, tapping a warning with his fingernails.

Jennifer was sitting naked on the edge of the bath, slumping forward, chin to chest.

'What's wrong?'

She lifted her eyes, which swilled with tears, shook her head, moaned again.

'Are you dry?' he asked.

She had not removed a towel from the rail. He began to rub broad back and shoulders. Fortunately her hair was not wet. He helped her to her feet and carefully completed the drying. She did not move; neither struggled. She stood like an animal. When he was certain he had done, he slipped her nightgown on and led her out. He made her lie and drew the covers to her throat.

'How's that?' he asked.

'This bed's warm,' she said.

'I put the electric blanket on.'

'It's only August.' That signified sanity. He straightened the bedclothes, and she snuggled down, the first time she had relaxed. He half-drew the curtains, asked if she wanted anything, and trotted downstairs to cook.

The next fortnight passed slowly. Breakfast

265

in bed, for her, then a bath, which she managed for herself. After the first week she came down for lunch, and watched cricket on the television, or once or twice sat on the garden seat. As long as she knew what to do—little enough—and was assisted, she seemed perfectly normal, spoke sensibly, read her mail, which he collected, dictated short answers— the quickest method, they found—and walked about the house, looking at his bookshelves or in the evening listening to the Proms. Once or twice she had been torn by crying jags, and complained of headaches, back pains, stomach disorder. She ate without much appetite, but could joke with him about his cooking. Feeble, tremulous as she was, she was recognisably Jennifer Speed.

At the end of the fortnight, he ran her to the doctor, who expressed satisfaction. The drugs were working, it seemed, but she must go steady. The doctor sent for him to join the consultation. Was it possible for Jennifer to continue living at his house, because they seemed to have hit on a winning régime?

'I take it you talk to each other a fair amount?' the doctor asked.

'Yes,' Jennifer said. 'I talk, he listens.'

'Good.' The doctor pushed her rimless glasses higher up her nose. 'More of the same. Go out if you wish, take some exercise, but don't overdo anything. Don't tire yourself needlessly.'

'How long shall I be on drugs?'

The doctor consulted her computer screen.

'You've been on these for three weeks. Perhaps another month. We'll have to see. It depends on how you shape.'

'And work?'

'Treat it as a nasty, four-letter word for the present.'

They left the surgery in a more cheerful frame of mind.

Helena visited once or twice a week. She and Jen talked at length, left to it by Henry. The day before the beginning of school Helena brought her professor to dinner. Jennifer planned the meal, and helped in shopping and preparation. Her behaviour seemed normal; she made suggestions, carried them into practice, bossed him about.

The evening proved successful. Jeremy Sanderson, 'Hel's prof' as Jennifer dubbed him, was tall and thin, rather diffident, younger than Henry, so Henry guessed, but appearing older, more solemn. He seemed much at home, admired Henry's house, and in the middle of the main course talked about Japan's motor industry, with verve and great clarity. The listeners enjoyed his exposition, delivered without superiority, so much so that the fetching-in of the pudding, profiteroles with thick cream, was delayed. Helena asked Henry for the etymology of profiterole; he did not know, but guessed it was connected with 'profit', the same word in French. They reached for dictionaries, which supported his hypothesis.

'Don't see it,' Helena grumbled.

'Filled with riches,' said Jeremy, pacifically.

Henry's French dictionary offered the sentence *les enfants profitent à vue d'oeil*, 'the children are visibly filling out'. 'There you are,' he said. While he fiddled with the Harrap, Jennifer asked him to look up choux pastry, telling them that was what profiteroles were made from. The dictionary wasn't much help, though generous with cabbage phrases in French, but Jen's question seemed sane to him, a sure sign that she was herself again, a social being, a member of society.

The visitors did not leave until midnight. Henry packed the dish-washer, rarely used, turned it on. Back in the dining room he found Jennifer folding the cloth, straightening the chairs. As soon as he came through the door, she beamed at him, then burst into tears. He could not get out of her what was wrong. 'Nothing,' she whispered. 'No reason.'

He led her upstairs, left her at the bathroom, cleaned himself up at his bedroom sink, undressed and put on his pyjamas. There was no sound from Jennifer, either in bathroom, corridor or bedroom. He shoved his head out of the door and called, once, twice. The second time, she replied, weakly, with his name. Her door was open; she sat fully dressed on the edge of her bed.

'Are you all right?'

She lifted her face to him, piteously, wept again.

'What is it?' he asked. She shook her head. 'You've overdone it.'

'Put me to bed, Henry.'

He undressed her, settled her comfortably, then climbed in beside her. With an arm around her, he lay still.

'Stroke me,' she whispered, 'but don't do anything else.'

Henry obeyed, guiding his hands. He fell asleep first.

When he began teaching she prepared meals for his return, and at the end of September seemed well enough to go back to her office for half-days.

She suggested that she return to her own house, but made no great fuss over his refusal to let her go. Her cat had been fetched and had settled to a routine. Both Jennifer and her pet seemed at home. Towards the end of the month, on the Saturday of Jennifer's first week back, they showed up at Helena's wedding. The ceremony was well attended, guests standing in rows, three deep, behind five lines of filled chairs. The meal, speeches, dancing, took place at a city-centre hotel, where Henry barely knew a soul. Jennifer sat still, apart from a couple of fox-trots, as if afraid that too much energy expended might put an end to her recovery. Neither had drunk alcohol, and they were home by ten. That night they made love, the first time since Tim Glover. It was a quiet performance, but Jennifer expressed her satisfaction.

'I wonder how Helena and Jeremy are getting on,' he ventured, as they lay quiet.

'They won't be in bed yet,' she answered. True, it was not yet midnight. 'But it won't be their first effort.'

'How do you know?'

'I know what Helena's like. She'd have tested him out. *You* know that. But it's been a great day for them. Did you see Jeremy's daughter?'

'Not to my knowledge.'

'No, she didn't come. Helly didn't know why.' Whether his ex had leaned on the girl to stay away, and whether it had upset Jeremy had seemed unknown to Helena. Jennifer sleepily outlined her own views. It appeared comforting, almost beautiful, to him to lie beside this naked woman, and listen to her sedately expressed views. Several times he drifted away, but when he jerked back to consciousness, she was still talking. He wondered if he'd answered sensibly from the boundaries of sleep, or whether she merely murmured to herself, happy to find herself in control, without anxiety.

On the doctor's advice, Jennifer did not hurry to go back to work full-time. She visited

270

her own house less frequently than Henry expected. Occasionally she sat at her desk there, but mostly she went to clean.

'Why don't you let the place out to some students?' he asked, once, again after copulation.

'It would be sensible,' she answered, 'but I don't like to do anything to upset the status quo. There'd be arrangements and agents and income tax, and I don't want anything extra.'

'You should marry me, then,' he said.

'I'll think about it.' Then, slyly, 'Isn't that extra?'

There they left it. She did not resume her study of Latin, and that seemed proper to him for the time being.

CHAPTER SEVENTEEN

Throughout the autumn Jennifer's condition steadily improved, though not without setbacks. She tried a week's full time at work, but could not continue. Her superiors, however, seemed content to allow her to come in for a few hours, and once she had understood this, and they had made suitable arrangements, she appeared to have settled that part of her life. On Tuesdays, Wednesdays and Thursdays she slept in her own home, but at the weekends and on Monday she lived with

Henry. Quite how this pattern had been established neither understood, but Henry laughed, claiming the cat didn't know where he lived without consulting the calendar.

At school Henry found relief. His subject seemed more popular, and Kinglake, the headmaster, consulted him frequently. The child who had claimed that her father abused her had been withdrawn from the school; no one knew why. Kinglake had unofficially consulted a police superintendent, who said nothing could be done, but who passed the information on privately to 'the right people'. Mrs Huntley had met the girl once, by chance, in the street, and had made sure she still had the Helpline telephone number. The child had seemed 'extraordinarily uninterested', so that the teacher had wondered about her own judgement of the case. In spite of the recession, the school prospered to such an extent that Kinglake considered a sixth form. Henry warned against it, but agreed to teach 'A'-level Latin to two girls, excellent linguists, who had left to study French and German at a sixth-form college that could not, or would not, offer Latin.

Henry made no further serious attempt to buy a house on the east coast, though he and Jennifer aired the subject from time to time, and house-agents sent occasional bunches of leaflets. He kept his folders up to date, and played about with them. At the same time he greatly enjoyed the sessions with his bank's finance adviser about his inheritance, which had been paid in full early in October. He took Jennifer out to dinner on that night, but she seemed grudging in her pleasure, as if she had hoped the dangerous money would never materialise. She could chaff him into buying two new suits, and shirts and shoes, but was nervous at the larger prospects.

They were invited to dinner at the house of the Sandersons, a house where the furniture, rather sparse, was brand-new Scandinavian. None of Helena's pictures, or her father's, hung on the walls, and when Henry questioned her she replied, very offhandedly, that they wouldn't suit the décor. They were tucked safely away in the attic. He said that when she decided to rid herself of them, he'd like a chance to buy two of the seascapes. She said she'd consider this, though at present she and Jeremy were run off their feet with work.

He questioned Jennifer and she expressed her dislike of the Sandersons' taste in furniture.

'It looked to me as if they'd gone into a shop and ordered matching tables and chairs, and then bought wallpaper and carpets to fit in.'

'Wouldn't that be a good way of doing it?'

'Yes, but I don't much like this light-coloured wood they've chosen, and the rest is all too bland. It looks like a picture in a posh magazine.'

'And who'd be responsible?'

'Helena, I expect,' Jennifer answered. 'He'll do as she tells him. And she won't have any ideas. No, that's wrong. No real ideas. She wants to be modern, up-to-date, clean and spare and square, and this is the way to do it. Or', she drew out the word, 'she remembers her old house in Stoke or wherever it was, which was big and full of huge black furniture handed down from her ex-husband's ancestors, and she wants a complete change. Or the job lot she'd acquired on the house in Stansfield Road.'

'Is this true?' he asked.

'No. I'm guessing. But I don't like houses which look like showrooms.'

'It might be Jeremy. He lived there first.'

'I don't think so. He's a wimp. He'll do as he's told. They're having a honeymoon proper in the Christmas holidays. To the Falklands. He wanted to go to some conference, but Helena wouldn't let him. You want to thank God you didn't marry her.'

'She's ambitious for him. She'll push him.'

Both laughed, before Jennifer straightened her face to say, 'I know all about you and Helena, and her mother.'

'Is it to my credit?' he asked.

'I'm no judge.'

One day in his half-term they started early to look at an 'ideal house' just beyond Sutton-on-Sea. A photocopied sheet had arrived, and they had read it eagerly. They had resumed regular sex some weeks before, and both were animated after the last night's burst.

'Read that,' he ordered. She obeyed. She looked up at him, then down, then scratched her head.

'Perfect,' she concluded, 'except we'll have to be careful.'

'I'll ring the agent today, and we'll start early tomorrow and case the joint.'

'And I'll spend the day outlining the drawbacks,' she said.

It was a two-storey farmhouse with four spacious bedrooms, early nineteenth-century, solidly built, with outbuildings and an acre of flat land. It boasted oil-fired central heating, a walled garden, a view of the sea at walking distance from the bedroom windows, and all in excellent order. The whole day they spent in excited discussion.

'There are certain to be snags,' Jennifer said.

'If one has money, then snags don't matter.'

'But it seems just as big as this house.'

'Give me space,' he said. 'Room to breathe.'

'You're barmy.'

They enjoyed the day, visiting the coast. The house was strongly walled, though the land round about was flat, drab.

'I like trees,' she said.

'Then we won't have it.'

'But the price. It's a bargain. It could be marvellous.'

'I'm scared', he said, 'of the responsibility.'

They moved round from room to room, testing the door handles, staring out of the windows, considering neighbours (there were few signs of habitation at all close), the commissariat, the points of the compass, what might be grown in the garden.

'What do you think?' he said. They were sitting upstairs on a discoloured, dampish ottoman, splashed by October sunlight.

'It's up to you.'

'I'll buy it if you'll marry me,' he said.

'That's not fair.'

'No. It's sudden. But you know it's what I've wanted for long enough.'

Jennifer stared into a far corner.

'I've blotted my copybook. You realise that.' It sounded only half-serious.

'I love you.'

'Kneel down, then.' She pointed imperiously, making a game of it. 'Propose properly.'

He went down, took hold of her hand, said, 'Jennifer Speed, will you marry me? I love you. I love you.'

'I will. Though that wasn't exactly eloquent, now, was it?'

They embraced, sat in rapt silence. Words seemed to him at a premium. He had expended the best to advantage already. They made love, precariously, not altogether satisfactorily on the narrow, sloping top of the ottoman, and then, still quietly, ate the picnic meal she had prepared: corned beef sandwiches and instant coffee from a vacuum flask.

'Let's walk round once more, and then we'll make our minds up,' he said. He glanced at his watch. Only one-fifteen. Thus the world is changed.

Afternoon sunshine brightened the main rooms; shadows stood sharp. They strolled hand-in-hand, touching each other, feeling the strength of the walls.

Back at the estate agent's in Skegness they began the business of purchase. The smart young man congratulated them, said he'd considered buying the property himself. All he had needed was money to spend to make the place a picture. But these days. He sighed.

The family who had owned it before, a builder in King's Lynn, who had put in a great deal of improvement, had had to sell because of the recession. 'It's a gem,' the agent said.

'If you don't mind living away from the world,' Henry answered.

'Nowhere is far from anywhere in these car-driving days.'

'Tell that to the doctor,' Jennifer answered.

Henry's solicitor advised careful search. Clearly he did not approve of middle-aged men of settled habits suddenly deciding to buy remote holiday homes in an unfashionable part of the country. His lecture left Jennifer down in the mouth, but Henry kept cheerful.

'With money,' he told her, 'we can ignore

277

good advice.'

Wealth was considered when they bought the engagement ring.

'I don't want you to spend more than you would have done as a part-time teacher.'

'Why not?'

She then lectured him on the pleasures of aesthetics and of choosing something beautiful that did not depend on cost. He was impressed, and even more so by the care she took to choose the engagement ring. They tried four jewellers', before returning after an hour and a half to the first to buy the token. It cost fifty-seven pounds over the limit she had set. That seemed a small triumph to him. She made no demur, but carried the ring away from the shop in a box, not on her finger. He did not mind; with its neat diamonds it was a symbol, and that was its importance. As far as he was concerned, he would have been content with the first specimen he was offered, as long as it wasn't an eyesore, in that it represented his promise. The promise held the consequence, not the gold. Jennifer walked from the shop, ring in box in handbag, as one beautified, beatified. They had travelled in by bus, and once they were seated for the return journey, he saw her dab at her eyes with a small lace-edged handkerchief. He felt proud.

On the next day, by appointment, they visited the registrar and fixed the wedding on the first free day of the Christmas vacation. It all appeared easy to arrange. Ten o'clock with their witnesses. Helena could not do it, as she would already be on the way to the Falklands. Kinglake and his wife would oblige, and a cousin of Jennifer's. Both bride and groom lacked parents and siblings, were orphans.

Jennifer put her house up for sale without any compunction. They would use her furniture for the Lincolnshire place, moving it the weekend before the wedding if her home was not sold. All these arrangements, vital changes, did not harm Jennifer; she seemed to blossom. She still did only part-time at her social work, but talked about it freely, as carefully as before her breakdown.

Henry thoroughly enjoyed his teaching, especially the 'A' level. He was, as he realised, rusty, and his pupils were bright, hard-working girls so that he needed to press himself. A challenge of this sort spurred him; he felt a real student again. He had studied all of their set texts at school and university, but it needed careful preparation to keep up with his pupils and their questions. He groaned about this to Jennifer, as well as the three early morning hours—eight-thirty start—he put in at their college, besides the whole of Wednesday afternoon at his home, and one further period on Thursday lunch-time at his school. The girls throve on it, made great progress, as did he. He seemed young again, energetic, though he was uncertain whether it was because of his pedagogic duties or the idea of his forthcoming marriage. The November weather matched his optimism, with misty mornings and nights, and bright, comparatively warm sunlight in the middle of the day.

Helena and Sanderson called in to see them. She worked herself half to death, she claimed now that she had made this branch utterly profitable, and had this week taken on a fully qualified young woman. The principal of the firm had offered her a full partnership from the New Year. Jeremy grew more content every day—that is, when she saw him—and had even ceased to complain about Christmas in the Falklands. He'd always be a moaner, but she'd change him.

'Unto him that hath shall be given,' she said. 'He's learning.'

They laughed out loud at her.

'I've got your wedding-present outside in the car. I don't know whether you'll think it suitable. It's very difficult to know what to buy people like you. You've two houses full of belongings already.'

'It's the thought that counts,' Jen said, smirking.

'Help me in with them,' Helena ordered Henry.

He guessed, as soon as he saw the two rectangular, flat, beautifully done-up parcels, what the presents were, and was not disappointed. Jennifer undid them, careful not to tear paper, folding it, to reveal two blue seascapes by Helena's father, Eric Blake. Jen, busy with the wrapping, seemed puzzled, but Henry said one word: 'Perfect.' He kissed Helena, who pressed her breasts into him.

'I wasn't sure.'

'Absolutely perfect. You couldn't have chosen anything more likely to give pleasure. Except you shouldn't. They're heirlooms.'

Jennifer joined the enthusiasm, delighted by her fiancé's gratification.

'We'll find a place of honour,' she said.

'In this house or the new one?'

'We'll decide after the wedding.'

The Sandersons drove them over to view the house. The contract had been signed, but the solicitor still continued his searches. It would be theirs by the last week in November. On the day of the trip—they went in Sanderson's Rover—the weather was dark, rainy, with low clouds. Walking round the almost empty rooms, Jennifer said, was about as pleasant as visiting the workhouse, but the four poked into corners, making suggestions to each other, pleased in a subdued way. They ate at a pub in Alford, visited Somersby at last, and drove back in the near-dark. The Sandersons dropped them at Henry's house, and refused to come in, pleading pressure of work. They seemed sad, subdued.

'They're a decent couple,' Henry said.

'It must have been boring.'

281

'You weren't bored, were you?'

'No. I'm an interested party. I listened to them nattering at each other.'

'There.'

In the weeks leading up to the wedding, Jennifer seemed subdued. She continued, at her own request, with anti-depressants, talked with a counsellor, an excellent woman, but never managed exactly to elude her anxiety. On the other hand, she made the arrangements for the transfer of her furniture—a few favourites to his house, the rest to Lincolnshire. They spent the weekend straightening the new place, which already had curtains and carpets, and then looked at each other in some sort of wonderment, that they owned this building, that soon they would be Mr and Mrs Shelton.

Henry bought a suit for the wedding, and Jennifer three outfits. Neatness was all. She had lost weight and looked well. Kinglake and his wife, together with Jennifer's cousin, attended the wedding, a simple ceremony that pleased Henry with his buttonhole carnation and the smell of new cloth about him. They spent the rest of the morning in the Kinglakes' house at the school before walking down to the George for the wedding lunch. All worked exactly to plan. The weather, though cold, was bright. They talked, and ate, and enjoyed Jennifer's company. The lack of congratulatory telegrams and cards seemed a bonus. The Sandersons, presumably *en route*

282

for Port Stanley, sent no word.

At two in the afternoon, the Kinglakes and the cousin saw them off for Lincolnshire. No confetti, hanging boots, facetious messages, spoilt their neatness of spirit. The cousin would take her car back to Henry's house, spend the night there before setting off for Sussex the next day. Christine was an efficient, trustworthy woman who would see all was well, programming the heating and alarms before she handed the key over to a designated neighbour. All had been efficiently arranged.

As the newly-weds drove towards the coast, they said little. Neither showed excitement.

'Well, Mrs Shelton,' he asked as they dawdled through crowded Grantham, 'does it feel any different?' Late shoppers flocked on pedestrian crossings, blocking their way.

'No. Should it?' But she smiled.

It was not quite dark when they arrived, but the house glowed warm. They plugged in a kettle and walked outside. They could not hear the sea. He stubbed his toe on a piece of builder's rubble. He, jolted, swore and laughed. Indoors they drank tea, watched the television—racing and football and depressing foreign news.

'How do you like it?' he asked.

'Fine. But I don't want to talk about it.'

He looked at her, his wife, with some apprehension. They ate a small meal, and walked about the house, as if unable to sit for any length of time, pacifically discussing changes. The cat, brought in a basket and not to be let outside for three days, followed them round mewing. When they read, he jumped on to Jennifer's lap, purred loudly, slept through this important evening. By eleven they were in bed in a strange, large room with a wardrobe and dressing table of hers for company. One of the seascapes graced the wall. They made the bed in tandem: the hot water boiled in its tank, and they bathed together, something they had never done before.

'Well, wife,' he said, drying her nakedness.

'Well, husband,' she replied. 'This is the first place I shall decorate.'

That seemed appropriate.

They were in no hurry to get up next morning, but lay in bed, drinking tea and talking. 'Christine will be on her way now. She's an early riser' or 'I wonder what Helena and Jeremy are doing this morning? And if they are enjoying it?' They touched each other with affection in the grey light of the bedroom. 'Can't see anybody about,' he reported from the window. 'Did you expect to?' she said, sprawling lewdly on the duvet.

At midday they drove into Skegness to buy newspapers. By one-thirty, as Jennifer served what she called a 'light collation', he explained the derivation of the word, the reading of the *Collationes Patrum* of Johannes Cassianus during repasts in monasteries.

'How did you know that?' she asked.

'I once looked it up. *Collatio* means a "subscription", a "collection", and it seemed a rum word for a meal.'

'And you remembered?'

'I remembered.'

She served a delicious bacon omelette. She asked if that was an interesting word.

'It', he said, 'is the result of a curious metathesis. The Latin *lamella* from *lamina* in time became *l'alemelle* from *la lemelle* and then *l'amelette*, a thin plate.'

She seemed delighted at his learning, and asked for explanations of metathesis and suffix, which he gave as they ate.

Jennifer congratulated him, but said he ought to wear his Sunday best when expounding such scholarship, not a white sweat-shirt and grey baggy trousers. When he cleared the dishes, he reported he could see rain on the window.

'I don't care,' she answered. 'We're warm and comfortable...'

'And married,' he said.

'And married, and replete, and with a pile of newspapers.'

'I'll put the car away.'

They read; he dozed; the fine rain became heavier. He woke once to find Jennifer altering the position of some of the smaller objects, photographs, flowers, a buffet, hanging the second seascape in a place of honour over the hearth. She grinned at him over her shoulder. 'I shall be doing this all the time,' she warned. 'You'll never find anything.' He groaned comically.

They stayed quite happily in brightening weather until after New Year's Day, walking out, driving once to Lincoln, and next day to Stamford. Jennifer seemed cheerful, and energetic, though Henry did not press her too hard. They never hurried any expedition, and spent the long evenings reading or talking. They were interrupted only once by a young German couple who wanted information about the countryside.

Henry had been standing by the outside gate when he heard the car approaching. It surprised him for it drew up, and the driver in check shirt and green trousers came towards him, and in excellent but foreign-sounding English made a few enquiries about the road. It soon became clear that the young man knew a great deal more of the coast than Henry, and was not averse to sharing the knowledge. He waved his hands, as he talked about erosion of the coast at Spurn Head and the subsequent enlargement of Gibraltar Point.

The German's wife, a small, dark, pretty woman, came out to listen to the conversation. Henry invited them in for a cup of tea. They accepted, wiping their shoes vigorously on the new doormat.

This was a part of England that they did not

know well. He was a university lecturer, in geography, she a teacher of languages. They were intending to drive up the east coast and back as far as Newcastle.

'It's dull, isn't it?' Henry asked.

'No. We'll stay in a town perhaps for two days, and stroll round, and talk to people.'

'It is a good way to find out what ordinary English people think. We listen to the radio, usually Radio Four, as we drive.'

'Is it important?'

'To learn about England and the English? I teach the language, and so it's good for me to read your newspapers as they appear, and hear the comments on radio, and watch your television programmes in our hotel rooms.'

Jennifer explained that they had just moved in, and said something of their plans.

'Why did you choose this spot if you think it's dull?' Herr Samstag asked.

'It's quiet. It's like us, not ostentatious. We can come out, and make ourselves comfortable in our own way, and not be everlastingly interrupted.'

'We are interrupting you?' Frau Samstag said.

'We are not hermits,' Jennifer answered. 'We enjoy company, within limits.'

'As I enjoy your cake,' said the young man.

Jennifer wrote down the recipe for the wife, and they discussed whether German ingredients would much affect the taste.

'For the better?' Henry joked.

'Oh, no.'

They walked the visitors round the house as if they were old friends, soliciting suggestions. Mrs Samstag feared damp, 'the curse of English buildings', while her husband seemed fascinated that they could hold such 'frank and friendly' conversations after so short an acquaintance.

'We drop, as it were, out of the sky on to you,' he said, 'and we find each other congenial. I cannot help wondering why this has happened.'

'By chance,' Henry said.

'Ah, yes, but such chances have their effect. They alter lives. You choose one street rather than another, and meet your future wife, as I did.' He took her hand, and raised it courteously.

'But we may not meet again,' Jennifer said, 'unless you come this way and we're in.'

'Even so, this pleasant hour, this delicious plum cake, may have an effect on our lives. An infinitesimal effect, you may say, but none the less there. And one can never be sure of the ultimate results of a small beginning.'

The Samstags finally drive off into the dark.

'That has been time well spent, profitably spent,' Samstag had said as they prepared to leave. 'I will tell you something which we have not mentioned before, because you might have been embarrassed. We are newly-weds. We have each been married before. I have a son, and my wife a daughter; they are staying over Christmas with respective grandparents. The time, the months up to the wedding have been difficult.'

'Hairy,' Jennifer suggested. She then had to explain the word.

'What with lawyers and families it has been a nightmare which troubles us still. The partings, the divorces, were accomplished only with infinite difficulty. We were made to feel like criminals or outcasts. Now we are recovering, and this afternoon has helped. We are human beings once again.'

Jennifer immediately invited them to stay overnight.

'No, thank you,' Samstag answered. 'We dare not.'

'We dare not tempt providence,' his wife elucidated.

'We have enjoyed two hours, three—time has passed so quickly—of English hospitality, of English happiness, and we are grateful. but we dare ask no more.'

After the visitors had gone, Jennifer and Henry stood by the closed gate in the darkness, although a cold breeze cut the face.

'A funny couple,' Henry said.

'Yes, but so are we. We never told them we were only just married.'

'We never told them anything much,' he answered. 'They did all the talking.'

'Fancy leaving the children behind over Christmas. And they didn't seem to be staying with parents, but grandparents, while this pair amble round the east coast of England.'

'You liked them?' he asked. 'Didn't you?'

'Oh, yes. I liked them right enough. But we didn't get half the story.'

'This is your professional training coming out. It makes you suspicious.'

'Well, yes. But. How old would they be? Mid-thirties? And they spoke such good English.'

Henry laughed.

'So you'll be looking in all the papers now, will you? "German couple found murdered in Lincs. Secret service involved"? Has Germany got the equivalent of MI5 or 6?'

'Don't know. These two were so knocked about that they couldn't begin to tell us their recent history in case it upset us and spoilt their hour or two of comfort. It's poor, isn't it, when you can only feel at ease with strangers, who know nothing about you?'

'You don't think they're murderers, do you?' Henry asked, gruesomely joking.

'Don't be ridiculous. They're what they said they were. A youngish couple who had married badly and had difficulty in escaping the shackles.'

'Why?'

'There's the secret. Perhaps their spouses wanted to hang on to them. For one reason or

290

another. The children, perhaps. Or status. Or money. One can't say. Marriage is a tricky business for some. They had managed to wriggle out of it at last, and get spliced to the right partner, but they didn't want to ruin it at the very beginning by raking over the old troubles.'

'I see,' Henry answered, scratching his head.

'The great advantage was that the discussion was in English. She loved that. They enjoyed their command of the language, and felt that they were learning more of it from us. They were on their toes, and clearly relished it. They were competitive.'

'Will they compete against each other?' Henry asked.

'I shouldn't be surprised. But they'll both be so busy with their jobs, we hope, or fitting the new family together, or escaping from all their troubles, they'll go carefully, damp the fires of ambition down a bit.'

'Cor.' He held his hands up in surrender.

Jennifer laughed at his comical expression. 'We shan't compete, shall we?' She sounded pathetic.

'I hope not,' he said. 'We haven't the time. I'm twenty years older than you, and that means we haven't the long vista of years most newly-weds have. Still, that might be an advantage. Many people can't stand a long course.'

She kissed him, patted his head.

'And all because two Germans dropped in.'

'Don't you wish they'd stayed the night?' she asked.

'No. I want you all on your own. I seem to be learning much more about you now we're married.'

'That's because you think now I'm your chattel.'

'It's a point,' he said.

They hugged, and began their lovemaking by the hearth, serious but smiling.

*   *   *

When they returned home to Beechnall Jennifer began to work full-time. Henry prepared the evening meal, and even cooked when they spent the weekends at the seaside place. The agents reported several serious enquiries about Jennifer's house, but no offers as yet. She was not to worry, since this was not the best time of year for house sales. Jennifer herself seemed in much better health, and best of all able to suit the amount of work to her present capability. She brought files home with her, and quite often she and Henry sat together at either end of the large dining-room table doing their preparation. She liked this, she said. If she had come across some error or difficulty she could call out 'Damn' at the top of her whispered voice, and her husband would look enquiringly but mildly up and ask what the trouble was. After a few words of explanation, to which he listened carefully, she felt better, she claimed. A trouble shared is a trouble halved. They laughed at this poker-work motto, but were pleased with the discovery, with themselves.

They heard nothing from Helena and her professor apart from a postcard of penguins from the Falklands. This did not surprise them; they were all busy. Jennifer twice and Henry once, at intervals, tried to phone her, but the answering machine gave the only satisfaction. They left no messages. On the fourth occasion, at the end of February, Jennifer spoke to Jeremy Sanderson, but reported that he seemed odd, embarrassed, and had hardly begun to talk when he broke off to answer, he said, the door. He promised he would ring back, but did not do so. Henry once drove past Helena's old house on Stansfield Road and noted that the agent's 'For Sale' board was still outside, but now announced that the place was sold.

At the beginning of March, as they sat at their 'homework' by the dining-room table, Helena telephoned. Jennifer took the call outside in the hall. When she returned she looked grim.

'That was short,' he said.

'Not sweet,' she answered. 'It was Helena. She and her husband have parted.'

'Eh?'

'What I said. They've separated.'

'They've only been married five minutes. Did she sound very down?'

'She wasn't exactly pleased. She said hardly anything. She was just going out. She will try to come round tomorrow evening. But I don't know anything about it except that they don't live together.'

'Didn't you ask any questions?' he pressed.

'No. I didn't.' He was surprised.

Over supper, in bed, at breakfast, they used their imagination. Jen, the professional, said they should wait for a few facts, but she enjoyed his flights of fancy as much as he did. He asked if she, in her professional life, had come across many marriages as short as this.

'Not very many. But some. In one case a wife left her husband on the wedding-night.'

'And never went back?'

'No. They were a young, immature, slightly disturbed couple.'

'Did you know any of Helena's age?'

'Yes. And the man committed suicide. Mark you, he'd never been married before, and I wasn't sure of his sexual inclinations.'

'I see.'

'Come on, then, just tell us what you think,' she urged.

'Well, I'm surprised. I thought they'd be highly suited.'

'You're not blaming Helena's menopause, then?'

'Has that started?'

'I shouldn't think so. What is she? Thirty-nine? Well, go on.'

'I tell you why I thought they'd be all right. Helena likes her own way, and speaks her mind, but I guessed he wouldn't object too much. Might even approve. Might like a strong-minded woman to decide for him on matters of no importance. As long as she left him plenty of time for his research, whatever that is, and his administration, then I guessed he wouldn't argue.'

'She's the villain of the piece?' Jennifer asked.

'She's, let's say, more outspoken, more likely to lose her temper, I'd have thought, but I don't know. I haven't seen enough of him.'

Helena rang to say she could not keep her appointment, but suggested the Friday evening following. She was living now in the Grosvenor Hotel, and was quite comfortable. No, she hadn't the time to visit the seaside with them, either on Saturday or Sunday. She thanked them, but she was run off her feet now the financial year was coming to an end, but she'd come Friday, after her dinner, for an hour. It might be a break for her.

Helena arrived looking particularly smart, as if she was about to appear at a high-class business conference. She showed no signs of ill-health, or lack of sleep; her skin glowed healthily. She kissed them both, on both

295

cheeks, effusively, holding them for inspection at arms' length in a faint cloud of expensive perfume.

'Well, thank God marriage is doing somebody some good.' She sounded brisk, half-humorous, pleased with herself, much in control. She sat down, accepted a glass of Derbyshire spa water, and enquired after their second home, asking all the right questions, telling them that if they invited her again she'd be delighted to look the new place over.

'I'm working all hours now. This is deliberate.'

'On account of your marriage?' Jennifer asked, suddenly but sympathetically blunt.

'Yes.'

They paused, fidgeted awkwardly, fiddled with cups or glass, looked at the floor. The silence stretched. Helena broke it.

'I suppose you wonder what on earth we have been up to.'

She held her head to one side like a child, caught in disobedience, trying to outface its mother. Neither listener spoke.

'It surprises me when I think about it. Not that it should. We were niggling even before we were married. I felt as if I'd found freedom, and then immediately thrown it away. And I suppose he was much the same.'

'Why did you persist, then?' Henry asked, timidly. 'Why didn't you break it off?'

'We did discuss it. But the line Jeremy took,

and it seemed sensible at the time, was that we'd become set in our ways, and it would take time to change them. When I asked why we should bother, he said he loved me. It seemed a fair answer at the time, and I never enquired what he meant. That was wrong, silly.' She looked them over. 'The sex was all right. We'd tried that. Not marvellous, but it passed muster. And we had our little experiments, choosing furniture and wallpaper. That sort of thing.'

Helena sipped, then rubbed her forehead hard.

'It was the Falklands that put the kibosh on it.' She smirked at her word. 'He didn't want to go. It was a waste of three weeks' working-time to him.'

'Did he say so?'

'Not in so many words, not when we first booked. I thought he'd enjoy it all once he'd got there but he didn't. He thought I was absolutely mad keen on it.'

'And were you?' Jen asked.

'Not to the exclusion of everything else. I was interested. I had a cousin killed at Goose Green. I did think it would be something quite different. You know, English islands in the South Atlantic with English people. Nearly in the Antarctic. And we'd gone to war over it. But if Jeremy had said straight out that he wasn't going, I wouldn't have made an issue out of it. But he just mumbled. He's a moaner.

He grumbles under his breath.'

'And did it come up to your expectations? The Falklands?' Henry asked.

'Yes, and more so. The long journey out there. The scenery. The bits of roughness. He didn't like that. He's a home bird, and when he's away he wants his comforts. Walking a few miles even in their summer weather creased him.'

'And?' Jennifer pressing.

'We quarrelled. Began to have open rows. I tried to be reasonable, but in the end I was bawling at him. It terrified him. I was better at it than he was. "The others will hear us," he used to say. "Let 'em" was my attitude.'

'And that was the end of it?' Jennifer asked. 'Of the marriage?'

'Not as far as I was concerned. I thought once we'd got back, and he had his job, and his students, and his graphs, and the bloody boring book he was writing, it would all shake down. But it didn't. He sulked, and I laced into him with my tongue. It was wrong of me, perhaps, but I hate these creeping Jesuses, with their long-suffering faces. It got worse. We wouldn't do anything for each other. If I was due in later than usual, he wouldn't put his meal back. He wanted me to go to some function with the vice-chancellor of his place, but I refused. I said I hadn't the time. It wasn't true, but...'

'Why, Hel?'

'I was getting pretty screwed up by this time. When I think of it now, it hardly seems rational, but I can easily understand why people take the carving knife to each other. And it got worse. Every day. And there was a crisis or two on at work. There always is. So in the end I just told him I was packing my bags and leaving.'

'When was that?'

'The last Saturday in January. I fixed myself up at the Grosvenor.'

'So you've been away from him over a month.'

'Yes. February's short.'

'And have you been in touch with him?'

'Yes. First to make arrangements to collect the rest of my clothes. And a fortnight ago I read that his mother had died.'

'Locally?'

'Yes. In the evening paper. She lived in Mansfield.'

'Had you met her?'

'Yes. We went over every week. He was the apple of her eye. The only child. Her clever boy.'

'Was she part of your trouble?' Jennifer queried.

'Only indirectly, as far as I know. She didn't approve of his first divorce. Probably didn't approve of anybody's divorce. She was an independent old lady, getting on for ninety. She was middle-aged, well up her forties, when

299

she had him. She'd lost two or three in miscarriages.'

'Was he like her?'

'No. She spoke her mind. He might be forthcoming on interest-rates or profit-margins or surpluses or whatever he lectures about, but not about everyday decisions at home. She was. She knew her mind. She knew her Jerry had married a suitable woman, because she had got used to the idea, and then he throws her over. So she looked on me with some suspicion. Not that I blame her. She disliked change.'

'Was she ill for long?' Henry asked.

'No. She had a heart-attack. A neighbour sent for the ambulance, but she was dead before they reached the hospital. Unexpected. At least to me. She may have been suffering from heart trouble for some time, and said nothing to anybody. That would be like her.'

'Was Jeremy upset?' Henry again.

'I expect so. Though you can never tell with him. He doesn't say much. And he's selfish, so that he'd be annoyed at having to put his work aside while he settled her estate, though it wouldn't be much. Anyhow, I wrote sympathetically. I made myself do it. He replied, and asked me to the funeral. I went. So did his first wife and his daughter. It was only a small affair. A few neighbours. No other relatives.'

'How did he seem towards you?'

'Polite. Not unfriendly. I walked in with him. But I was busy and so didn't go back home.'

'And there was no mention of reconciliation?' Jennifer asked.

'No. All formal. I felt as awkward as hell. I couldn't have discussed anything with him even if he'd wanted it. He telephoned next day, and thanked me.'

'And never said anything about your marriage?'

'No. Nor did I.'

'And that's where it stands?'

Helena shrugged. Henry refilled cups and the glass. Again the clumsy silence, which again Helena was the first to break.

'When I think about all this I can hardly believe it's happened. Talk about immaturity. Why we were in such a hurry to get married baffles me now. Or why he was. He can't usually make up his mind whether or not he wants another cup of tea. But we arranged it, like a couple of love-crazed teenagers. But it was the speed with which we fell out that mystifies me most. You'd think at our age we'd have the sense to keep our mouths shut, and let things shake down or blow over, but it wasn't so. I felt utterly frustrated, and before we'd finished I was everlastingly looking for opportunities to get after him.'

'Was he aggressive?'

'In the end. Not physically. That's not him.

301

But he was clearly waiting and prepared for every next squall. And he did nothing to make up. I thought he might creep out of the way. I can hardly believe the lunatic antics we got up to. We were like small children with no control over our tempers.'

'Were you as bad as he was?' Henry asked.

'Worse, probably. Put me in sight of him, and I went mad. Out at work I got on quite well, acted normally, did all I should, sorted things out. Now, you'd have thought that would have settled things down for me, but it didn't. In the middle of some piece of work I'd suddenly have a two minutes' burst of rage, and I'd fist my desk, but it would disappear and I could carry on again, level-headed as you like.' She looked accusingly at her listeners, as if they did not accord her sufficient attention.

'What I can't understand', Henry stuttered out, 'is the nature of your dislike, loathing, hate.'

'I can't describe it plainly because it wasn't rational. Even if he said something sensible, I'd oppose it because *he*'d said it. Loathing is as near as I can get. Whatever he did I hated. It frightened me because I could understand that my feeling was greater, deeper, more violent than the cause demanded. Inside a few weeks I came to despise anything he wanted, or thought, or, even, was. He was a source of dislike.'

'Is this how your first marriage broke up?'

302

'No. That was a longer-drawn-out tale altogether. In time Geoff and I found that we wanted to do different things, and said so. And this became so marked that there wasn't much to be said for living together. And Geoff was a bit of a philanderer, and that didn't endear me to him. So we gradually grew apart, and then I had the offer of this move to Beechnall, and he thought he wanted to marry somebody else, though that in fact came to nothing. But the break-up was understandable. We grew away from each other, and in time did the sensible thing, divorced.'

'And that was different from the present difficulties?'

'Utterly. I'd heard of incompatibility, but I just thought of it as a vague term for getting tired of each other. But with Jeremy I just could not stand his physical presence, or even, for instance, a note from him.'

'Did you feel this loathing when you went to his mother's funeral?' Jennifer asked.

'Hardly. I don't know why I went. Perhaps I was annoyed with myself, or scared, and so I got in touch with him. He wasn't himself. His mother, his doting, bossy, darling mother had died, and he was frozen trying to come to terms with that. It was like meeting a statue. I suppose he was gratified that I had put our differences aside for this public occasion so that people wouldn't talk. I don't know. We didn't meet in private. We spoke on the phone.

303

I haven't been to many funerals, and it was all so strange that I'd no time nor relish for personal dislikes.'

'Did you never think', Jennifer asked, 'of separating for a fixed time to see if you felt differently after a period free from each other?'

'He never suggested it. And I was sure that no absence would alter me. I was—am—terrified at myself. I had acted in a manner that I would have thought impossible. Oh, I know I like my own way, and blurt out what I think when it would be wiser to keep my trap shut, but I'm thirty-nine, and at that age it was a surprise suddenly to find out a nasty secret like this about myself.'

'You don't put it down to your age?' Jennifer asked.

'The menopause, you mean? There aren't any other symptoms.'

'If it was all so violent,' Henry asked, 'why did you not feel anything of it when you first met, when you went about together before you were married?'

'I don't know. I just can't account for it. We met, were interested enough to meet again, to begin talk about marriage, to buy a house and furnish it. I did most of the work there. But, no, I must admit that I had no foreknowledge of how violently I was going to change. It's been a surprise, and unpleasant at that, and so bad that I have wondered whether or not I was sane. Only the fact that I could hold down a fairly stressful job without difficulty and meet other people socially, convinced me I was not off my head.'

'What happens next?' Jennifer asked.

'Nothing. We go our own ways. We'll divorce in time, I imagine.'

'Will he sell the house?'

'I don't know. I shan't press him. He's paying the mortgage. That was one of the things he insisted on, though I guess I earn more than he does.'

'Don't you know?'

'No.'

'And there's no chance of reconciliation?'

'No. Not a hope.'

'But', Henry interrupted schoolmasterly, 'if you changed so violently in so short a time, couldn't the reverse happen?'

Helena snorted with rough laughter.

'No. I can't really understand why things turned out as they did, but I've not lost my wits completely. No. We shan't live together again. I don't want it, and I don't suppose he does.'

'But you came together for his mother's funeral, and acted with courtesy, and circumspection?'

'One-off. Less than an hour involved.'

Helena now sat much at ease as if she had either justified herself or eased guilt out of her system by confession. She had spoken without heat, never losing her temper. It appeared that she had mulled it over in her mind, sorted it out, fixed her story so that she could now tell it without loss of composure. She began in return to ask questions about their marriage.

Jennifer claimed that her new relationship had settled her down, made it possible to work full-time.

'We go every weekend to the coast, sometimes Friday night, sometimes Saturday morning. We take work if we have to, but we have at least one long walk by the shore, a minimum of two hours. And we stroll down the garden and we're right by the North Sea. Any time of the day or night.'

'Doesn't the place get dirty?'

'We found a very good woman who cleans it once a week, more than I would. And her husband, who drives her up, does a couple of half-days on the garden. We can afford it now that Henry's well-to-do. It's all marvellous with spring coming, and these huge white clouds piling up in the sky. You can't describe it, but it's ours every week.'

'Buying the new house has made a difference?'

'Yes. It has. We love it. Henry says that in two or three years' time we might well think we could have done better, but he has money to throw about. Having two houses has its drawbacks, but its's surprising how money smoothes difficulties away.'

'And you get on well together?'

'Look, Hel, I went through a bad time.

Henry coaxed me out of it. I know I had doctors and psychiatrists and counsellors and drugs, but he lived by me, and made it possible. I'll tell you, I still don't know whether I've done with it. Sometimes I feel so depressed that I think it's starting all over again, and I'm in pain, physical pain, headaches, visual disturbances, a crippling back, but I've clambered out each time, so that I'm beginning to think I've mastered it. And it's Henry with his Latin and Greek and his books and odd ways that's mainly managed it for me.'

'Will it last?' Helena asked cruelly.

'That's what I don't know, what I'm afraid of. And while that fear exists, my depression is likely to come back. I suppose I'm genetically disposed that way, or that it was set up early in my childhood.'

'Aren't you just depressed because of what happens now?'

'I'd say not. I'm like you in that the final explosion is a lot bigger than that of the fuse that sets it off.'

'Is my trouble innate, genetic, do you think?' Helena asked.

Jennifer shook her head.

She and Henry talked this passively over, at meals, at times of leisure, in bed, getting up. They laughed in the end at their obsession with the topic; 'the ever-interesting subject' Jen called it. Henry could not believe that Helena had so suddenly come to loathe Jeremy. 'She's

307

too normal,' he argued. 'For anyone to act as she says she did, she would need to be insane. That, Helena is not. She's quick-tempered, boisterous, not over-tactful, but never mad.' His theory was that Hel and Jeremy had for one reason or another got across one another, that she had cleared out, on fairly trivial grounds, and now she had made up this account, accurate only in minor detail, to explain her behaviour. 'I'd like to talk to him,' Henry said, 'hear his side of the story.'

Jennifer wondered if Helena's family were stable. 'Her mother was pretty intense, sometimes,' Henry answered. 'But such of the family that I knew, admittedly not very well, seemed ordinary enough. No murderers, child-abusers, criminals. Decent working-class people. Helena likes her independence. So did her mother, but Helena has made her way up in a man's world, and doesn't see fit to kowtow to Jeremy and his mother's darling's whims. I didn't know either her father or the stepfather and how they behaved at home.'

Thus they argued. In the end Henry decided he did not believe Helena's account. Jennifer was more genuinely puzzled. She had dealt with people on the extremes of behaviour, and claimed that human beings with only slight stimuli or apparently insignificant changes of temperament could act like demented animals. 'We don't know enough about it. Humankind is a mystery. The range of behaviour, even in quite normal people, is staggeringly wide.'

In the end they exhausted themselves and the topic, but could not leave it.

'We'll just have to see how it pans out, and then assign causes if we can,' Jennifer concluded. 'Meanwhile...'

Helena spent a weekend with them, Friday night to Sunday night, on the coast. She was good company, tired as all three were from a week's hard work, but able to relax, full of joking conversation, the life-and-soul of small exchanges.

On Friday and again on Saturday night they strolled down to the beach.

The sea lay flat, shallow and cold, magnificent on a cloudless, late Saturday with silver and smooth, blue darkness intermingled. The air bit cool, windless, keen.

'No chance of a paddle?' Helena asked.

'It would freeze your feet off,' Jennifer warned.

'The sea, even in the pools here, is desperately cold in the winter.'

'Is it ever fit to swim in?'

'You have to go a long way out for it to be deep enough. Perhaps with a hot summer it might be suitable by the end of August.'

'Just when holidays are ending?' Helena grieved.

'Well, yes.'

They stood together—Henry wearing a woollen scarf—looking over the plain, steely expanse of water.

'We seem to have it to ourselves,' Jennifer said. 'It's selfish, but it gives me terrific satisfaction to think that this beautiful stretch of the North Sea belongs just to me and my friends. We own it.'

'You don't,' Helena answered. 'Do you?'

'But I can think I do.'

'Do you encourage your wife in these fantasies?' Helena asked Henry.

'I share them,' he answered. 'I'm much in favour of self-deception.'

'There is something about the place,' she said. 'You're lucky.'

'Let's hope the luck continues,' Jennifer breathed. 'For all of us.'

'We don't deserve this.' Henry spoke firmly, grimly perhaps. 'And I can't convince myself that I do'

'I'm always on the look-out for the next catastrophe,' Jen said.

'What's responsible? Job or temperament?' Helena asked.

'Both.'

'We'll bluff our way through,' Henry said. 'Not perhaps exactly as we would want to. But with days and nights like this, we'll manage. Just.'

'But for how long?' Helena's voice nagged at his cautious optimism.

'Ten years. Then I shall be over seventy.'

'Poor old fellow,' Helena mocked.

'Three years, then.' Jennifer's voice had an edge of desperation.

Three years hence, she would have partially recovered from another bout of depression, would still be married to Henry, who still taught Latin at his school. They owned the same two houses, and in spring would walk down to this shore in the moonlight, tentative of life, fearful, unsure of themselves, but not defeated. They knew each other well enough to realise that they could yet win something, some brief pleasure out of the days of darkness. That contented. It had to. In the three years, Helena had left Beechnall and worked, they guessed, at the head office of her firm. They had lost touch, did not even bother with Christmas cards or casual telephone calls. Nothing remained of the friendship, of the intimacy of this night, of shared confidences. The Sheltons did not know whether Helena had remarried, she had signed herself at the first Christmas after her departure Helena Gough, on a card that they had not kept. They were unlikely ever to meet again, or for Helena to note the small obituary notice for her husband which Jennifer had put into the local evening papers on Henry's expected death nine years on. Thoughts of the loss of friendship rarely concerned them. They were inured to small changes, expected them, refused to be excited or put out. Periods closed; to make a song and dance over it merely demanded trouble. Once when by chance

311

Henry saw Helena's professor in the street, the two men nodded, not even smiling, in recognition, and passed each other without a word. It took Henry three days to remember it and tell his wife, who asked what they had said, and, learning, had never mentioned Jeremy again. They exchanged dinner-engagements with the Kinglakes and with the Reeves-Joneses, Jen's latest head of department and his lady-wife; they spoke to friends at concerts or lectures; every day seemed full, without boredom. In the summer they went abroad, to Venice, Rome, Vienna, to Prague and Budapest, once to India, but all without Helena. Once or twice they mentioned her, and her swiftly broken marriage, as one who had done something remarkable, out of the ordinary, like swimming the Channel or winning the pools. Henry always concluded these short exchanges with a schoolmasterly end-of-term report: I never believed a word she said about it.

Tonight they walked hand-in-hand, Helena, Jennifer and Henry, casting humped shadows in the clear of the moon, under the large arch of the sky and the heavier metal of the flat sea, quiet but unsubdued, breathing deeply, three humans in mortal pleasure.

'It's wonderful,' Helena said. 'I shall never forget this evening.'

'No,' Henry answered. 'That's right.'

They stood on the flat sand, fingers and

figures bound in an ephemeral friendship.

' 'It was night",' Henry intoned, ' "and throughout the world wearied bodies were enjoying peaceful sleep." Virgil.'

'Exactly,' Jen said, and they walked on. In ignorance.